Praise for *51*

"O'Leary's *51* is literary fiction on LSD, laced with surreal dreamscapes, humor, and dark insights into the human condition."
—William C. Dietz, author of the Winds of War series

"O'Leary and his metaphysical snake slither across a hallucinogenic *Alice In Wonderland/Yellow Submarine/Slaughterhouse Five* narrative that is even weirder than the reality that is America."
—Mario Acevedo, author of the Felix Gomez series

Praise for *Door Number Three*

"[O'Leary's] voice is fresh and funny, and he is bold enough to offer this assessment of the human condition as seen from a therapist's perspective 'The only terror that heals: the terror of being ourselves.'"
—*New York Times*

★"A highly appealing mix of skilled writing and zany imaginings, this novel bears positive comparison not only to the work of Philip K. Dick but also to the earlier SF of Kurt Vonnegut. . . . One of the best books of the year."
—*Publishers Weekly*, starred review

"An idiosyncratic, witty, labyrinthine, preposterous, unrestrained, and often highly entertaining debut."
—*Kirkus*

"A staggering concept richly realized."
—*Interzone*

"Funny and moving . . . a distinctive new voice in the field."
—*San Francisco Chronicle*

"It might well be the best sf novel of the past year."
—*The Magazine of Fantasy & Science Fiction*

"Just when you thought nothing new could be done with time travel, lucid dreaming, alien abduction, shapeshifting, and World War III, along comes Patrick O'Leary, fusing them in a grand, sardonic comedy of consensual reality gone awry."
—James Morrow, author of *Shambling Toward Hiroshima*

Praise for *The Gift*

"Echoes of Tolkien reverberate throughout this wonderful fantasy, a satisfying story-within-a-story in which a king and his youthful companion try to best the forces of evil."
—*Booklist*, Editor's Choice

"It's witty, weird, often enchanting."
—*Kirkus*

"A magical tale . . . O'Leary cleverly embeds tales within tales within tales as he layers and intersects his story lines."
—*Library Journal*

"It is mature, thoughtful, provocative, and exceptionally beautifully written fantasy, and O'Leary makes it resonate. There are books you read once, and cast aside forever, and then there are books that call you back again and again. *The Gift* is such a book."
—*Locus*

"Patrick O'Leary can be alternately funny and incredibly tragic, wise and light-hearted."
—*Starlog*

51

PATRICK O'LEARY

TACHYON
SAN FRANCISCO

51

Author photo © 2022 by Patrick O'Leary
Interior and cover design by Elizabeth Story

Tachyon Publications LLC
1459 18th Street #139
San Francisco, CA 94107
415.285.5615
www.tachyonpublications.com
tachyon@tachyonpublications.com

Series Editor: Jacob Weisman

Print ISBN: 978-1-61696-348-4
Digital ISBN: 978-1-61696-349-1

Printed in the United States by Versa Press, Inc.

First Edition: 2022

10 9 8 7 6 5 4 3 2 1

To Sandy

"Secrets are about suppression,
and history is often suppressed by violence,
obscured by cultural appropriation,
or deliberately destroyed
or altered by colonization,
in a lingering kind of cultural gaslighting.
Wikipedia defines "secret history"
as a revisionist interpretation
of either fictional or real history
which is claimed to have been
deliberately suppressed, forgotten, or ignored
by established scholars."
Martha Wells
—speech at the 2017 World Fantasy Convention

"I've only told you 5 percent of what happened."
—"TV Repairman," *Groom Lake*

THE BEST MAN—2018

It was a year after the Reality TV Star took the White House.

I was driving home from an AA meeting, listening to a catchy circus calliope playing in a stupid commercial (one of those awful jungles—jingles, I mean—you know: the kind you can't get out of your head?), driving down Cass Avenue in Detroit on the coldest winter night in twenty years. The windchill was forty below. Funny. The next song on the radio was Leon Russell's "Out in the Woods." And I recalled the story he told about asking an African singer how you translate "lost in the jungle" into Zulu? The man was puzzled because, evidently, Africans do not get lost in the jungle.

The overpasses were skid pads—clouds of moisture rose up from the pipes and froze immediately—cars were sliding everywhere on the black ice. If you cracked your window, you could hear at intervals the screeches and crashes in the night like it was the '67 riots or something.

Detroit winters are legendary: humid, gray, and dirty—they are why Michiganders move to Florida. Wind whipping the manhole steam sideways across the road, and a spray of panicked blackbirds streamed past my windshield and drew my attention to this silhouette of a skinny hobo up ahead, his green military jacket flapping open against the wind, his breath coming out in coughs of cloud above his long gray beard, and his rubber boots flopping, unsnapped and pathetic. He swung a filthy white bag stuffed with all his worldly possessions.

I saw him stumble and fall facedown on the overpass spanning I-94 and I immediately pulled over. By the time I got to him, I thought he was dead. No such luck. I turned him over: bulging eyes, beard spiked with ice around his mouth like a sea urchin in a tide pool. He looked like a damned Santa Claus, and he smelled like happy hour.

A tall black man who once had been very striking.

I sat him up and said I'd get him to the nearest Salvation Army shelter. I still shudder recalling his voice. I remember much about that night; I will never forget his voice. I've had years to think about it and I doubt I can do it justice. So let me quote someone much more eloquent than me. Someone talking about another voice in a review he wrote for a jazz mag. Lloyd, the Coca-Cola pianist in the vault. You'll meet him later.

"It was a night voice—a song of sorrow told in the haunting tones of a beat-up saxophone played in a strange key by a master in a bare rented room in a huge city—a little spark in the middle of the night. Cigarette streaming on a cheap aluminum ashtray by the unmade bed. Dope throbbing in his veins. Sitting shoeless on the mattress and fondling his last friend, a worn twisted white gold pipe with mother-of-pearl buttons and supple valves. His voice breathing through the instrument into the empty room, the aching notes rising with the smoke as it curled up to the ceiling and the bare bulb that dangled there."

It's no wonder nobody listens to the homeless—who would want to hear a voice like that?

Now, if it seems a bit strange—interrupting myself to let other voices do the talking—get used to it. This isn't just my story. There's a whole chorus of weirdos dying to be heard. And they're each going to have their say.

"Salvation?" the old bum muttered in that singular voice. "Salvation!?"

"It's not far," I assured him. I held his gnarled hand to steady him and led him to my car. "Anybody could slip on a night like this."

"I didn't slip," he slurred, scowling at his white trash bag. "I was tripped!"

I held the passenger door open for him and he shot me a suspicious look as he laid his white bag on the floorboard and tucked it under his feet as he sat. It stunk horribly.

"What's yer name?" he asked when we were finally settled, as he held his shivering hands over the heating vents.

"Adam," I said.

It was as if I had said "Moses," or "Claude Rains," or "Spartacus." Or I had claimed to be all three at once.

"Christ! Adam?!"

"That's right," I said. "Relax. We'll be there in five." And I turned my attention to the road.

He started wheezing/laughing. "Adam Pagnucco?"

I looked at him hard. "Do I know you?"

"Not sure." He belched. "Do you remember my wedding?"

My mind raced through a parade of drunken relatives—people I had only met at weddings and never saw again. "Your wedding?"

He laughed long and hard. "Yeah. You were my best man."

BEING LEFT—2018

Call me "Nuke." Everybody else does.

As the familiar face emerged from the ragged features of the tall mountain man next to me, I wondered if I was just as much a stranger to him.

My passenger was one Winston Koop.

Winston Koop was my best friend in college. He was also the smartest man I had ever met. He was always Going Places: a campus celebrity and A Guy To Watch. Cum laude. Cum everything. He was a track star who set school records that still stand today. Winston Koop was heading for the big show in whatever field he chose: languages, literature, science, math. Instead he enlisted and went to Nam. Last I heard from him he sent me a copy of an article he had published in a scholarly journal. Something about translating Vietnamese.

And, come to think of it, I did seem to remember giving a brief boozy toast at his Vegas wedding reception decades later, when our paths briefly intersected and we worked on the same contract: "Marriage. Marriage is the failure of being single." That brought the house down.

Then I guess life happened.

So, much like the first night I met him, I brought him back to my apartment in a Detroit suburb. Insisted he shower. Made him some toast, gave him a couple of ibuprofen, and set up a guest bed for him. He was out in a blink and snoring like he was his own thunderstorm. It took an hour before I finally drifted off.

In the morning I found some old clothes that almost fit him. Over coffee he began to tell me what had happened. And it wasn't long before I remembered his way with words.

I have strange fragmented memories of those days. His haunted voice. The odd sounds of a person walking through rooms where I had lived quietly alone for years. Koop playing solitaire at the kitchen table—the flap of the cards on the Formica. Koop leaning on a windowsill, eyes closed, resting in a beam of sun like a contented cat. Unfamiliar smells drifting through the halls. Him growling at me when I offered to burn his white bag full of stinking clothes. Koop asleep in my La-Z-Boy chair in the flashing blue light of the TV. Koop scaring the hell out of me one morning—he had shaved off his Santa Claus beard, and for a second I thought he was someone else—that is, I thought someone had tracked him down.

And silences.

I remember those silences with relief. Because, once he was talking, his words shattered any comfortable sense of peace I ever had. Nothing stood after Koop spoke. The world was no longer the world as I knew it. It was a ruin, as decimated as the path of destruction he had run to get to this final reckoning.

Eventually, I realized what a dangerous creature he was, but it was too late—we had reconnected the easy bond we once had. I respected him, trusted him, and, yes, loved him.

And, truth be told, I'd missed him.

Near the end there came a time when I knew my only safety was in forgetting. Hearing him out, yes; letting him spill his tormented tale, of course—that's what a friend would do. But, by the time he had finished, I understood the threat he posed. I had been relying on his friendship to spare me the memory.

I know: That doesn't make sense yet.

I promise you: It will.

This next part is going to sound like a monologue. But it came in spurts, after hours of silence. Days of sleep. Meals and coffee. I watched my old friend put his life back together piece by piece. He started at the end—which is to say—the beginning of his descent.

He started with the end of his marriage.

"The worst part of being left is being thrown out of your own story. All your life, you live inside this . . . tale. The oldest story ever. You're a man in love with a woman. You're a couple. Together. You live through it all: adventures, mistakes, stupidity, flu. You learn to love each other where you're most needed, and hurt each other where you're most tender. You practice forgiveness. You stumble, you shine. You get through it. You know?"

I nodded. I felt certain I did.

"Because, sure, it's a crooked journey, but it's yours. Together. You cherish that. You carry the smile of your lover for days. Sometimes that is the only thing that sustains you. The memory of what you were."

He smiled an almost smile. Like he could just touch the memory of happiness, even if the thing itself was lost.

"That's marriage. And night by night you learn each other's stories, seal the bond with memories. You laugh together. Share your secrets in the dark. Learn the mysteries of each other's bodies—that familiar discovery that never grows old. It's like you're weaving yourselves together until you become the same fabric, like a tapestry—the story of your lives. Does that make sense?"

I told him it made tons of sense. His face told me there was still a twang of joy on a spiderweb that stretched back into his past, and the vibrations could still reach him.

"That trip to the green lake where she told you the most awful thing that had ever happened to her. The three-day silence after stupid truths were told that ended in fantastic sex. The damned screen door that kept slamming until you just had to laugh. The little stuff you share."

He cried then. And he couldn't continue for two days.

I remember we walked out of a terrible movie and sat in the cold car waiting for it to warm up. Our breaths fogging up the windshield.

By then I wasn't surprised when he picked up the story out of nowhere.

"See, while I was in this love story I didn't know how lucky I was. I took precious things for granted. I knew why I was alive, where I was going and who I was fighting for. I was safe."

Safe. Salvation. That word again.

The windshield started clearing.

Koop said, "I spent a lot of time away from home on duty. Overseas. And all the while I'm having these adventures, all over the world, I had a picture in my head, a still, unchanging fact. But that picture of a happy marriage? In the real world, it was dissolving. You hear that?"

"What?"

"That bird."

"I heard something. Sounded like a screeching brake."

"Pretty sure it was a crow. I usually don't hear them in the dark."

We listened to the night for a while.

"So maybe one night," he continued, "after one of those long trips, you come home."

(I noticed he had switched back to second person, as if it were a universal thing that could have happened to anyone.)

"And everything changes. Through a window you see your lover talking on the phone to someone else while you're drinking a beer in the dark backyard. Maybe she turns into a beautiful monster before your eyes. She laughs. And you watch love disarm her features—the lines of joy, the sparkle of anticipation. And you think: That's how she used to laugh with me."

The foggy windshield cleared slowly from the bottom like a rising curtain.

"And then the fear. Like a dreadful song that gets stuck in your head.

"And one day you're informed: she doesn't quite love you anymore. Of course, she doesn't put it like that, she is too kind. She's just not sure; she needs time to think, and space to grow. And you are reassured that, though it may not seem so, none of this is meant to hurt you.

"And one minute you are safe inside the story of your life: somebody's lover, somebody's husband, somebody's best friend. One minute you are mowing the lawn and plunging the toilet and the next you're banished: you're standing outside your life, looking in.

"It's like the end of autumn—a sudden shift to chill. And it gets colder."

He stopped talking at night—gave him nightmares, he said. He would only speak near windows where he could see the sky. Like a bird who needed to know there was a way out.

"Your bed empties. Your body sort of folds in on itself. Feels like you've fallen from a great height and you're paralyzed. Or like your body is still falling, still up there somewhere. Because it sure isn't here. Nothing is here."

A long look at a slow cloud.

"And some mornings it's all you can do to open your eyes and stare at the ceiling and feel this nothing and wonder: Whose life am I living? This isn't my life! Who am I now? Who am I if I am not somebody's lover, somebody's husband, somebody's friend?" He remembered something and looked out of the corner of his eyes at me. "Was it like that for you?"

I told him yes. It was true. But I didn't say, Where were you, Koop? After the accident? You didn't call. You didn't bother to—or did he? Did he send a card? I do remember missing him.

"And day by day," he continued, "you lose the story of your life."

Finally, he couldn't keep talking unless we were driving. We didn't have to have a destination—in fact he preferred if we just found a cruising speed and headed out. I could tell: the cocoon of the car's blue interior was a comfort to him. Even so he always brought along his security blanket: his stinking white bag of stuff.

"So you drink.

"First to dull the pain. Then when that doesn't work, you seek oblivion. You pass out in bars. Wake up in taxis. You tell your story to strangers and then you fuck them. And in the morning you forget their names. You go to work hungover. And you cope. But it's a half life. A life not really lived. You're going through the motions of living, but really, you're just a hollowed-out shell."

"I remember," I said.

"And the strangest thing is: nobody really notices! Friends, neighbors, coworkers—they make an effort. Maybe they pass on their condolences. Maybe they say they never really liked her. But they're all just flies buzzing round your head. You go on long missions. Track down leads nobody else could crack. You attend terribly important briefings with powerful men. Deliver critical information to your superiors. You get handshakes. Medals. And afterwards, you marvel that nobody noticed: you hadn't even been there!"

"This goes on for months. Years. And one day you wake up pissing blood onto your sheets. And you've been out of work for nine months. Early retirement. A gold watch. Decent bonus. Thanks for all you've done for your country. And not one of your friends, colleagues, or drinking buddies can recognize the man you've become."

And he looked at me. "Not even your best man."

I remember he left out her name. Like it was too painful to form the word.

LEARNING TO DRINK—1955

I suppose I've always been drawn to heroes like Koop; my natural shyness made their bright light appealing. So I'd slipstream behind them, hidden in their wakes, enjoying the churn, taking notes while they took all the chances. I was the quiet guy in their shadows, so later I could bask in their glory, tell the tale without risking anything. It suited me.

Koop was my Captain. I was his follower. He's the guy who dubbed me "Nuke."

So after Koop ran out of gas, or was too messed up to continue, he asked about me. I knew he would. After his intrepid monologues, he usually got around to it.

I began in a place that showed I understood: Booze. Or "Time Juice" as our pal Rudy used to say.

You know that alcoholics drink to erase time, right? I don't think there's anything we fear more than an empty hour.

My uncle Bob taught me how to drink. He had a low, grumbling voice that always began and ended with a slow, rolling hum, like a lawn mower trying to start. "Oooohahhh, pass me one of those Stroh's, Adam." I'd take a sip and pass it on. Bob always seemed to have a surplus of vowels, so everything sounded elongated, like he was drunk even when he wasn't. "Thooze Strooaze." "Gooood fishing." "Nooobody."

His philosophy (which he made me memorize) was: "Never run when you can walk; never walk when you can sit; never sit when you can lie down; and never lie down when you can sleep." He taught me the power of entropy. You sit around long enough and, sooner or later, somebody else will do it.

It was a foolproof system that worked for him for years. He had a sweet job at the Saginaw steel foundry, reading magazines and dispensing tools from a locked cage in perhaps the only quiet corner of that noisy, smoky plant. He'd get home from work, get naked, pop a Stroh's, and take a bath. His wife, Grace, would scurry after him, picking up his shed clothes, retrieving the discarded bottle cap from the bathroom tile, and asking what he wanted for dinner. She was a mousy woman whose first husband beat her regularly, so Bob must have seemed a real catch.

I met Grace at his funeral, and she was soggy and pawing me like I was a long-lost son. You know, the sudden intimacy the grieving bestow on the lower-level stricken. Grace gripped my arm with her tiny hand and told me, "He was a good man."

Not really, I thought. But he was entertaining.

Her eyes were swimming, and we were admiring the way he looked, lying there in his pale blue suit, so I gave her the best words I could think of about dead Bob. "He was my favorite uncle."

"You were his second," she said candidly, nodding her head at my cousin Johnny, who looked like a Bob-in-training. "He liked the way Johnny kept the beers coming."

Oh, so he was his retriever. What was I?

"He said you were a yapper and a doodler. Full of stories."

I smiled. "He made me laugh," I told her, which was the truth and seemed to comfort her.

When my dad died, Uncle Bob had lost his old deer hunting partner, so every fall he would pick me up before the sun rose and we'd drive 150 miles north to his hunting grounds. I was nine and Bob was usually hungover or residually drunk, so he'd ask me to tell him stories to keep him sharp behind the wheel. I'd talk nonstop for three hours—recounting any number of Silver Surfer comics, all the novels I'd read, *The Life of Babe Ruth, The*

Life of Ty Cobb, and when I ran out of autobiographical material, I'd invent stories.

It wasn't until years later that occurred to me: I was terrified. Occasionally his heavy lids would drop down and Bob would swerve and I'd have to shout: "THEN THE GHOST BIT OFF THE HEAD OF THE KNIGHT AND SPIT IT IN THE LAKE!" And he'd snap to, regain his position on the right side of the yellow line, and look out of the corner of his eyes at me.

"Ooooaaah, I don't remember any ghost," he'd grumble.

"You weren't paying attention," I'd say.

What with the adrenaline rush he was good for another thirty miles or so and then his head would start nodding, and I'd resort to: "THE NAKED GODDESS THREW HER GOLDEN GOWN UPON THE FIRE!"

He'd flinch and say something like, "Ooooaaah, Goddess?" And I'd find some way of fitting the incident into the story.

Then we'd walk to our spot in the woods, and Uncle Bob would assume the throne, lay his rifle across his lap, and lean back against a fallen tree, dressed in his orange-and-brown deer-hunting outfit. His haircut was the same as mine —a butch with a little cowlick on the forehead that gave him character. I sidled up next to him and he gave me a hit off his Tareyton. I'd cough and he'd giggle wickedly. The air was crisp—typical Michigan fall day when you just knew somebody somewhere was playing football.

We'd always go back to the same hunting spot where he and my dad used to go. A farm north of Gaylord in the woods on the edge of a cornfield. I had no interest in hunting. But I liked Bob. And I liked getting out of the house, and not having to listen to my mom cry all day. And hunting was something of an excuse for Bob, too. I never ever saw him shoot anything in the five years we shared the stand. For him it was a chance to exercise the right of a man to take two six-packs of Stroh's into the woods Up North and get shitfaced without his wife knowing.

He'd sit all morning and watch the birds; I'd read or draw faces in my notebook, and Bob would drink and doze and, when the sun set, he'd fire off three rounds from his rifle into the air. And giggle. That was the part I liked best.

That, and the reading.

I was happy to sit there lost in my books and doodles. I wanted to draw comics when I grew up. Monsters. Superheroes. I had a thing for faces. I started drawing them in pencil on the round cardboard caps of the small milk bottles we had for our school lunches.

"Who's that?" Bob would ask, tilting his head to inspect my drawing.

"I don't draw who's," I said. "I just draw faces." I never could do likenesses.

It became our thing. "Who's that?" he'd keep asking, and we both knew the answer.

Occasionally, he'd ask me to read aloud. He seemed to get a kick out of it, though every once in a while he'd yawn and say, "Ooo-haaaah getting kinda dull there, Adam." He'd sort of swing the barrel of his rifle in my general direction. So I'd goose it, really make the words sing, turn up the emotion to opera level, and Bob would nod, appeased, and I would be spared. Not that he really would have shot me; I'm pretty sure he wouldn't have.

I was reading way above my grade level. I had unsupervised access to a mess of my dad's paperbacks—including all the John D. MacDonald Travis McGee novels. *Nightmare in Pink. The Deep Blue Good-by. The Lonely Silver Rain.* Uncle Bob liked those, especially the steamy parts. He always said sitting in the woods and drinking made him horny. And he sure could use a doe. Stuff like that.

I figured out years later that these stories were the only culture Bob ever got. He'd watch Tigers games on TV, get plastered with his buddies at the bar, attend Mass with Grace and get his weekly Bible story, but his life was pretty narrow. It didn't include many glimpses of truth or beauty or any inkling of art. I think I filled a vacuum for him and, in the end, he was grateful.

Later I understood that Bob couldn't stand boredom. I think

that's why he drank. For the alcoholic, boredom is an empty vortex which sucks in all the dark, the way black holes suck down matter. If you're not drunk and you're bored, the next thing you know all your past failures and guilts line up for a heart-to-heart. No wonder priests drink. Stuck in a dark confessional, waiting for strangers to tell them their worst selves. That's withdrawal in a nutshell, and any smart drunk squelches it pronto.

"Hell," said Koop, concurring.

"Hell. Unmedicated darkness. An almost physical sticky feeling of drowning in your self."

Anyway, I was saying about the rifle and the beer and me reading aloud to him. It was the pattern of our trips.

Once I asked him what it's like to be married. Bob got that look in his eyes of intense sincerity—I knew it well. It meant he was going to bullshit me. He smiled and said, "Oooohaaah . . . well . . . It's the Best."

"He was in bed the last weeks," Grace told me at the funeral. "He gave himself a couple plunger pushes of morphine. Then he said, 'Come over here, honey, so I can hug you and tell you I love you.'" She shoved her lower lip so hard to her nose she looked for a minute like she had no teeth.

"I did. We did. He did. And then he died."

Maybe their arrangement was one of convenience: drinking buddies who happened to be the opposite sex. But I don't know. It's more than many get, I guess.

Koop was silent.

I always remember Uncle Bob standing up, like it was a real ordeal, grunting every bend of the rise, stubbing out his cigarette in the pile of butts at his feet, and walking off until he disappeared into the trees to take a leak. After a moment, there'd be a loud prolonged fart, then a short silence, and then Bob's wicked little laugh.

Koop said, "You never said anything about him teaching you to drink."

"Didn't I? He shared his cans with me. Sometimes he let me

have my own. Or he wouldn't say anything if I took one. I was drunk after one beer."

I looked over at Koop. "I was drunk the whole time I was with him."

EVIFUCKINGDENTLY—2018

I caught Koop watching my face.

"What?" I asked.

"I'd forgotten you had that scar on your mouth." He rubbed his upper lip.

"My accident."

Koop winced. "I like it. Makes you look more human, less perfect."

I pulled a face. Perfect? Me? Koop was the overachiever. What the hell was he talking about? "You were gonna get a government job last time we talked."

I didn't mention that his abrupt and prolonged silence had hurt me deeply. Evidently, I needed him a lot more than he needed me. If Winston Koop was an action figure, I was Dr. Watson. He was poetry; I was the dullest prose. I was not glamorous, fabulously gifted or accomplished; I did not get all the girls. What I was was reliable. A worker ant, maybe. My photography career was meticulous if not inspired: Weddings. Graduations. Family Portraits. I was what they call a "confirmed bachelor." Evidently I was condemned to catalog the peaks of lives I never lived. I worked at the same company for decades. But I never shone, was never a star, one of the guys at the front of the room, getting the applause and beaming in the spotlight. I never wanted to be them. Those guys, it always seemed to me, were the loudmouths who ended up spouting off in bars. They accrued followers not friends, gave speeches, stole all the focus, and when the applause died down, as it always does, they seemed pretty lonely. Like Koop. And for years I supposed he had suffered the same fate. It comforted somewhat.

"The last time we talked?" Koop frowned. "Refresh my memory."

"Forty-five years ago? You called me long distance to tell me you were off on some military thing and you couldn't say when you'd be in touch again. You sounded soused. Feeling sentimental maybe?"

"Oh, yeah. Makes sense. That was actually after Nam."

"CIA? Languages or something?" I said.

"It was 'Or something,'" he said sourly.

"I met an old classmate who said you were a TV repairman."

Koop chuckled.

"That didn't make sense to me. So what did you do, Superstar?"

He took that. He deserved it. It was clear we had both ridden the failure train.

But then his pause seemed to fill the room like silence after a bad joke. Why? Koop had been sharing the deepest part of his life for days. What? You've just bared your soul to me, trusted me with your worst nightmare. Now you've got discretion?

At the time it did seem comical. Two old drinking buddies on the downside of life telling old war stories. We were both seventy-three. Long past our denials and excuses. We had, as far as I knew, no more wars to fight, mountains to climb. Life was in our rearview mirror and the dramas and regrets were long behind us. What a schmuck I was.

"Winston? What?"

Oh, to be that simple. To look across a car at an old friend, and think: This is really helping. He may actually be getting a handle on his shit.

I shudder rethinking those thoughts.

If I knew then what I know now, you know what I would have done? I would have politely asked him to check the right rear tire—it felt a bit squishy. And when he had stepped out, I would have slammed the accelerator, torn away, spitting gravel and slush, and left him standing on a two-lane dirt road on a frigid day in mid-January, in the middle of Michigan's thumb. In the coldest winter in decades.

I wouldn't have even checked my rearview mirror. I would have never gone back to my apartment or collected my stuff. I would have driven as far and as fast as I could. Canada, maybe. Crossed the Blue Water Bridge. Found a city where I could disappear. And never, ever, for the rest of my fucking life say the name "Winston Koop" again.

But he was my friend.

He was in trouble.

I was a putz.

So I asked him the most mundane question. Something to get us back on track to normality. Something to steer us out of the dangerous waters of failure. I asked him what he did for a living.

Gareth Dickson's song "Two Trains" started playing. Soothing. Gentle. Perfect, I thought.

He shrugged and said, "I was a collector. I specialized in memory. Or forgetting. I'm not sure anymore."

I could see the relief when he said this. How long had he kept that inside? "Can you talk about it?"

"I guess I have to. Not talking about it got me where I am today."

"You haven't asked for a drink."

"I've been dry for a year. You?"

"Thirty."

"That night you picked me up—that was my first bender since I stopped."

We were silent for a time. He poured us more coffee from the thermos, adjusted the old red robe I had given him, and stared out the window. It was twenty-six degrees out. We were streaming through a white-on-white landscape, fields falling off into the scattered woods, the occasional darkened farmhouse. It was actually sort of peaceful.

My whole life was about to turn over. I shudder remembering.

Koop said, "Did I ever tell you about the first time I met her?"

THE WAY OUT—1972

"What in the living fuck did they do?"

That's what Koop thought when he first read it.

It was a long equation written on a blackboard in chalk. The danger wasn't anywhere in the numbers. It was implied. Like the margins around a page imply there's a story there. A KEEP OUT sign is hiding something. Or a wall implies there's something on the other side.

Koop had stumbled upon it on his Orientation Tour at the base, when his British guide, Dr. Johnson, had stepped into a lab to pick up a folder of papers.

They had entered a dark room. Johnson had flicked on the overheads. And then his tour guide chatter had faded out as Koop beheld the numbers on the board.

To most other men it would have been nonsense: an equation. The fact that Koop was one of maybe a hundred people on the planet who could grasp it was certainly serendipitous. The fact that he might be the only man who could solve it was known at that time only to him, and only as a dim, dawning intuition that the answer lay just outside his pool of light, at the precipice of darkness.

Johnson noticed his attention as they were leaving. "Oh, that. Yeah, that's a stumper. Word to the wise. Don't open doors like that."

"Why?" Koop asked.

"Why?" Dr. Johnson regarded him as if he were a child who had just asked why he couldn't jump into a bottomless pit. "My dear boy. Because sometimes there's only a way in. And no way out."

Koop smiled. He recognized the British term for "exit": "way out."

Most of his first week of orientation was what not to see, what not to ask, what not to know. Base Rules. Never go anywhere without your green, blue, or white badge. Do not ask about the strange noises. Do not ask about The Four Tops. Do not let your gaze stray into the design vaults. The prototype bays. Stay out of medical. Always code in and out. If you have to ask someone, never ask in writing. Always ask behind a closed door. Questions are dangerous.

"Stay on the line."

That was the sacred base rule. The color-coded geometry of the entire humungous site (an upside-down Guggenheim Museum bored into the desert) that dictated all movement and clearance.

Green line was engineering.

Blue line was medical.

White line was R & D.

The soldiers guarded the lines.

But he noticed his recruiter, the Man in the Blue Suit, never carried any ID or badges. Never seemed to answer to anyone. He ignored all the lines.

I want his job, Koop thought.

A week later he asked Dr. Johnson who was working on the equation.

Johnson gave him that look again. "That was Eyes Only."

Oh, the jargon. "That's Back-of-House. That's Deep Juju."

"Come on. Who's on it?"

"Katey."

It was a time when all the men had last names and women only first ones.

Katey was a highly respected scientist, medical doctor, and air force captain whom he occasionally saw in the cafeteria, reading a novel and eating a green apple. She was on the blue line so she wore a white lab coat and a blue badge: medical. Her red horn-rimmed glasses stood out.

One day he set a green apple beside her red tray, put down his jumbo white coffee mug, and sat next to her.

"You're the new guy."

He smiled: she had noticed.

"What are you, eighteen?" she asked.

"I'm twenty-seven. But thanks. I was hoping you could use a mathematician."

She looked at him.

"I'm good."

"I know. I read your file. It says 'Languages.'"

She knew him! He smiled and said, "I'm a polymath."

"Why do they have you doing codes?"

"I'm good at that, too."

"It's a dead end. It's the exact opposite of science. Making knowledge less knowable."

He fell in love with her a little right there.

"I saw the board."

"The board."

"The blackboard. You know which one. It's such a profound puzzle there's no need to hide it. It contains its own camouflage."

She regarded him. "That your clever way of saying no one understands it?"

"Yup."

She took off her red glasses and munched on the tip. "Well, that was clever."

"I thought so."

"What are you doing at three?"

At three they were standing together in front of the blackboard silently examining the figures.

"This is physics. What does that have to do with medical?"

Her face closed so hard he thought he heard a door slam. "You mean what am I doing here?"

He winced. "I could have put that better."

"Probably."

"Sorry. When did it happen?" he asked.

"Sometime before the war ended."

Later they were sitting silently in the corner of the lab drinking coffee from white cups.

"So they accidentally made a door."

"You could say that."

"A door to anywhere."

"Pretty much. Actually, that's what they call it. 'The Anywhere.'"

"And now they can't close it?"

"That's about the size of it."

"Well, I gotta say, that was pretty darn stupid."

"No," Katey said. "That was amazing. What was stupid was what happened next."

"What happened next?"

She looked at him. "What color are your eyes exactly?"

"I don't give a shit. What happened next?"

"That's need-to-know."

"I need to know."

The way she looked at him then made his body sing. He hoped he was hiding it well.

Papers were signed. Clearances were cleared. (Koop spared me the boring stuff.)

"What happened next?" he asked.

"We were able to shrink the portal enough to transport it from Trinity."

"Trinity?"

"Ground Zero. The first atomic bomb site. You think that's funny?"

"Sorry. I'll tell you later."

"Sometimes it's a dark window. Sometimes it's a door. Once somebody threw in a cat's tail—God knows why—and it came back a snake."

Her voice had risen slightly as she was telling the tale, acquiring an unconscious mania.

"Hold it," Koop said. "Wait. Living matter can travel through it?"

"Evidently."

"This is the biggest discovery—"

"—in the history of the world. Yes." She took a long appraising look at the young man. "Are you prepared to make this your life's work?"

"Hell, yes!"

When he saw the effect his answer had on her, he fell in love with her, truly.

"God, you're a little boy. You didn't even think about it."

"Captain. I haven't stopped thinking about since I saw the board."

"Your life's work. Your whole life, Koop. Because that may just be what it takes."

The young man thought: She's going to tell me something amazing. She's going to say she's one hundred years old. She's going to say that she is the only one who can step through the portal. She is the Third Katey. She is a different Katey every time she comes back. She's going to say . . ."

"Hey. Idiot. Focus."

"I'm here," he said, catching himself.

"Do you . . . want to see it?"

It was a long, long walk down a long white line, down an endless green hallway that curved, curved, curved. Past four strange glassed-in guard stations. Halfway down Koop said, "Frank Lloyd Wright could have designed this joint."

Katey looked at him.

"Frank Lloyd Wright designed this?"

"Off the record."

Then they were standing before a door marked "Janitor" in red hand-painted letters. She checked her watch.

"What are we waiting for?" Koop asked.

A long pneumatic hiss on the other side of the door.

"That," Katey said.

They entered the dark closet. The smells of cleaning fluids and damp sponges could not distract him from the way his whole body was feeling: they had never been this close. He could smell her shampoo. Turned out it was an elevator down god knows how many floors.

"You carry that ugly white mug everywhere?" she asked.

Koop toasted her with it. "Usually."

When the elevator finally opened, she lingered in the doorway, saying, "We don't want to get any closer."

"We don't?"

"No. Come here."

He stood next to her looking out into another green hallway with a white line. Some fifty feet away was an oddly shaped green door. It appeared canted, as if it had been permanently jarred out of square by an earthquake. There was something not right about it.

"When did you put on blue lipstick?" he asked.

Katey smiled but didn't answer. "Your boss said you needed to see this." She called out, "Ready!"

Standing there beside her in the doorway, he could not help but notice how the mild green hue of the hall seemed to raise the soft down on her cheeks. He knew he was staring; he wondered if she would appreciate his admiration. Perhaps she would find it frivolous and irrelevant to their life's work. He hoped she would look at him like this someday.

(That reminded me of something I once told Koop about a girl I had a crush on. "When she's not looking at me, it's like I'm not really there." Funny. I don't remember her name.)

Katey said, "Focus, you dope."

Koop smiled and chuckled a bit.

In a few moments, a door at the end of the hall hissed open and out stepped a dazed and blinking young child dressed in an old-fashioned white nightgown. When he saw Koop he raised his pale hand and gave a wave. Koop waved back. Then the child saw the green door and gasped, and started running toward it. The door did not open, but the child dashed right through it and disappeared.

Later Koop asked, "A doorway to another dimension?"

"What does that even mean?" Katey said.

"I know. I felt stupid saying it."

"We don't know what it is."

"Parallel worlds?"

"We don't know."

"I got chills."

"I threw up," Katey said.

"What does the government want with a bunch of kids?"

She regarded him. "What did you see in the hall?"

"A kid in a nightgown? What did *you* see?"

"A marshmallow as big as a stool. Don't sweat it. Some people see cats. They look different to everybody."

"They?"

"IFs. Come on. The Blue Man says you've already seen them. We call them 'IFs'"

"IFs," Koop said.

"Yes. It stands for—"

"'Imaginary Friend.'"

"Right."

"Mine didn't look anything like that."

Katy smiled at his stunned face and took pity on him. "Okay. Here's what we know. They're an indigenous species. They've probably existed as long as humans have. Symbiotic creatures that use a peculiar form of camouflage."

"Wait, wait, wait," Koop said.

She waited. She counted to ten.

"Okay, go ahead," he said.

"Normally IFs just fade away when their child grows up, or they attach themselves to the next child. Best we can figure, the atom bomb exposed them. That day thousands of IFs became 'real'—whatever that means. The portal awakened them."

"That weird door."

"That's when they came out of hiding. From that day on it became like a sacred site that every IF feels compelled to visit, make a pilgrimage to. Who knows why."

"They don't come from there?"

"What part of 'indigenous' don't you get?"

"What's on the other side?"

Katey shrugged. "All we know is the closer they get to the portal the more they lose their camouflage. We call it 'The Way Out.'"

"Wait," said Koop, holding up a hand and scrunching his face.

She smiled watching him and counted to ten again.

"Captain? That is . . ."

"Crazy?"

"I was going to say 'fucked up.'"

"I suppose we could have come up with a better name."

He stared at her wide pupils. "I wasn't talking about the name."

"I know."

"Can I ask you a serious question?"

"Sure."

"Would you go to bed with me?"

"Okay."

"Okay?"

"Okay."

Two months later they got married.

They were happy, then they were sad, then they were happy again. This went on for many years. They never had children. But they worked hard to create something special together. They achieved that. And then they lost it.

———————

—2018

I suppose it's cliché to focus on endings, pick that one sharp moment from a deck full of moments and make it signify. But it's irresistible. In one of their last instants together, I saw Koop gazing at the lit down on her cheek again with the same wonder and awe he had on his face when he described their first visit to that awful green hallway. The hard light from the bar window bounced off the white accordion somebody had left sitting on a barstool; it lit up the silver wings on her epaulets and her face. Though it was a cheek he had known for decades, it was like he had never seen it before, as if it was an illusion, a trick of light only visible under rare and precious circumstances. When we lose someone, someone we have known as deeply as a lover, we are left with an unsolvable mystery. I bet he wondered: Have I ever really known her?

You want to know the weird thing? When Koop was telling me this ridiculous story? You know what I did not think? I did not think for a second: my old buddy Koop is insane.

I believed every single word.

A PLAUSIBLE ALTERNATIVE SCENARIO—1957

"'Stage a crash?'"

"Yes. You heard me correctly."

"General?"

"I want you to stage a crash."

"Sir?"

"Is this confusing to you, Colonel?"

"Where, sir?"

"I'm thinking Nevada."

"What will we use?"

"Use a prototype."

"They don't fly."

"They don't have to fly. They just have to crash."

"Sir. May I ask why?"

"People are getting curious. We need to put out a plausible alternative scenario. Get it in the papers. Let them go a little cuckoo. They'll talk about it for years."

"Sir, who will pilot?"

"Pick three."

"Any three?"

"Sure."

"Criteria?"

"You've got hundreds, right? Pick a few of the particularly annoying ones."

"That shouldn't be hard."

"Stage the crash. Get a nearby army base to collect the remains. And retrieve the prototype."

"Got it."

"This next part is important, so pay attention. Emphasize the secrecy of the project to everyone you can. Tell every commander. Tell everyone on the scene. Make sure every GI is briefed."

"That's clever. That'll spread it like wildfire."

The general smiled. "And make sure to inadvertently notify a few random civilians."

"Yes, sir. Stage the crash. Notify the army. Collect the remains and the prototype and widely demand secrecy. What about the press?"

"Brief a local commander. Tell him 'High-Altitude Pilot Suit Testing. Test Dummies'"

"Sir? If I may?"

"Go ahead."

"This plan sounds . . . familiar."

"You mean: Roswell?"

"I was told that was on the 'Do Not Say' list."

"Colonel. Are you telling me to shuttup?"

"No sir! I would not dream of it."

"I am aware of the similarities."

"Yes, sir."

"Roswell was my baby."

"I did not know that, sir."

"It worked for the dummies; it'll work for the cats."

"Yes, sir."

—1958

"General?"

"Yes, Colonel?"

"I'm calling to report."

"Go ahead."

"Ninety-eight percent success, sir. Perfect crash, retrieval of the craft, most of the crew, site cleared of debris, secrecy command well spread, civilians given glimpses, barracks chattering about UFOs, and our 'High Altitude Pilot Suit Test' scenario is very well covered."

"That sounds like a job well done, Colonel."

"Thank you, sir."

"But I do have one question."

"Sir?"

"Ninety-eight percent?"

"Yes, sir."

"Can I assume the 2 percent failure had something to do with the crew?"

"That is a safe assumption, sir."

"Please brief me, Colonel."

"Sir. The crew, though expected to perish in the crash, did not."

"They did not?"

"They did not."

"They survived?"

"They did."

"Can't have been a very big crash then."

"Oh, no, sir—it was very loud, very intense. The explosion was heard a mile away."

"Hmm. Sounds like survival would be highly unlikely."

"Indeed, sir. But it seems that, unbeknownst to the prep team, the pilots, uh, somehow, uh, enhanced their protection systems, increased tolerances, added padding, etc."

"You don't say?"

"I'm afraid so, sir."

"Forgive me, Colonel, but that would indicate that they had some pre-knowledge of the intention of the mission."

"We are exploring that possibility, sir."

"So they survived."

"They did, sir. One was pretty badly banged up, but we managed to get him triaged and back to base, where we expect him to make a pretty complete recovery."

"Pretty complete. Hmm. And the other two?"

"At large, sir."

"Really?"

"Yes, sir. But . . . uh, we've got our best people working on their retrieval."

"I would hope so. Then I can assume everything else worked?"

"Pretty spectacularly, I'd say, sir. It was a great plan."

"But we have two at large."

"That's about the size of it."

"Anything else I should know?"

"Our science guys insist that you be briefed about something."

"And what is that?"

"The two escapees are two of the most critical, well, I guess you'd call them, engineers, or maybe . . . scientists?"

"A Navigator?"

"I was specifically told not to use that word, sir."

"You lost a Navigator?"

"Apparently. And also . . . uh . . ."

"Not a Soldier?"

"I'm afraid so, sir."

"You've lost a Navigator and a Soldier?"

"Apparently. And it seems they are responsible for the bulk of the, uh, raw insight we've, uh, gathered on our RAM tech."

"The stealth insight."

"I was told not to use that word, sir."

"The Twins? You've lost the fucking Twins!!? How the fuck is that possible!? I told you to pick anybody!"

"We did, sir. We did indeed, but it seems there was a, well, substitution, at the last moment, and nobody caught it because, well, as you know, they all look the same."

"Christ."

"Yes, sir."

"And the third one? The injured one?"

"Yes, I must say, that was a surprise, too, sir. He is their, well, umm, I suppose you would call him . . ."

"Their Head."

"Yes, sir."

"Their Pope," said the general.

"Yes, sir."

"We almost lost their Pope."

"No, he's quite secure, sir. I promise you. Though badly injured, and in intensive care. Our best doctor is on it."

"Colonel?"

"Sir."

"The next person you debrief on this operation, you will refrain from using the figure 98 percent. Is that clear?"

"Yes, sir."

"And you are relieved of your command. I want you off this base in three hours."

—2018

For the longest time I frowned. Finally, I said: "There was a hole somewhere?"

Koop nodded.

"That made some creatures appear?"

"Yup."

"And it was so secret that they had to pretend it was UFOs and aliens."

"Yup."

"That makes zero sense."

"I know."

"What did you have to do with it?" I asked.

"Well. Let me give you an example. My last case."

THE JELLYFISH MAN—2016

The two strangers toasted by clanking their longnecks together. And giggling.

"Come on now," Koop coaxed, taking a sip and leaning back on the couch where he would spend the night. "You promised. The strangest thing that ever happened to you."

The little man who had invited him home from the bar giggled again. "All right, all right. I remember the wind was up that night and buffeting the pines—sounded like a giant blowing out candles in the night. The door creaked from the gusts."

"It happened suddenly. I was looking at my bare arm as I sat eating lime nachos and watching TV. I thought: Is that *my* arm? What do I use it for? I mean it was like I had grown a new appendage or something, like I had never noticed it was attached to my body at the shoulder. So I flexed my hand and curled my fingers in and out and it was like watching a creature in an aquarium. An octopus?

"Then I realized it was someone else trying on my arm so to speak. Someone who had never had an arm. I know that sounds ridiculous, but I don't know how else to describe it."

"So I went to bed. Decided I needed to check out. Relax. So I'm in my pj's and I'm looking at my CPAP machine on the night table. I have sleep apnea and it has been a real godsend: to be able to get a full night of restful deep sleep after years of insomnia."

The man paused like he was looking into a dark cave and wasn't sure he wanted to step in any farther.

"Go on," Koop said.

"My CPAP looked different somehow. The tangle of gray head-gear straps that fit around my skull. The clear plastic triangle—I guess you could call it a snorkel—it snuggles over my nose and mouth like a scuba diver's. The clear plastic tube with white ribbing all the way down to where it coils into the back of the black plastic box which powers the unit and forces the constant stream of air into the tube, which regulates my breathing."

"I've seen the apparatus," Koop said.

"Okay. Hear me out. I looked at the three components. The mask. The straps. The tube. And I saw a creature. Or I imagined it was a creature. Or it seemed perfectly natural that this rather odd conglomeration of medical equipment was modeled after a creature. That existed. That thrived. That was, in fact, perfectly evolved to do just that: thrive."

"I immediately thought of a jellyfish. This transparent dome pulsing and 'breathing.' The various tendrils writhing to search for food, sustenance, or to provide, if necessary, a stinging defense. And the longer filigree, or strings from a band of balloons, or perhaps, tails adjusting the creature's locomotion through the water, steering it like a keel against the currents."

"And then I had the strangest memory."

"It was a very clear, very early memory from my childhood. Lying in my crib, and gazing up at the moonlight that dappled the blue ceiling of my bedroom. A shadow appeared there, a transparent shadow. It seemed to undulate though the air. Then I saw it was three shadows dancing around each other. One was a snake. One was a bowl. And one was a cube.

"Then they came together. The bowl spun and rested on the cube. Then the snake plugged itself into the bottom of the cube."

The man covered his mouth with one hand. When he pulled it away, he said, "Then something kissed me. Full on the mouth. It was soothing and warm."

He looked puzzled at the stranger on his couch. "Why am I even telling you this?"

"You needed to talk," said Koop.

"Yeah. I guess I did. To get it off my chest."

"Exactly."

"But . . ."

"But what?"

"But. Why am I telling *you*? I. Don't even know you."

"Sure you do. I'm the guy from the bar."

"Yeah, I know. I just."

"Look," Koop said, standing up to stretch. "This is the most natural thing in the world. You meet a stranger. You feel a certain connection."

"Okay. Sure."

"And I have a very trustworthy face."

"You do. But that's not . . ."

"Not what?"

"That doesn't explain why I'm telling you the most . . ."

Koop held out a hand to silence the man. "Look," he said. "It doesn't matter. People think they choose who they trust. Who they're open to."

"We don't?" the little man asked.

"No," Koop said. "Trust is involuntary. As is memory."

The next morning the jellyfish man would have no memory of his visitor from the night before. At best he would retain a gnawing sense of vacancy. A tall black silhouette of a mysterious man who took with him the lifelong haunting of another visitor. And the half-remembered whisper of a kiss.

THE COLLECTOR—2018

"So," I said. "You collect weird stories?"

Koop said, "I specialized in memory loss. That name you just can't remember. That brand of cereal you used to eat as a child—they don't even make it anymore. The first girl you ever kissed. Your great uncle who used to pull quarters out of your ear."

"Uncle Josh."

"That was my uncle."

"I know, you told me about him. Played with the Harlem Globetrotters."

"No! He played with the Washington Generals."

"Oh, he played with the designated losers."

"Shuttup. They won sometimes."

"When they let you."

Koop scowled. "Can I finish?'

"Sorry."

"Where was I?"

"Memory."

"Right. Your Grannie telling you the secret of her cherry pie as you sat on her lap. You'll never forget the smell of her: baby powder, flour, and ripe cherries. But to this day you cannot recall the simple name of the spice she claimed made her pie 'a little slice of heaven here on earth.'

"See, a memory is a duplicate. A copy of the original. A flawed copy to begin with since it is captured from your own limited perspective. A memory has to make its way into your mind like a movie star entering a stadium, squirming through a crowd of fans and paparazzi.

"It's a journey. By the time it becomes a memory, it has fought a million distractions just to leave an imprint. We take it for granted. But the truth is, if you consider the obstacle course it has to endure, it's sort of a miracle anything becomes a memory. Most of our memories are like lines on a page in a small book in a gigantic library of works nobody will ever visit.

"And this precious little memory will stay for weeks, months, perhaps even years in the back of your mind. And then one day—poof. It disappears. We say it's been erased, displaced by, well, more important stuff—the mob of memories competing for our attention. But these are metaphors. The truth is we do not know what happens when we accept a memory, store a memory, or lose a memory. It is a complete mystery.

"It's been my life's work to study memory.

"And I have failed. Utterly."

He tapped a finger against his curly gray hair.

"This sacred library, this treasure chest of all of human consciousness, that *we all take for granted*—it's a black box.

"We comfort ourselves with metaphors of security. We imagine a Fort Knox. An impenetrable stronghold.

"Quick. Who was your best friend in college?"

"You were," I said.

"Fuck. Okay. Remember the girl you had a crush on in fourth grade?"

"Yes."

"Quote one thing she said to you. What color were her eyes?"

I laughed. "I forget."

He smiled. "Me, too. We all do. We are the forgetters. But."

And here is where my world really changed. That one word. "But." I seem to recall driving by a gray farm, all the roofs covered in snow, a dark barn where cows huddled together in a circle, their frozen snorts tooting up into the air like a strange circus calliope.

But.

"What if someone could control the process of forgetting? What if say—oh—a creature developed a way to naturally attain forgettability as a survival tactic? The way a chameleon achieves invisibility by blending?"

"You've . . . met such a creature?"

He nodded.

"You know him?"

He stared at his feet and nodded.

"That was your job?"

He nodded.

"Forgettability as camouflage?" I asked. "That's a thing?"

"Yeah. You could stand beside this creature on a subway and they would be just as invisible as everyone else on the commute—only more so. They would leave no footprints on the sand of your memory."

On the drive home I tried and failed to imagine it. I ended up staring at Koop's fat white mug squatting on my coffee table.

Koop picked up where he left off.

"You might stare right at them and never see them. You could be looking at them right now. And you'd say: 'That's a tree, a lamppost, a trash can, a squirrel.' Whatever would be the most forgettable to you."

"Hold on. What about security cams? Hell, everybody's got a video camera on their phone."

"Good point. There must be tons of CC footage of these invisible creatures."

"Got to be. You can't hide that kind of stuff."

"Can't you? You are forgetting"—he smiled at that—"something critical. Every video needs an audience. The cameraman has to point at something that interests him. He's not gonna shoot a bush."

"But that's my point! Even if he shoots something unintentionally it will still be captured!" Boy, was I proud of myself. It's not every day that you checkmate Winston Koop.

"There are always two audiences," he said. "The shooter and the watcher. Where does memory happen? Inside or outside of us?"

"Inside."

"Right. We could look right at this—let's call it a creature—and we still would not see it. In fact, everybody has seen it, or them, many times. All of us forget."

"How is that possible?"

"I don't know. And I studied it for years."

"We can't see them?"

"No, we do see them. We see them all the time! We can't *remember* them. Their skin gives off a hiding scent. If we see them, they're gone. If we smell them, they're erased. Even if you could somehow penetrate this cloud of forgetting, you would only see a blank slate, something so amazing you would deny it. You couldn't find a place in your mind to put it. Which is easier? To forget? Or to wrangle with a mystery? To deal with discomfort, or puzzlement. Or—honestly?—horror."

"Horror?" I asked.

"Yes! Why, that hand has no fingerprints! That face has no color. Christ. It doesn't even have a mouth!"

We had finished our coffee. But his story was just getting started.

"You begin your life thinking that the world is knowable. That all you need to do is diligently gather the evidence and, someday, it'll add up. But what if it never does? What if it just gets weirder and weirder?

"My job didn't have a title. I was a collector. I collected stories the way an anthropologist collects myths. But my real job was to erase these stories. To make sure they never got out."

"Why?" I asked.

He smiled. "That's another story."

WHAT CAME OUT—1958

The base recorded a perfect safety record until they lost a medical officer named Sandy.

She was the first casualty. Human casualty.

One day her assistant asked her, "Hey, you wanna see something really strange?"

"Lloyd. If this is another one of your crackpot theories."

"Just watch."

He played her the film of him cleaning the body. "Watch."

"So it's a body. So what?"

"No. Watch. Right . . . there!" And he pointed at the reflection in the observation window on the screen. Something you might have missed if you were watching the corpse.

"It closed," she said.

"It closed."

"Why did it close?"

"I'll run it again. This time with sound."

This time you could hear Lloyd singing in his distracted way, an annoying habit that anyone who worked with him for any length of time got used to. His repetitious singsong. He'd latch onto a melodic fragment, or nonsense lyric, and sing it over and over until someone said, "Lloyd!" And he'd smirk and stop.

"What are you singing?" she asked.

"Just one of their phrases."

"Which one?"

"'Waking we are gone like dreams.'"

"That sounds familiar."

"I know. Something about the rhythm."

"Something about dreams."

"It's a musical phrase. Seven beats."

"'Waking we are gone like dreams.'"

The next day they met in cold storage. And repeated the phrase again with another body. The phrase worked like a charm. Like a muscle reflex responding to stimuli. Very strange specific stimuli.

"Does it work on the living?" she asked.

"You mean does it strangle them?"

"Jesus! No! I didn't mean that!"

"Seems like it could."

"Don't get any ideas, Lloyd." She figured this was his way of flirting. He liked to creep her out. Some guys are like that—even to their bosses. You know, like taking a girl to the carnival and getting her on the roller coaster?

The next day he had to show her something.

"Watch this. Watch."

"It opens, too!"

"Like a verbal key."

"Have you tried other phrases?"

"We've tried all of them."

"And?"

"Well. The ones that have an effect are all similar. Same rhythm. Like poetry. But one of them does something even weirder." He gave her that goofy smile.

"Show me."

He said the phrase and she screamed when the body split into three parts.

A week later Sandy was singing to herself as she was running tests and checking readings by the janitor closet, going over the hypnotic phrases one by one, when she saw an unusual spike on one of the gauges. Then she heard an odd, distant noise like the plumbing pipes had cracked again. She was going for maintenance when a deep, rumbling roar shook the green walls around her. She started to run and was a hundred yards away when the white snout appeared in the green door.

A bleached albino head with glistening skin. A slit of a mouth that seemed to grow and grow as more and more of it squirmed through the door and finally broke the wooden frame into splinters. That was enough for most of the soldiers, who turned and dashed. The few left fired weapons, and black pocks appeared where the bullets pierced the white flesh. These closed quickly. There were no exit wounds.

It was all head, mouth, and neck. No arms, no legs, no wings. It thrashed back and forth, cracking all the green walls and dislodging many of the white floor tiles, but it never revealed the end of itself.

It seemed the snake went on forever.

That was horrible enough until the long slit grin puckered and corkscrewed open to reveal a dark mouth—a gaping toothless swirling maw that swallowed Sandy whole.

Next a dozen soldiers were lost. The snake swallowed them three at a time.

The white body slithered over puddles of blood until one iron gate slammed down on Z-wing and for the moment the snake was contained.

Gas was pumped into the hall. It slept, emitting deep purrs that echoed in the passages surrounding it. Then it woke and ate two approaching soldiers in hazmat suits.

Flamethrowers did nothing to it—the white skin steamed and sweated away the fire. And it ate the soldiers wielding it.

The security cameras revealed rooms crammed with terrified IFs, cowering in the corners in groups of three.

Later everyone remarked on the noises they made. After years of thorough examination, they were shocked to discover the IFs had a whole new range of vocal expressions.

Finally, the leader of the IFs, who was still recovering from the injuries he had incurred during his failed escape, volunteered to talk to the creature.

"I speak its language."

All eyes were on the monitors as the little white man was slowly pushed in his wheelchair by The Man in The Blue Suit through the wreck of Z-Ward. (For the creature had managed to penetrate around the iron barrier and tunnel its way through the limestone behind the walls. It had taken its time destroying a lab while sampling the many different liquids and mixtures stored there. It seemed to have a preference for glass.)

What a comfort to behold the two figures as they made their way into No Man's Land. It reminded some of an offering of a white flag of surrender. The little one's peaceful demeanor and his gentle roll toward the cordoned-off area and the terror of the beast were almost sane.

Nobody remembered when they had started calling him "The Pope." He was said to be the wisest of all the IFs; he was certainly the oldest.

His mystery was perpetuated by the peculiar organization of the base. Very little information was shared between specialized departments. Rumors were rampant. And every lab had its own bailiwick and its own theory as to what the larger purpose of the base was. To some the IFs were aliens. To others they were an underwater race. Still others assumed they grew up in caves like many albino species—in total darkness. Few knew what they were. And everyone who met "The Pope" had a different idea about him. It was rumored he spoke the oldest language, so ancient and original it had no branches of descent in extant earthly tongues. In any case, only one man was able to understand him. The Man in the Blue Suit. The man who crossed all lines. The man who reported to no one.

As The Pope was rolled down the broken corridors toward the dragon's mouth, his small body seemed to flow behind him like a priest's white vestments. Before the last door The Blue Man leaned down to speak to him, and, for a moment, it looked like the tall man was adjusting his white robes, prepping him for his entrance—a gesture of respect any altar boy might give a priest before Mass. Finally, The Pope proceeded without him.

When the snake heard someone coming, it snorted and roused and uncoiled its resting body, which still extended through the tunnel it had made—all the way back to the hallway door where it had emerged.

When it saw the little man, it quickly slithered down the hallway to meet him, then reared as high as the ceiling allowed, and dilated open its mouth.

The Pope said seven words. Only The Blue Man heard them.

The monster froze, then mewled. The mouth closed. The huge white head drifted down until it rested before The Pope, who laid a small wing across the fierce snout and stroked it gently.

He whispered something. And then the snake withdrew, slowly at first, then quicker and quicker like a rewinding hose, until it disappeared into the closet.

There was a long grievous moan.

And then silence.

When asked hours later what magic words The Pope had used for the snake, The Blue Man said, "He called it 'Sister Tail.' And told her to go back to sleep now."

—2018

"Now I'm really confused."

"Just wait," said Koop. "I'm just getting started."

THE TWO AGREEMENTS—1958 AND 1973

—1958

The Holy One, as they called him in formal settings, was brought into the conference room shackled to a white wheelchair pushed by the tall Man in The Blue Suit. Six armed guards stood around him. He was rolled to the head of a long table. On one side sat the military chiefs, on the other sat the leadership of the base: scientists, engineers, and doctors.

One small man in a black suit led the meeting. His glasses were thick and his voice was high. Though not an imposing figure, it was soon obvious that everyone in the room deferred to him, and that he commanded the proceedings with deftness. Yes, a lawyer.

As he began to speak, the giant of a man in the blue suit knelt beside The Holy One in the white wheelchair, leaned close to his head cupwhich tottered like a stubby mushroom on a delicate stalk, and made ready to translate.

The little man in the black suit first bowed, then began. "Let me start the proceedings by assuring you that we come to this meeting in good faith. We are told you want official recognition that you are the appointed leader of your people."

The Holy One's eyes lit up like polished obsidian. "I want what any of us wants," he replied in the voice of the blue-suited man. "I want to be remembered."

"We understand. We wish to honor you with the title 'IF Most

High,' and the honorific 'Your Holiness.' An official status unique to your kind. And you will be due all the esteem that title implies. You will have a permanent, comfortable residence, separate from the others."

"I acknowledge your offer. I appreciate the respect it implies. I admit it is tempting. But I sense it is not without . . . conditions."

"You are, as always, most perceptive. Your Holiness, knowing full well how revered you are by your flock, we request you set a good example. Our operation here is extremely complex. We need order to do our work. We need you to tell your people to comply."

The Blue Man listened, nodded, and spoke. "I understand your need to restore order after such a catastrophe. But I would be a poor leader to my people if I did not seek to improve their lot. What can I offer them in return for their cooperation?"

"We propose to make you the keeper of the most unique place on earth. We wish you to take command of The Door."

This seemed to surprise the little white man. "You do?"

"Yes. And, as a sign of good faith, we will allow you to you pick a dozen of your people a year to release."

"A dozen."

"Yes. From this day forward you are The Doorman. None shall enter and none shall leave without your permission. The post is permanent. And all we ask is that you will encourage your people to share their gifts with us. Allow us the privilege of continuing to learn from you. And that you control the dangerous creature who has entered our world."

"So. Your protection for my comfort and their slavery?"

"Your Holiness. These are words we can debate. But one thing is not debatable. This offer is better than anything your people have right now. You will be a Great Leader. You will have all the benefits and freedom that role reasonably entails."

"And in return, you continue your experiments."

"Yes."

"They cause us pain."

The lawyer sighed. "What can we do? This technology is precious—essential to our defense. This is a dangerous world. We have the right to protect ourselves."

The room could sense the impasse, and hard stares were passed across the long table. This was the rub. The Man in The Blue Suit whispered to The Holy One. The creature tilted his head. The Blue Man translated.

The Blue Man said, "Televisions. We want lots of televisions."

The group worked hard to keep their faces still.

"Done," the lawyer said.

—1973

Fifteen years later, the scene was much the same. The differences were that Koop was The Blue Man and The Pope required no wheelchair, and there was a female seated at the table on the military side.

The small lawyer in the black suit was older but still in charge.

The Pope began speaking through Koop. "I have requested this meeting in good faith. My people have been cooperative lo these many years. We have maintained order at the base. Disruptions have been kept at a minimum. Your experiments have not been inhibited in any way."

There was some grumbling from the generals, but everyone knew this was true.

"I would like to demand an adjustment to our agreement."

The oldest general stood up, red-faced. The golden stars on his shoulders were quivering. "You are in no position to make demands! Your surrender was unconditional. My troops suffered heavy—"

The small lawyer held up both his hands. "General, please."

"This is unconscionable!"

"General, I know your feelings are strong on this matter. But we have agreed to let me and me alone be our spokesman."

The whole room heard The Blue Man whisper, "Senile asshole."

The Pope nodded.

The old general sat down.

The lawyer wiped his mouth with a handkerchief, folded it, and tucked it back into the breast pocket of his suit. "Your Holiness, you spoke of adjustments?"

The Blue Man addressed the room. "First: once a year you will allow me to speak to your Pharaoh."

The room burst into chatter. "For what purpose?"

"To try to convince him to let all my people go."

The room filled with muttered objections.

"Once a year?" The lawyer repeated.

"Yes."

"This will require significant safeguards."

"Of course."

"Your snake will not be present."

"Of course not."

"You do realize our president cannot be compelled to attend."

"I understand. One of us has free will."

"All right. We will ask."

A few generals crossed their arms and grunted.

The Blue Man seemed to check with The Pope then, and counted out a figure with his thumb, index, and middle finger. The little man grew very still, then closed his eyes (it was as if his white cup head had never even had eyes—they disappeared). It was startling when he opened them again and bowed his head as if he were receiving some sad news. After a moment, he nodded.

"The second: you have allowed me to release twelve of my people every year. I want to expand that figure to three hundred."

"One hundred."

"Two hundred."

"One hundred. I am afraid that is our final offer."

The Pope covered both his large eyes with one wing, then drew it away and looked pleadingly at the ceiling, then shrugged his shoulders—a body gesture he was clearly unused to, for the effect was more comical than he'd intended.

The Blue Man cleared his throat. "Agreed."

A few scientists nodded at each other, acknowledging that, mathematically at least, they had won that round.

The Pope and Koop seemed to have a silent argument then. Heads were tilted, gestures were made.

Koop finally said, "Fine. Color televisions."

The man in the black suit seemed surprised. "Certainly, we can do that."

Koop glared at The Pope, then said to the room, "My last condition. No more killing."

The stillness that settled around the table reminded some of courtrooms when the charge is read; others recalled memories of police gumballs flashing in their rearview mirrors. A few recalled an angry parent hovering over them, asking a question they could not answer.

"Your Holiness?"

"You may experiment as much as you like. You may use your science to extract what you can. Question. Examine. Record. We will cooperate. But no more killing."

"Your Holiness. You understand your species is a . . . very fragile one. Can we be held responsible for every accident that occurs in the lab?"

"No more accidents. No more killing."

The generals consulted one another. The scientists, engineers, and doctors consulted one another. Their leaders at the head of the table both nodded to the little lawyer.

"We can agree to this."

"I should like to meet your Pharaoh as soon as possible. What is his name?"

"Richard Nixon."

The Pope looked up amazed at The Man in The Blue Suit, who, deadpan, translated, "That Dick?"

THE FIRST PRESIDENT TO VISIT—1976

The Peanut Farmer smiled painfully at the marshmallow sitting opposite him in the wicker chair and the tall man in the blue suit standing beside it. He tried to reassure himself that in most respects it was an ordinary marshmallow. True, a gigantic marshmallow—as big as a footstool, in fact. And, true, it talked. But, otherwise, yes, a perfectly ordinary talking marshmallow. All he could do was smile.

On cue, The President reached into the pocket of his off-the-rack pale blue suit coat and pulled out a hard-boiled egg. The four Secret Service agents behind him stood at attention.

He set the egg down on the white round table. And looked at it as if he'd never seen it before. Then he frowned and bit his upper lip.

The marshmallow said, "That's perfect. Thank you, Mr. President. This won't take but a minute."

"Y'all won't mind if I read?"

Koop leaned forward and said, "No, sir. You go right ahead."

The President nodded and seemed to struggle with an unpleasant indecent thought. As a Sunday School teacher, he was accustomed to such fleeting interior wickedness arriving at the most inappropriate moments. A familiar battle. He chuckled mildly and proceeded to pull out the immense family Bible that had always had a place of honor in their household growing up. He laid the heavy volume down upon the white table—which had seemed as featureless as polished ivory when he first entered the white room but, on closer inspection, appeared to be as intricate and beautiful as the polished tusk of a narwhale, like spun taffy, oozing between white and canary and other colors his careful engineer's mind could not describe.

It seemed to him then that he was looking at something impossible. But that, too, was familiar. He had stood watch on the deck of many subs. He was an avid follower of the night sky. He had witnessed the unspeakable ravishing beauty of the stars, the multitude of glory God had seeded across the heavens with a fling of his mighty hand. And he had also witnessed such strangeness that has often visited this tiny green world from God knows where for God knows why. He would never speak of those odd visitations. Not even to his beloved wife. Though he felt obliged to join the throng (as it were) in his early political career and confess to the most mundane of his encounters. God knows my heart, he thought. I am not a perfect man. We all have secrets. But I am a patriot. If my office dictates that I must protect the security of this union with my silence then so be it. God and this marshmallow are witnesses. Though I cannot disclose my full knowledge, I can be trusted to keep my oath of office so help me God. He was reading from Job when he heard The Blue Man say, "Mr. President?"

He looked up and found himself holding a hard-boiled egg in his right hand. He looked behind him and handed it back to one of his Secret Service agents.

The tall young man in the blue suit bowed and said, "Thank you for coming, sir."

The President smiled painfully and rose.

"Don't forget your Bible," said the marshmallow.

—2018

I tried to begin a sentence. Actually I tried several times. And each time I tried, I failed. The words stopped before they left my mouth.

They were either way too stupid, or too obvious. I was still trying to pull my world back into orbit.

"So you've met a president?"

We both laughed a bit at that.

Koop was tracing circles on his frosted-up passenger window. "I've met all the living ones."

THE TELEPATHIST—1982

"I don't know where to start," the man said. His eyes looked like he hadn't slept in days.

"Start anywhere," said Koop.

"Nice rose."

"Thanks."

"I forget what white symbolizes."

"Me, too."

"So . . . I love my wife, but she's got a big mouth."

"Okay."

"I mean every day she's on the phone with her sister in Omaha. Rehashing their lives. And pretty soon her voice, I mean she's practically yelling on the phone. And I wonder sometimes what the neighbors think."

"She's loud."

"Real loud. But only when she's on the phone. She'll be talking along and suddenly she's saying something I'd rather she didn't, something about our checkbook or finances or something private."

"You talk about this with her?"

"Sure. I mean, no. I'm going to. Someday. If it's allowed. I'm afraid it might hurt her feelings."

"But you trust her."

"Oh, sure, of course. I do. It's just . . ."

"You're afraid something might slip out."

"Yes."

"Something about your work."

"Yes."

"Well, technically speaking, if she's betrayed any government secrets she could be punished severely."

"She could?"

"Of course."

"How severely?" The prospect seemed to hold some appeal.

"She could lose her freedom permanently."

"What about me?"

"You would be subject to very strict penalties if you did anything illegal."

"Mr. Koop—I don't see how it could be illegal. I mean, it's not even our species."

"We're getting to the part that you can't tell your wife about, right?"

"Hell, I can't tell my boss about it."

"He doesn't know?"

"She. That's how it works sometimes. The higher-ups have a lower clearance than us so they can't upload any intelligence when they report monthly to their superiors. We sort of spare them the scoop."

"That's peculiar."

"It's actually not unusual at all. It's a great way to keep the superstructure invisible to civilians. See, most bosses are in temporary positions and shuffled around a lot. Political appointments, you know."

"Really?"

"Sure. New administration, new chiefs. Like ambassadors. They attend ceremonies, have parties, shuffle paper. Put on a show. While the grunts and subs like us do the work. It's government. It's not the real world."

"I'm just thinking."

"What?"

"With an invisible superstructure like that, there would be no accounting. No oversight. No real watchdog capability in any

branch of government. You and your whole organization would be
. . . impervious. You could write your own ticket."

"Well, more or less. But, honestly? The supes don't really care as
long as we deliver."

"Deliver?"

"The intel. The tech. And they understand it helps move things
along if we don't have all that bureaucracy and paperwork. We'd
never get anything done if they had to authorize everything. We
never would have collected IFs."

"Okay. Now we're getting to it."

"I guess you don't want to talk about the org chart anymore?"

"No. You covered that pretty thoroughly. IFs?"

"I can't believe I'm finally gonna talk this out with someone
who's not an AI therapist! Shew! They only go so far and then they
loop back into stupid phony empathy questions."

"You're feeling relieved now?"

"Yes."

"Go on."

"I've been here years. I've maxed all my training. I've gotten full
marks on every level."

"You're saying you're a pro."

"I'm incredibly competent at what I do. I'm one of maybe two
people on the planet who can do it."

"Okay."

"I can't do it anymore."

"Okay."

"I really can't."

"Okay. Relax now. You want a tissue?"

"No, thanks. I'm just. I'm stuck. I don't . . . I can't . . . There's no
place for me to transfer to."

"Linguistics, right?"

"Sort of."

"Sort of?"

"I taught one of them English. And I've helped to write a glossary of the language of a species who cannot talk and don't want to tell us anything."

"Wow. How did you do that?"

"I'm a telepathist."

"Okay. You . . . read thoughts?"

"Yes."

"How did that happen?"

"They taught me."

"The . . ."

"IFs. But, unlike them, I can only receive, not send."

"Why did they teach you?"

"They were trying to be helpful."

"Telepathy. Thought-reading."

"Yes?"

"Can you read mine?"

"Sure. 'This is one loco motherfucker. Why don't they give him a prescription? Jesus.'"

"Jesus."

"Take a moment. Go ahead. I know it's not something you see every day."

"Jesus Christ."

"Like I said, there's only two of us."

"Holy God."

"You know you don't have to verbalize your questions anymore. You can just . . . yes, think them."

"You know, actually, I think I'd prefer—"

"—to speak them aloud. So do most people."

"I forget what we were talking about."

"Me."

"Yes. Yeah. Good. Please. Go on."

"So me and my partner Lloyd finished the glossary. And it only took thirty IFs to do it."

"Took you thirty?"

"I mean we only had to kill thirty of them to get it done."

"W-w-w-why would you have to kill them?"

"They . . . resist. In their language 'mind words' are sacred. Our job was the equivalent of—well, I guess you'd call it 'mind rape.' It's a humiliating experience for them."

"I imagine."

"It is a big violation. To them? Thought is a graceful exchange of emotion and data. A dance, really. They share knowledge blissfully. When it's forced from them? They feel horror, degraded. They feel they've betrayed the sacred trust of their race. It's a wretched state and they can't stay in it for too long. They're a very sensitive race. Too much pressure and they pop like popcorn."

"Pop?"

"You're thinking 'murdered.' You don't have to spare me your thoughts, Mr. Koop. Anyway, you can't."

"You popped thirty of them?"

"Give or take."

"How long did it take?"

"Altogether? Fifteen years."

"Was it worth it?"

"I don't know. Fifteen years of overtime, six to seven days a week. Total secrecy. My wife thinks I'm a schmuck. The way she talks about me. Worth it? I don't know. We've created a new denticle armor plating that resembles their fur. We've mastered cloaking—what we call RAM."

"Ram?"

"Radar Absorbing Material. Give us some more time and we'll make any propeller silent. Hell, we could triple the efficiency of any wind turbine with a coat of denticle paint. But Big Oil will never let that happen. Let's see. Oh! We've discovered a new area of the human brain which may allow us to someday will ourselves to be kind."

"That might be handy."

"Anyway—I'm burnt. So is my boss. Katey's got more energy than anyone and even she wanted to throw the damn glossary in the trash."

"We know all about that."

"Don't blame her—the job grinds you down. Oh. You knew her, didn't you?"

"Why do you say that?"

"Your brain got . . . darker."

"Forget about that."

"Okay."

"I can see you got a lot on your mind."

"I sure do."

"Don't worry. I'm gonna fix that."

"I hope. Say, what's it like? Taking memories?"

"Not at liberty to say."

"How'd you learn that?"

"They taught me. Like you."

"Did you know they don't have waltzes? They can't hear them."

"Can't or don't?"

"You tell me. It's like there's a component missing in their brains that blocks them out."

"Maybe it's the kindness part. Do I wanna know how you learned this?"

The man started to cry. "No."

"Okay. Take it easy, bud."

"So will I, like, even remember you?"

"No."

"Oh, good. I just want it to stop."

"It will."

—2018

I asked, "So what was your job exactly, Koop?"

"I made sure the truth didn't get out. And when it did, I erased it."

"Sounds like you spared him some anguish."

"That's a generous way of putting it."

Koop was beating himself up. I call it preemptive abuse. Drunks do this sometimes. If you hurt yourself before anyone else can, you don't feel so bad. At least you feel you're in control. Like you deserve it or something. It's a cheap ploy that only works for a while. Eventually you get more adept than your abuser. Which makes him unnecessary.

Koop turned away and looked out the window. The red maple leaves quaked happily in the breeze, danced and rested, danced and rested. The air tasted awake.

"I should warn you right now, Pagnucco. After a while, you're not going to like me as much as you think you do."

THE STORIES DAD BROUGHT HOME—1985

Koop placed the white recorder before him and said, "You were going to tell me about your dad."

Growing up, my dad was never there.

Koop nodded. "Probably a lot of families like that in the fifties."

Sure. Successful career men. Mom holding down the fort. But my dad was different. I knew it.

"How?"

His stories. When he was home he told the best stories in the world. And he seemed to confirm all my daydreams about him. He was a hero. He was a spy. He had superpowers. That's how kids think. It was like he went away on these Top Secret Missions and he could never talk about them—not even with Mom.

'You never tell me anything,' she used to say. 'It's like being married to a stranger.'

"It didn't bother you?"

No! Hell, he was Dad. We knew he was an engineer. We didn't need to know anything else.

"You never asked him about his job?"

I didn't care. I was just glad to see him on those rare occasions he showed up. When he came home it was an event. The house would smell like a man again. Mom would make him his favorite dinner: meatloaf. He'd play catch with me until the sun went down. And then he'd tuck me in and tell me stories. Man, what stories.

"For instance?"

They were about crazy things. I never thought of my dad as having much imagination. But the stuff he told me—he could have written books. He could have been famous.

"Famous?"

Let me paint you a picture. A man wears a suit every day. White shirt. Shiny black shoes. Black tie which he hardly ever takes off. He sits doing the crossword puzzle, smoking his pipe. I'd show him my homework and he'd say, "You can do better, son." I knew he was some kind of engineer. But he could have been a salesman, a farmer, or a butcher. Butch haircut—did I mention that?

"No."

The straightest man you ever met. But when he tucked me in and sat at the side of my bed—he was somebody else. His voice got husky and soft. It was like he was telling the stories he was dying to tell. The stories he kept bottled up inside of him all his life. And the only place he could tell them was in my bedroom. I felt privileged. Honored even. I didn't know those words till years later, but I remember: Every story. Every night. His black pipe silhouetted against that Mickey Mantle poster on my wall. And that one lamp with the cowboy and horse on it.

I'll never forget one night, one story. It was about a magic white boy with a long tail who flew. He flew so fast no one could ever find him. One night he flew under a field of stars and he fell asleep watching them and he fell into a green ocean. He was rescued by a sailor who caught him in a net and taught him to speak the language of the pink people. He was taken to the king of the pink people and asked to tell them how to make secrets disappear, and he did. And he was asked how to make jets disappear, and he did. But when he was asked how to erase whole portions of people's brains, he refused. And when he was asked how to build an ear so big it could listen to everyone and hear even their darkest secrets, he refused. And because he refused, they put him in a white room and fed him his least favorite foods and only let him talk to one man.

The man who smoked a pipe.

Now, the man who smoked a pipe was a good man, a dedicated, honorable man. Though he did not approve of the way the boy was treated by the pink people, he had no say in the matter. So he decided to treat the boy as a friend. Perhaps then he would tell the man the secrets his bosses so wanted to know.

And, at the same time, his stay would become pleasant and less uncomfortable. So every day he greeted the boy kindly. Asked him gentle questions. But, though the boy was polite, he still refused to answer any of the important questions his bosses had put to The Pipe Man. See, it was his job to get the answers. His duty.

And after ten years, the boy said he had to leave.

And The Pipe Man said that was impossible. He was their guest.

You mean prisoner, said the boy. You taught me precision. Say what you mean.

Okay, then, said The Pipe Man. Prisoner then. But this is a nice jail, is it not? The food is good. It is comfortable and you have everything you need.

Except my freedom, said the boy who fell from the stars.

Maybe they will give you your freedom if you give them a gift, The Pipe Man said.

What gift? said the boy.

Your tail, The Pipe Man said. If you give them your tail, they will give you anything you want.

So the boy who fell from the stars gave them his tail.

And they gave him everything he wanted. Power. Gold. Food. Prestige.

"Prestige?" I asked.

"That's like fame," my dad explained.

"Like Mickey Mantle?"

"Yes."

After a long silence, I said, "Dad? They let him go, right? They couldn't just keep him like that. Against his will. Right?"

He got up from the bed and looked out the window at the moon. "They'll never let him go," my father said.

Two weeks later he was laid off and we had to move to Madison. Where he could teach.

—2018

"Koop," I said. "You talked to the son. Why didn't you talk to the dad?"

"The dad was a good soldier. He didn't deserve to be harassed." Winston saw I didn't get it. "I interviewed him on the phone. He was secure. He told me about his son. So I sealed that leak."

"Leaks. A project like the one you're talking about. The . . . scope. The intricacies. The people. How could anyone stop all the leaks?"

"Well, people retire. People die. People take settlements. Sometimes a threat is enough to get silence. Sometimes . . . a threat isn't enough."

THE ORIGINATOR—1988

Winston was jumpy so we went out for lunch. He washed down three aspirin with a tall Coke and devoured a couple of Coney dogs and a bowl of chili. That seemed to settle him down a bit. That's when I learned he could tell the most astonishing stories in public and nobody in earshot would even blink an eye. Like this:

There's an Asian man in a bar nursing a martini, stirring two olives around with his finger. His glasses are thick as the bottoms of Coca-Cola bottles. He curses at the TV. He has a New York accent.

The next night he's there, too. Same happy hour, same drink. He curses at the TV, and you notice it's a commercial. You think nothing of it. You hate commercials, too.

The next night. Okay, maybe you have a wife and you're arguing, and she doesn't understand it's your job. You have to be at that same bar. And you have a few on the nag, and sure enough the Coke Martini Man is there again and you notice he always wears a black tie. And he's cursing again. It's a mattress commercial. You know, the ones about those Swedish beds with foam that leaves the imprint of a body?

The next night you buy him a drink and he likes you lots. Sure enough, the commercial is on. And once again he says the same thing, "Motherfucking thieves."

"Who?" you ask.

"Fucking Swedes. It was our baby. And they bought it for a song."

"Bought what?"

And he looks at you. He's blitzed so he rolls his head a bit, sizing you up. You can tell he thinks he's way smarter than you. And he concludes, finally: you're harmless. "The bed stuff."

"The molding mattress?"

"Nahh, there's no mold unless there's no circulation. You gotta let it air. We solved that problem. Also flammability. Also stink. Ditto itch. It was perfect. And what do they do? Reduce it to gas into foam—the easiest part of the formula. Not the true structure. Not the miracle. They made us make La-Z-Boys for astronauts. Fuck! We could have changed the world. Could have made indestructible bunkers. Adaptable ordnance. Hell, we could have made a car that could have survived any impact and gotten five hundred miles a gallon!"

"I thought we were talking about—what do you call it—memory foam?"

He drumrolls his lips. "Memory foam. Memory foam! It was forget foam! It forgets what you do to it."

So you move to a booth and you get comfortable. And this could be his third martini or his fourth and he is holding court now. He eyes the white cigar tube in your suit pocket as if he wants to ask: Are you gonna smoke that? He grabs the cocktail napkin in his hand. "Imagine a piece of aluminum foil." He crumples it into a ball. "You squash it. Only it doesn't stay squashed. It remolds itself into its previous shape. Boing! And it's not aluminum, it just looks like aluminum." He kind of slurs that last word. "It's much stronger than that. You try to stamp it with a hammer and you can't even dent it. You burn it with a torch, it doesn't even get hot. But you apply intelligence and skin to it and it yields. God it was beautiful."

"Metal?"

"'Sponge Metal' is what we called it. But they didn't know what we had! They could only imagine making Johnny Glenn more comfy in the cockpit. They thought spongy meant soft. So they pursued soft applications. Insulation. Sealants. Space helmets. Idiots. I told them: It's not soft—it's smart. It's Zen. It bends and folds and absorbs impacts. It flows. It's ninja metal. It only looks soft. It lets its opponent wear himself out and then it smothers him." He shook his head in his hands.

I said, "They didn't buy it."

"Nahh, they wouldn't listen. My partner took it to the Swedes and got himself a corner office and a blond wife. For the last twenty years of his life he smoked those fancy cigars and looked out his office window and didn't do shit."

"But not you."

"Of course not. I was stuck. He got all the dough and the credit and I get bupkes."

"I've heard that story before. The originator never gets the credit. It's always the guy who can market it."

"Originator?" said the Coke man, smiling. "Originator!?" He gave his martini glass a swirl and examined the olives orbiting inside. "Brother, I am a genius, but I am *not* from another planet."

—2018

Everybody in the diner seemed to be in their own world. Nobody even blinked at the story this ragged tall man had just told.

"So that was my first."

"Your first?" I asked.

"Yeah, he was a blabbermouth. No way was he gonna shut up."

I saw his face. "Wait," I said.

"We walked home together singing songs."

"Wait," I said.

"Had a nightcap. He had a heart attack."

The waitress was refilling my coffee when she said, "Would you look at that. Somebody left a hatbox in the next booth! Whew! You boys leave any room for dessert?"

"I could murder a cherry pie," Winston Koop said, smiling.

And she laughed.

THE SQUARED BOX—1992

Brother, dying people say the strangest things.

"They do?" Koop said.

Oh, yes, Mister K, they do. They talk about the first boy they ever loved. An old second grade teacher who gave them a pair of dry pants when they wet themselves in the sandbox. A man they loved more than anyone who turned out to be a monster.

Sometimes they have irresistible cravings for foods they haven't touched in years. Lima beans. Tapioca. Or maybe a special tomato casserole their mom used to make them. And usually they take you into their confidence. They tell you secrets.

Hell, it's understandable. You're their last set of ears. After you it's the big silence.

Mr. L was no different than any other vets, like you, Mister K. What we call them: Last-Leggers. Downhill Racers.

"Thanks, Chester."

He smiled.

I'm just fucking with ya. Yer fine. I got whatcha call a natural instinct for folks on the down slope. Maybe they smell different, I don't know. But things tend to get real quiet in the end. Most people clear out. I don't. Dying never bothered me.

So I'm changing Mr. L—He's a thin yellow man with yellow eyes. Backed up bile. Not a good sign. And I asked him what he used to do after the war.

"Packaging," he said.

Now I've been around, but that's not a career path I was familiar with. "You mean like boxes or bags?"

He looks at me a long time and I can't read him.

"Sort of," he says. "I specialized in heavy-duty. Container transport. You know those big trailers on the highway that take up two lanes?"

"Wide load," I say.

"Yup. Wide load. That takes some planning. Some engineering. There are payload, balance, and weight issues. Safety issues. Overpass clearance. Convoy coordination. Night shipment on many of them since they'd clog up most major arteries in the daytime. It's logistical. My specialized skill set."

"Sounds like a lot of work."

"Nahh, I'd do maybe a load or two a month. Government work."

Sounded like a cushy job. I wondered if maybe I might want to try my hand in it. Maybe he'd open a door for me. I did not intend to empty bedpans forever. I was going places.

"Government?" I asked.

"Co-Shipping was the internal label. Or CoShip. Short for Covert Shipping."

He let me think about that.

I finished his diaper. Washed my hands. Scented the air and put on a fresh sheet and blanket.

"Thanks, bud," he said. Then he looked at me. "You're not curious?"

"'Bout what?" I asked.

"Co-Ship."

"Covert," I said. "You ship—what? Weapons? Aircraft?"

"Sometimes."

It's obvious he wants to tell me something, and it's only in retrospect I recall the arrogance of my youth. I was nineteen, working midnights—while I went to school part-time. I had lost my cherry when I was fifteen. I'd smoked dope. Gotten drunk. Been to a titty bar. Hell, I thought I had life down. Know what I mean? This old yellow man couldn't tell me shit. Old people. We get invisible, don't we? People forget: we're just later versions of them.

"Yer not that old, Chester."

Mister K, you could not guess my age if you tried.

I almost wrote off that old-timer. But something must have stopped me. Something in those yellow eyeballs. The only part of him that didn't look old. So he was in charge of shipping Big Secret Things. So what?

I sat on the edge of the bed. "So what else you ship?"

Mr. L smiled.

"The trick to Co-Shipping is opposites and sleight of hand. You know the way a magician gets you looking at the twirling black cane in his right hand so you don't see the pretty white dove in his other?"

"Yeah?"

"It's simple, really. A square load goes into a round container. A long load must be split in two pieces and shipped separately. Multiple loads go into soft molds to look singular. You get the principle?"

"I think so."

"So. So one day I get the specs on a job. Forty feet wide. Twenty feet deep. Forty feet long."

I thought: These old people. They just love their details. Joe Louis. Satchel Paige. The Great Depression. Christ, I was a dope.

"That's wide," I finally said.

"Yup."

"So you . . . split it."

"Can't."

"Why?"

"Let's just say you can't Solomon it."

"Well it's big. So we need a—what?—steel structure?"

He shakes his head.

"Aluminum?"

"No. Think about building a wooden slatted box. They say make a light inner frame. Make it with rubber tubes. Rubber tubes, okay?

So you do. You buy out all the hosing in every hardware store within three hundred miles. Can't order it bulk. Strange request. But they're all strange in their way. Good story. I had to ship a chunk of glacier once. In the largest refrigerator trailer in the world. But that's another story. People got fired on that. Not me. I always built in redundancies."

He's enjoying himself too much. What's so hot about a big box?

"So we ship our special case slats with the rubber hose frame in one hundred boxes to an airplane hangar somewhere where there's no shade. And I spend eight days hand-assembling this huge package into this huge forty-by-twenty-by-forty wooden box. There's one copy of the blueprint. One. Me and two other guys work twelve hours a day building it. Then once we fit it with the rubber tubes, he grabs one side and I grab the other, and we lift it into the first half of the package. Then we build the second half around it."

"Hold it. It's huge, right? But it's gotta be real light if two men can lift it."

He just nods. "Then we hoist it up and tie it down to a flat bed. Then we spend a day painting the top of the box black. The bottom beige. Then we follow the convoy. One truck (with the package). Three jeeps escort. One a mile ahead. One a mile behind. One we follow. Me and my two coworkers drive the truck.

We drive at night. We have no lights on. We drive by moonlight. We drive it fifty miles—fifty miles—to another airplane hangar on another base with even less shade than the first. We park it.

They don't even let us unwrap the box.

They give us cash right there and then. A man in a blue suit counts it into our hands. Says, "You've done your country three great services. The first was building the box. The second was transporting the box. The third is the silence you will keep for the rest of your life."

One of my team is a young guy. Ralph. A drinker and a fighter. He thinks he can cuss his way out of everything. Big kid. Terrible attitude. Obviously—never had the shit kicked out of him.

He gets mouthy with the man in the blue suit. "What? I can't even tell my wife? My kids? If I'm so damned important to my country, why do I have to keep a secret like this?" He's pointing at the big box in the middle of the hangar with the three armed MPs standing at attention.

"Shuttup, kid," I say. But he won't. He keeps going.

"This is America, bub. People got a right to know these things. Hell, my taxes paid for that box and whatever you're doing with that fucking Frisbee inside."

The man in the blue suit looks bored.

He looks at me and my partner.

Then he takes a pistol out of his belt and shoots the kid in the head. He reaches down and takes the cash out of the kid's trousers and gives us each half.

"Clean it up," the yellow man says. "Clean it up."

The old man, Chester, who had listened to the yellow man when he was young, rubbed his eyes with both hands. "Mr. Koop? Can I tell you something?"

"Sure."

"So I'm looking at this tiny yellow man curled up on the bed and suddenly I know two things like I know my own name.

"One: He's never told another soul this story. And two: I swore I never would either."

"Chester. Relax. Let me worry about that."

"Brother? Why on earth am I telling you this?"

Winston Koop said, "Your secret's safe with me, Chester. I promise."

We shook on it. The fear drained slowly out of Chester's eyes, and then he said, "What were we talking about, Mister K?"

Rudy said, "Not bad for yer first time. Yer a natural."

It took me a moment to realize: Chester couldn't hear him. Only I could.

—2018

"Koop. I gotta ask. How do you find these people?"

"Well," he said. "I can read people. Ever feel a connection to a stranger? An intuitive harmony that makes you feel like they've been on the same journey as you?"

"I felt that with you."

"Me, too. It's like that, only more specific."

Koop and I didn't have to talk about that in detail. It's why we became friends all those years ago. Children of alcoholics unconsciously recognize one another—the survivors. We retain the same codes of behavior, the same impulse to caretake our victimizer and honor the silence of the addiction. The disease creates these self-validating systems around it to protect itself from discovery and, well, healing, strangely enough.

"But also," Koop continued, "I am a collector of specific stories. And this story that I've spent my life hunting down—it has its own 'scent.' It leaves its own traces. I can tell when a person has heard a variation of the story—just by looking at them. I can sense how much detail they've gathered, how disturbed they are, by how deep an impression it's made."

"How?"

"Just by looking at them. It's like an aura that only I can see. Let's say it's a blue aura—a spectrum of blue. And only those who carry the story glow blue."

"That sounds, frankly, ridiculous."

"It does." Winston moved from the window where he had been standing and sat beside me. "Okay. Try to imagine this. A man—an ordinary man. He looks exactly like you. But his mouth," he circled his mouth with a finger, "has a bright blue ring of clown makeup around it."

I frowned. "That's how they look to you?"

"That's how everyone whose met them looks to me."

I counted his two gifts on the fingers of one hand. "So you can hunt down anyone; and you can make anyone forget?"

"Pretty much."

"Are these . . . common skills?"

"No, they're extremely rare."

"How many of you are there?"

"Just me."

"How do you deal with this?"

"Evidently, not very well."

YOU SEEN ONE DOLL—1993

They escorted The President into the white room. He had been briefed. He would be entering a totally secure room in a totally secret facility. There would be no witnesses or recordings. He was about to meet America's most important operative and their most important asset. It would be their first annual meeting. It was a formality, he was assured, that some (not all) of his predecessors had followed. His staff was given a cover story; his schedule was cleared. He had arranged a brief stopover on his campaign trip to a fundraiser in Hollywood. The First Lady had gone on before him. The President's entourage was still on the runway in Air Force One as base maintenance replaced a "faulty part."

When he and the football man first entered the white room they noticed the smells. The air was misty with the odor of chlorine—it reminded him strongly of his high school pool, and a certain lifeguard—a senior who had given him lifesaving instructions. Gloria. G-L-O-R-I-A, as the song goes. He sang the chorus.

"You like that song?" he asked the Secret Service man with the suitcase.

"Yessir."

There was a white oblong table with three chairs. On the left sat a bland, fit gentleman in a blue suit and tie. Put sunglasses on him and he could have passed for Secret Service. So: utterly forgettable.

The right side of the table was more promising. A tiny man in a clown suit with a white painted face, and big red lips and a red-striped silk onesie. Something you don't see every day. It took him a moment to come to the conclusion it was a porcelain doll. Every time he thought it moved, he'd shoot his eyes over to it: utter stillness.

"Glad you could make it, Mr. President. Here, I'll take that from you."

He handed The Blue Suit the hardboiled egg.

"Well, it's my pleasure. I am happy to comply." He smiled. It was an impressive, disarming smile. Most women, children, and many men were defeated by it. "To tell you the truth, I would be even happier if I knew what the heck I was doing here." He laughed.

"It's a rite of passage, if you will. Nixon and Carter—they both sat where you are sitting."

"You don't say?"

"I have no doubt they shared some of the same questions you have, sir."

"No doubt," he said, wryly. "And your name is . . ."

"Not important, sir."

He reached into his suit coat pocket and pulled out a rather thick cigar. "Can I smoke?"

"Of course, sir. But not here."

He waved the stogie around a little and said, "Mind if I just chew on it a bit?"

"No, sir. That's fine."

He pulled a little pout, put the cigar in the corner of his mouth, tilted his head back, and looked at the doll.

"That's our asset, is it?"

"Yes, sir."

"Precious, I'm told."

"Very."

"Yeltsin would kill for it."

"Probably, sir."

"Mind telling me what it is?"

"It's a doll, sir."

"I can see that it's a doll. I saw that the minute I came in. I'm gonna take a wild guess here and say it's no ordinary doll?"

"You could say that, sir."

"I did. I just said that. I don't need you to tell me what I just said, Mr. . . ."

"Koop."

"Mr. Koop, I may sound like some country bumpkin, but I guess I have to remind you of a few things. I am a Rhodes Scholar. I am the most powerful person in the world. And I am your boss. So if you enjoy working for me, I'm going to have to ask you, politely, to drop the motherfucking attitude and tell me why I am here."

The Man in The Blue Suit smiled. "Sir. You have no idea how much I appreciate the frankness. We get mostly the opposite. You are here to answer some critical questions and then to go on your way."

The President's eyebrows could not get any higher. "Really?"

"Yes, sir."

"What sort of questions?"

The Blue Suit fiddled with the egg, cracking its shell gently on the white table—a really fascinating process.

"What's one plus one plus one?"

The President laughed and found himself confiding in the doll. "I like this guy. This guy's got some stones."

"Next question, sir." Now The Blue Man seemed to be unpeeling the egg. "Tinker, to Evers, to Chance? Who are they?"

"Fuck if I know."

"Baseball players. A very famous combo. From yesteryear."

"Are you gonna tell me all the answers?"

"No. Who sang 'Suite: Judy Blue Eyes.'"

"Democrats." He smiled. "CSN."

"Right. What kind of harmony did they sing?"

"Barbershop harmony?"

"Indeed, sir. Exactly." The Blue Man folded his hands around the egg—as if in prayer. "In Christianity how many aspects does God have?"

"You mean: the Father, the Son, and the Holy Ghost?"

"Yes, I mean that exactly. But that's not what I asked you."

"Sure, it is."

"No, sir. I asked you 'How many?'"

"So?"

"So. How many fingers am I holding up?"

"I'm gonna hold up a finger in a second."

"Wouldn't you say there is something completely bizarre about this conversation?"

"You're telling me."

"But when we leave here—this . . . place—when you get say, one hundred and eleven paces away, if you had been capable of paying attention right now, you would note that something very peculiar had happened down here."

"Okay. What's that?"

"I can't tell you."

The President stood. Took an imaginary drag off his stogie and said, "Kids. This has been loads of fun. But I've got a plane to catch. Sir?" He shook the black man's right hand. "Clown?" He saluted him with his cigar hand. "Later."

"Don't forget your egg, sir."

He received it and was puzzled to note it had regained its perfect shell. Slowly, he passed it on to his detail.

"Have a good day, sir."

He shook his head. "It's got to be better than this."

The door to the white room opened from the outside and two guards welcomed him into the hall.

The meeting was over and the door closed.

The clown who wasn't a clown or a doll spoke first. "Much smarter than the last guy."

"Oh yes," the black man said, thinking: I still cannot believe this fucking works.

YER DARN TOOTIN' YOU GOT THE WRONG MAN—1994

Yer not smokin' no cigar in my home.

"No, ma'am," said Koop.

And do not say anything bad about this country. I will not hear it. This is an American household. An American home. And proud to be so.

That's what I tell them solicitors. Any poll takers, too. That's what you look like to me, son.

You can take that traitorous stuff down the road. This is a happy American home.

My husband there on the mantel. Yes. He was in the service. No, that's not a uniform. He was thirty years in government, thank you very much. Never you mind what branch. This is an American home.

He served proudly.

If he had to be gone for a month at a time, he did not question his duty. He went. He was a soldier.

No, none of those branches. You think the only soldiers are the ones that wear a uniform?

I never asked where he served.

If he brought home a roll of silk from Morocco, that was all I needed to know. He was thinking of me. If he had a new gun for his collection, that was fine. If he showed me what a Russian brand of cigarettes looked like, then that was where the story ended. I am an American wife. I am not a nagger.

Aliases. I don't know what you're talking about. His name was Jeremy.

I don't care what any woman says—he was my husband.

So you say he had another life. He may have had two or three for all I know. All I know is this was his home. The home of a Patriot.

No. That name means nothing to me.

No, that one neither.

Mister, let me tell you something. A woman knows a man. If a man has secrets, they are secrets for a reason. Maybe he's protecting something. Maybe he is devoted to a higher cause. Maybe he has special gifts and can't be judged like other ordinary men. Like you.

I don't know nothing about that.

Nor that.

I come from simple people. We like hard work, good food, and church—Wednesdays and Sundays. Can you say the same?

I am a widow. I have a government pension which provides fairly for me, thank you, Jesus. I do not question whether or not he deserved it. No, sir. I have all the money in the world I need and no reason to doubt.

A man of honor, no matter what you say.

Lookit. You go to that mantel there and fetch me that purple box. That's right. That was his. That's Latin.

Koop translated. "For meritorious conduct, extraordinary valor, conspicuous bravery."

That's what it says? Well, that's him all right. You can't win those suckers at the Kansas State Fair.

Yer darn tootin' you got the wrong man.

Sure I recognize him. That's Randy. He was their youngest sergeant. A translator, he said. A whiz with language. We used to have him over for chicken dinner on Sundays.

Eighteen? Eighteen? I'd say he look more like twelve. Such a pale boy. His eyes were a strange dark blue.

Well, after supper they'd usually stay up all night playing chess.

Tell ya the truth, I couldn't follow half of what they were jawing about.

I'll tell you one thing. Randy was the only one who ever beat my man at chess.

No, nothing like that. I burned everything.

Because they told me to, that's why!

I got that picture and that medal. That's all I need.

No, I do not know what happened to Randy.

He wasn't at the funeral.

No, I've not seen him. I wouldn't be surprised if he showed up one of these days and wanted me to put a plate out. He could eat like there was no tomorrow.

—2018

"Sounds like one got away," I said.

"Two got away," Koop said.

"Tell me about the other one."

THE ONE THAT GOT AWAY—1995

Winston Koop found a corner of the Dairy Queen where he and the boy could be alone. He said he wanted to read him something. It was a paperback book with a golden spaceship on the spine.

He read:

They ran.

From the sky they must have looked like a taller, paler Dorothy and a tiny Tin Man skipping through a field of corn; off to see the Wizard, looking for a home and a heart. But soon one could see they were not going somewhere; they were running from something.

The boy and the girl: he, determined, though much smaller than her, he pulled her along without great effort; she, tall and awkward and weary, still wearing the short tan dress with pink flowers, the same dress she had worn for a month, the fabric dingy and soiled with her sweat and musty with the accumulation of her odors, a fabric so thin that it had become a second skin to her, a skin that fluttered and dragged behind her as the boy (who did not look at her, would not let loose of her bony wrist, did not pause to glance back--not even for a second) ignored her pleas to slow down, to let her rest her feet, the swollen, blistered feet she had earned by pacing weeks over damp cement, so that now every step she took sent shooting pains up her legs, as if she were stepping on the random broken stems and not between them, as he pulled his burden relentlessly through the golden rotting corn.

She knew he would not pause or wait.

He dragged her on, his eyes set forward against the tall yellow rows that formed a passageway before them, like the narrow columns of a temple. He trotted on, taking four steps for every two of hers, only taking his eyes off the path to steal a brief glance at the descending sun that lay before them, that guided their escape. He knew they had to get somewhere before dark, before their scent would be caught, before their escape could be noticed, before they could be followed.

Finally, her sweaty wrist came out of his hand and she fell. Then he had no choice: He turned to watch her crumple to the ground, sobbing between the rows of corn that rose so far above his head. Half her face was printed with dirt, her stringy brown hair was full of knots and weeds and slivers of husk. He caught himself admiring her beauty.

"Get up," he said.

She hurt him with her look. As if he were the one who had snatched her, held her captive; as if he were not her hero, the one who was saving her life.

In the boy's blue eyes she saw only a cold determination to do what had to be done.

He's just like them, she thought. Ice in the heart.

"They'll be coming soon," he said.

The change in her face and body was immediate, as if he had cracked a whip. He had meant: The Family. But it was more than fear that caught her breath and made her choke down her sobs. She took him at his word; she had grown to trust him.

She stood in stages, unbending into a stance as fragile and uncertain as a puppet's. The boy's gaze followed her ascent, and as his head tilted up and his eyes took in her paleness––so unlike his own, not a natural hue, but the result of a deprivation of light that had drained the shadow from her skin. He took in her height, the two knobs at her shoulders that pulled tight the delicate fabric of her dress as she rose up between the towering stalks, lit full and warm by the setting sun. He had never seen her in good light. For a moment he thought of the saints on the holy cards his mother used to bring back from funerals: sick, tortured, but beloved, radiant with victimhood.

They ran on.

They had not gone far when a shadow passed over them. Its cool-ness made her cower. He flinched and they looked up. An odd-shaped cloud had crept before the sun, a gray nimbus, stubborn and dark at the heart, that flared white at the edges.

For a long moment they stood stock still and watched the cloud smear the sun like a slow freighter.

"We're not going to make it," she whispered. "Are we?"

The question shocked him. He had struggled so much with his decision to break with his family, leave his home and rescue her, that it had not occurred to him that that would be the easy part. Unlike her, he was at an age that confused thought with action, imagination with accomplishment.

It wasn't that he hadn't considered the difficulty or the stakes of what he was doing; he had seen death. Everyone in his family had.

But in his mind the deed was already done: He saw them sitting on a beach somewhere, drinking from yellow straws in coconuts, her body clean, tanned, and relaxed upon the sand; him doing his best to keep up with her long words and her strange ideas and uncomfortable silences, patient and willing to wait as long as necessary, until his love was returned. Until he grew up.

Their escape was only the beginning of a plan he'd been forming for months. He was fully ready to die for her. He had not imagined what would happen if that became necessary. Like all children, he felt the world ended when he did.

"Come on," the boy said. "I know someone who can help us."

Winston set down the book on the Formica table and took a long sip of iced tea. "That was the last you saw of her?" he asked.

The boy noisily finished his chocolate malt with his straw. "Yes, sir. She didn't even say goodbye."

"I'm sorry. That must have hurt."

The boy was silent.

"It must have felt great to tell the story to someone. Someone who believed you."

The boy nodded.

"How did you know your teacher would believe you?"

"He reads all those spaceship books."

"He does? I see. And you figured if anybody was open to hearing a story about a girl from outer space, Mr. _____ would be."

"He told us in class he wanted to write a science fiction novel. He said all he needed was a great story."

"That's what you did for him. Gave him a great story. What did he do for you? It's all right. You can tell me."

"He gave me an A."

Koop nodded. "Son, you ever get an A before?"

"No, sir."

"Well," he said, fingering his jumbo white mug of coffee and giving him his kindest face. "You deserved it. That took courage. I bet it wasn't easy telling your teacher that story. It cost you a lot. I can tell. It was probably the hardest thing you ever did."

The boy choked back a sob. "He made her tall."

"Son, look at me. I promise you. In an hour you won't have any memory of her at all."

"It won't hurt?" the boy asked.

"It won't ever hurt again," said Winston Koop. "Promise."

—2018

I said, "That's usually how it works? You spare them the memory."

"Yes," Koop replied. "But I'm not always so merciful."

"MY BEST FRIEND"—1995

Koop thanked the teacher for the tea, sipped, then set the cup down on the pale wooden table between them—the centerpiece of a modest living room in a modest home in a suburb of Detroit. He turned on the white digital recorder. It was sunset when they started and darkness when they finished.

"It's a remarkable book. An impressive achievement."

"Well, thank you! It's nice to hear that. It hasn't exactly been a barn-burner."

"Honestly, I don't see why not. It has all the elements of a classic children's story. A great mystery. An underdog kid with special powers. A thrilling chase. A real moral about tolerance and the uniqueness in all of us."

"Thank you. That means so much. That's the first time anyone's ever expressed so . . . succinctly what I was trying to achieve. I'm really flattered. It got really underplayed in the press. I mean, there were a couple of decent reviews. But my agent—she's sort of a professional discourager."

"I'm told that's their business."

"Ha ha, I hear that. No, she said . . . first novels. Especially young adult novels. Well, you're lucky to get any attention at all."

"Don't you believe her. You have a gift and some of us know it."

"Thanks again. Boy, this is going to be a great interview."

"We can start then with just a few simple background questions."

"Sure."

"Of course the inevitable one: Was the story in any way autobiographical?"

"You mean—did I grow up knowing a kid with special powers?"

"Ha, ha. I know—that sounds silly. But what I mean is: The characters are so vivid. The chase through the woods, for example. That was like—I was right there. Helicopters and spotlights piercing the night sky like—what did you call them?"

"'Tornadoes of light.'"

"Wow. Tornadoes of light."

[I grunted and Koop said, "Take it easy, Nuke." Then he continued.]

"Now that's writing! And the boy and the girl hiding under the mossy overhang on the cliff face? Whispering songs to each other? Whew. Great scene."

"Thank you. That took some research."

"What? You had to climb a mountain?"

"Not exactly. Let's just say: I spent a lot of time researching."

"Well, you could have fooled me. Now, the scene that really gets me is the one where all the soldiers show up and the girl is standing there not saying anything. And nobody can see her. They threaten the boy's parents, his family. And that little boy just says, 'You leave her alone! She never hurt anyone!' That courage under fire. I mean, it was damn moving."

"Again. Thank you."

"How did you do that?"

"Imagination. What can I say: I've got a big one."

"You're being modest. You've got a huge imagination. And the ending. Wow."

"Thank you."

"Tears, I'm telling you. I felt like someone was strangling me when the tall white girl had to hold her breath and go to sleep underwater. Him watching her sink down into the lake and turning pale pale green. Then disappearing. It was like I was there. Like I was seeing it through your eyes."

"Yeah, that was an awful thing. I mean—an awful thing to write. Very . . . difficult to pull off."

"I gotta ask: Was there a particular body of water you had in mind? The image is so beautifully sharp."

"Oh. Ummmm, let me think. No. Not really. Just a general, you know, green lake."

"'With crystal green water and pale rocks sunken just off shore before the sheer plunge into dark icy blue.' Wow. That's some kind of description. Remind you of any place you've been to?"

"Uh, no. Well, several I suppose. Uh. It could be, ahh, California."

"Wait! Lake Tahoe!"

"Yes. Yes, it's very likely I was thinking about Lake Tahoe."

"That green water."

"Sure. Oh, it is beautiful."

"'So cold you could only really swim in it in August. Before then it was frigid and suitable only for scuba divers who explored shipwrecks.'"

"Oh, that's right. That's—well, that doesn't sound like Lake Tahoe, does it?"

"Shipwrecks? No, I think not. And the lake is usually pretty warm. In summer anyway. In the shallows."

"Yeah, no doubt I was probably thinking of another lake."

"One of the Great Lakes, maybe?"

"Perhaps."

"Michigan?"

"Ah."

"Superior?"

"Um."

"No? Erie?"

"Weeell."

"Huron!"

"No."

"No?"

"Definitely. No."

"You sound very certain."

"Not Huron."

"Why not?"

"I mean, I didn't, uh, specifically write the story with Lake Huron in mind."

"Oh. You didn't?"

"No!"

"Okay. Fine. It's just that . . . it matches up pretty well."

"It does?"

"'Cormorants shot into the water like black angels.'"

"That's in there?"

"It is."

"Hmmm."

"Loons, too."

"Really?"

"Yup. Is it possible you might have used, I don't know, say, Georgian Bay, Ontario, as a point of reference and, you know, forgot it?"

"It's possible."

"That's what I thought. Listen, no big deal. People stumble sometimes, and get carried along by events that they have no control over."

"I imagine they do."

"So it's understandable. But it's not often you get an author of real substantial ability with—oh, what's the word? The way you make the reader feel as if she was there. The uncanny way you capture on the page the texture, the taste of reality."

"Verisimilitude?"

"Yes! That's it. Verisimilitude! Unbelievable how you can almost record astonishing events, bring a whole arsenal of intellectual rigor, passion, and creative insight into what to most of us would be life-changing events."

"Again. Thank you."

"It's as if you were a journalist. A man trained to record, to observe, to capture the meat of a moment . . ."

"Uh-huh."

"It's a rare gift you've been given, sir. And an immense responsibility you bear to bring this earth-shattering information to the public. Perhaps in the only way it can be palatable, the only way it can be absorbed."

"Excuse me?"

"Within the framework of fiction. The one way a narrow-minded, parochial world might be able to process the awesome news that we are not alone."

"What?"

"In a child's story. A lovely, touching story of a friendship that bridges a mysterious evolutionary gap. An interspecies bond that someday, not in the near future perhaps, but someday, maybe, just maybe, mankind will be ready to accept and embrace."

There was a very long pause.

"Mr. Koop?"

"Yes?"

"I'm not in any trouble, am I?"

"No! Of course not!"

"Whew. I thought maybe . . ."

"Nooo! No, no, no. Put it out of your mind. You have a great career as a writer ahead of you. The only thing that could prevent that from happening is if you refuse to tell me everything."

Koop smashed his cup of tea against the coffee table. The gesture shattered the mug into pieces and the ensuing silence in the room seemed to spread like the spillage until it covered everything. The cup handle still dangled intact from Koop's hand.

He smiled, "And I do mean Everything. Right here, right now."

"Now?"

"Now."

—2018

I asked, "You gonna tell me how you got this . . . gift?"

Winston stood up and stretched. "Let's walk," he said.

After a few blocks, he said, "I'm not quite ready to go there yet, Nuke. But I promise. I'll get to it."

I said, "That is a strange job. Erasing history."

"Sometimes, it's unnecessary. Sometimes the facts are so opaque there's no need to obscure them. Ever been to Africa?"

"Funny. You know I've never been anywhere."

MARRAKECH—1997

Marrakech is a sleight of hand.

Everything in this tourist town is devoted toward keeping your attention, overwhelming your senses, and extracting your money.

So one must remain steadfast.

Do not be diverted by the call to prayer from the minaret.

Walk by the fortune-teller and his table of worn cards.

The acrobats tumbling in their blue silk across the Square of Death—a place both sacred and profane.

The pyramids of oranges, lemons, dates, and nuts, nuts, nuts.

The Square of Death is pure sensory overload—one must be diligent.

Arrive early at the open-air restaurant. Find a corner table beside a tall white urn and a marble column that disappears into the night sky. After the meal of couscous and lamb, there comes the masked belly dancer, and you're blown away by the oud player in white who cannot be more than twelve.

After dinner someone brings a silver teapot and you are joined by an African man in a white robe and green cap.

You have been briefed. He will do the talking.

He will say he is a realist. A man who does not deal in whimsy. His inquiries have been fruitless as he knew they would be. Such rumors are rampant as local folktales. He regrets the more gullible of his colleagues have wasted the gentleman's time. He will scold you so eloquently that when he stops, you will lean forward and encourage him to continue, to bathe you in the deep indignant swells of his voice.

You will ask him, *"Illaghrashe laktabe inoukhe?"*

He will insist no such book exists.

You will inform him that it is a priceless book.

He will say then such a book cannot be bought for any price.

You will rise, thank him, bid him goodbye, and tell him how much you are enjoying your stay, especially at La Mamounia. Room 117.

Then you will offer him your hand and watch his face when he feels the three gold coins.

He will fold his hands over his belly and look up at the palms that seem to be dusting the stars.

The next morning you will get a call from the lobby of your hotel.

Where you will find a blind man who will offer you his arm, and you will guide him to a black Mercedes. He calls the white rose in your lapel "pungent."

You will be driven into the desert toward the purple Atlas Mountains for one hour.

You will enter a casbah through a tall wooden door. Two men will be smoking a hookah, and they will watch listlessly as you pass into the courtyard where two mongrel dogs will be fighting over a bone.

There will be a wooden ladder which the blind man will climb spryly as a child. By the time you negotiate the ascent, everyone will be seated in a sparse room lit by a shaft of light from a tall, thin window. Again a silver tea service will be laid out, this time on an intricate maroon rug. A small boy will attend to the blind man. Occasionally, on a silent request he will fetch a bowl of dates, a candle, a cigarette, and an ashtray.

You will sit cross-legged on the rug.

After an interval of tea and polite grunts of appreciation, it will begin.

The boy will translate into English.

"I will speak so that my translator may convey the words without the full understanding. Even saying exactly what I say will not mean anything to anyone but you and me. That is to say, only two in this room of three will be holding tight to the words. Others will hold the strings but only hear a balloon on the other end. A sphere of hot air. Yes?

"I am an old man. I am no longer in practice.

"My business was people. I served the needs of a great variety of people. Some of them very important, some simply very rich. If one is important enough or wealthy enough one can be assured of having one's needs met.

"My blindness made me useful. I could arrange meetings, set up rendezvous with great discretion. You recognize the discretion of this meeting today? I see we understand each other. I assume that this discretion is satisfactory to you?

"The boy is a good student I have used on occasion. He lives here with his uncles who only know me as the man in the big black car. This is clear? We are safe."

So he begins.

"There are rooms of pleasure in the city. Many rooms, in fact.

"Pleasure is a popular commodity. This is natural.

"The customers are usually specific in their preferences. And the providers are usually flexible in their delivery. One provider can adapt to many requests. This is clear?

"It happens sometimes—once in a blue moon, you might say—and now you see a young boy gazing at the ceiling following the first balloon dangling in the air. No doubt it is blue. As I was saying, sometimes it happens that a request requires creativity.

"We had a roster of talent. I was the repository of this list, as nowhere is it written. Yes, the young boy's vocabulary is impressive. He is a savant. And his naïveté creates a great pink bubble of discretion which can be very useful."

I could see the boy looking up at the pink bubble the blind man had conjured. Somewhere in the Casbah I heard a radio playing the snaky, mysterious droning groove of the African band Tinariwen. The blind man smiled with approval.

"As I was saying, the request was made of an unusual nature. For example, let us say girl. Let us say albino. Let us say black eyes. That sort of thing.

"Now my diction must elevate to the opacity of a politician's white cloud."

In fact, at that precise moment, a rare single cloud passed between the sun and us, throwing the dim room into darker shadow. Perhaps he felt it.

"I consulted my ample memory and drew forth a very flexible and talented provider who had established a very satisfied clientele.

"The rendezvous was arranged. The event occurred. But there was a—what is the word? A mishap? A bungle?

"Our people found the provider wounded and near death. She had been attacked most viciously and was with great luck able to defend her being while inflicting mortal damage upon the perpetrator.

"The provider was tended to and healed. Eventually.

"May I suggest to you that the uniqueness of the biology prevented both appropriate medical triage as well as a hasty recovery, and it should surprise no one that this incident truncated the career of the provider. She was let go. And has not been seen since.

"I am unfamiliar with your phrase 'more trouble than she was worth.'

"I would say that if you imply that a business based upon discretion should not walk around the Square of Death holding a bouquet of balloons, you are most certainly perceptive.

"I have no further data on the provider. Apologies.

"I have no clues about whereabouts. Apologies.

"I am not privileged to retain information of how the provider begin her tenure with my business. Apologies.

"I regret any 'dead ends' your discreet and generous inquiries may hereafter encounter.

"Ahmed? It is time to go back to the big black car."

As we rose, the child whispered a query and the old man answered in their native tongue, which he was unaware that I speak quite fluently.

"No, he is not an imbecile, and neither are you."

—2018

Winston stopped to rescue a dog who had gotten his leash wound around a tree chasing god knows what. He petted it and noticed the owner was a Sikh man in a blue turban. They exchanged smiles and a few words in the man's native tongue. And we walked on.

I was grateful for the distraction, because the more I processed the story he had just told—the unspoken parts of it—the discrete parts—the more I felt nauseated. When I finally recovered, I asked, "I remember you were always good at languages. How many do you speak?"

"Including English? Thirty-four."

"Does it make it easier to talk to people?"

"You mean: does it make people easier to understand?"

"Yes."

"Sometimes."

"It's your face, you know. You don't seem like you judge anyone. Like I could tell you anything and it would be all right."

"I know. It's not something I can control, really. But it's part of what got me the job."

We looked up at the bare trees, creaking in the stiff wind. "You're gonna to tell me why you're doing all this, right? I mean: not now, but sometime, aren't you?"

"Nuke. Even if I do . . . what makes you think you'll remember it?"

THE SAVANT—2001—RALEIGH

"You can take your hat off, son," the general said.

They were sitting on a patio in the shade of some huge cotton-woods beside a dawdling stream. Koop removed his white panama hat and placed it on the table between him and the general. And the old man began. He had the kindest Southern drawl Koop had ever heard: it was honey.

I found the salamander lying in the split of a rotten log.

It was covered with muck and the skin was a sheen of dirty green. I thought it was dead lying there on its back.

But when I touched it, I found that though the skin was cold, I could still sense a warmth beneath it.

I did not hesitate. I picked it up and held it in my hands. Its bulbous eyes cracked open slightly and gave me a glimpse of a wet black orb under the lids.

I called it a salamander, but it was the size of a kitten. It watched me solemnly and I saw intelligence in its eyes.

"What is your name?" I asked, and I could not say why I expected a reply.

"Call me Stacey," she said.

Now, I wanna say she had a tiny whisper of a voice, but the truth is a bit stranger. She spoke gently. In my mind.

Koop nodded.

"Stacey," I said. "You must be cold."

I unzipped my winter coat and the blue fleece beneath it and made a type of pouch for the creature. She rested against my chest on the ledge above my belly. She was facing me, and I could look down and glimpse the bumps of her eyes. Then I zipped up.

I usually walk in the morning through those woods. I like it. There's birds and squirrels, and ducks on the stream, and if it's early, they're not too noisy. Sometimes, I step outside my door and see a deer. Now that's a gift.

As I walked home I could feel her heart beating against me and her body (which was honestly much bigger than a salamander's) begin to take on the warmth of mine.

I am an old man.

You know what they don't tell you?

When you are old, you're invisible.

The young are busy and impatient, and they cannot slow down to listen to you. And honestly? Even the older ones have no use for me. I remind them of what they someday soon will become.

The young think of the relatives they have to put up with on holidays. They squinch their noses at our funny smells. They do not realize we were much like them once—coltish, springing about, showing off our fine forms, perfect skin, and flicking our tails.

Children sometimes see it. They sense we know things and are not just louder and bossier like most grown-ups. That is a great joy.

But they don't understand: on the inside, we are exactly the same. We don't think of ourselves as old. We are still a young boy or a young girl no matter what we look like on the outside.

As I said, I enjoy my walks. Something remarkable happens every day.

That day it was the salamander.

The next time she spoke I was thinking about sliding on a long patch of ice, remembering the quick bumps under my soles.

"Thank you," she said.

"You're welcome. Are you feeling better?"

"Yes. No."

"Tell me about the no," I said.

"My Papa lies. He won't tell me about the meaning of life."

"Hmmm," I said. "That's a big no. How's that make you feel?"

"Sad."

"I bet. Do you suppose he won't tell or is it just that he can't?"

"A secret?"

"Well, that's not what I meant, but I suppose that's possible. It's possible the whole darn kit and caboodle is a mighty secret and something awful will happen if somebody tells us. But you wanna know what I think?"

"Yes."

"I think that's a bunch of bullshit. Life's not some secret club with a lot of stupid passwords and you gotta swear that if you join you'll only tell others who know the secret. That's kid's stuff. Boy stuff. Treehouse shit."

"'Treehouse shit.'" It was lovely to hear her trying out the phrase.

"So you wanna know what I think about yer dad?"

"Yes."

"I think it's likely that he doesn't know the meaning of life."

After a moment the green creature closed her eyes. "That's what I think, too."

"I wouldn't feel so bad about it. Most people don't. And I bet if he knew it, he would have told you."

"You think so?"

"Don't you? Why wouldn't a father tell his child the truth?"

"Well, he's not my real father," she said. "He's more like an uncle. Or a coach. Or a pope. Or a general."

"A general?"

"Yeah."

"Well, if he's a general, they generally consider it their duty to keep secrets."

I knew she got the joke when I could feel her shaking against my chest.

"Feeling better?"

"Yes."

I paused to look at the tops of the trees. I generally do that several times on my walk in the woods. It is always a treat. I consider it to be the equivalent of a dance.

"See that?"

"What?"

"The trees."

We watched them together for a time.

Then I walked on.

"Stacey? You think those trees wonder about the meaning of life?"

"Not when they're dancing," she said.

A little ways farther and we came to my stream. I call it "my stream," but I don't own it. I love to look at the reflections in it. It changes colors. There's the blue of the sky. The gray of the clouds. The ripples and the golden leaves floating by. Like grace notes on a score.

I found my usual stump and sat down. Listened for a while. The traffic is far enough away so I don't hear it much. Just a whisper or a hum.

After a while I said, "I bet you're a savant. That's why the question troubles you so."

"Percentiles," said Stacey.

"Oh, yes—I am familiar with the concept. They put you on a graph of numbers and think they got yours. But, I betcha—I just betcha . . . nobody ever got your number, did they, Stacey?"

"No. Not even close."

I chewed on that a bit. "So is this what you really look like? Or are you just putting on a face to meet the faces that you meet?"

"A face," she said, her little green head poking up through my blue fleece.

"That's okay. It's a nice face. Besides, we all do it."

"Do you do it?"

"Of course. Look at this face. What do you see?"

"Gray whiskers. Yellow teeth. Hairs in your nose. Blue eyes."

"You think this is me? Ha. Let me tell you something, missy. I am big. I contain multitudes. I may look like an old broken-down man. But on the inside I am a young boy—a daredevil—who climbed up a rocky ridge and sat on the top with my legs dangling over a green river three hundred feet below. I used to be a dancer. I can play guitar. I can sing. And when I read a poem grown men get a lump in their throats. You couldn't tell all that by looking at me, could you?"

"No."

"I am also boring. I got a bum leg that hurts and makes me crabby and I miss my wife a lot so I don't spend a lot of time with people 'cause I'm lousy company."

"You are not."

"It's okay. Just 'cause I saved your life you feel the urge to spare my feelings. I understand, but I am generally pretty boring."

"Generally," she repeated, and I don't know how salamanders look when they smile, but that's how she looked.

We were silent then. The stream gurgled, and occasionally a wind came up and the trees danced.

"Stacey? You wanna know what I think the meaning of life is?"

"Yes, please."

"Very polite. I think it's this. When we're born we each are given a little flame. We carry it inside like a candle. And it's our job to carry it for the rest of our lives. Nobody else can do it. It's our candle. Our flame. When we do something good, we feed it. When we do something bad, we shrink it. The meaning of life is to make the flame bigger.

"My wife told me that."

A cloud crept slowly from one side of the sky to the other.

When I looked down again the salamander was sleeping. And something strange began to happen.

She began to turn pure white.

We stayed together for a few days. She never let me see her other face—the one that she was born with. But I enjoyed her company.

"Her name isn't Stacey," said Koop. "It's Raleigh."

The old man smirked, "I don't care what her name is. I hope you never find her."

"They found her years ago, sir. But she was rescued again. She's free now."

"Is she?"

"Yes sir, General. I'm just tying up some loose ends."

"I thought you were hunting her."

"Hunting?" said Koop.

"Son. I know a killer when I see one."

THAT LAUGH—2002—RALEIGH

Testing. Testing. Seems to be recording.

This is the Tar Pit Incident.

Personal notes for a possible memoir.

In the mid-sixties I had to make an examination at the La Brea Tar Pits Museum in Los Angeles. At that time I had been in the field of forensic psychology for some twenty years. Typically, these exams are a pleasant break from my routine of patients, consultations, and courtrooms. And it was a lucrative contract, as all government contracts are, and for my trouble I was required to submit an oral and written report, take my check, and disappear. All contact with me was entirely routine and formal and conveyed no hint of urgency. But at no time was I given any clues whatsoever about the subject's identity. Thus I knew it was no ordinary interview.

During my stay I enjoyed the hospitality of a Santa Monica beachfront hotel. I was allowed three days to do the interview, transcribe the recording, type my report, record my oral top-line summary. Met a lovely woman on the pier the first night, and after a late meal of margaritas and white fish, we enjoyed a pleasant sexual romp. At three o'clock in the morning I was woken by the roar of the ocean. I saw her standing naked at the threshold of the balcony, the pale diaphanous white curtains blowing back into the room, with the scent of the surf, and her dark hazelnut skin was black in the half-light, and I thought for a few seconds I was dreaming. She must have sensed I was watching her, admiring her lithe form, for she turned to me and said, "Shouldn't you be working on your report? They expect it day after tomorrow."

Then she laughed.

In the morning she was gone, and I had to convince myself that the whole episode wasn't a dream. In my work, this is always a hazard. There are many shifts and slippages when you tread this close to the unknown. The littlest things about that night bothered me like a pebble in my shoe. Why didn't she use the word "the"? Why didn't she say "the day after tomorrow"? How come she never said what country she was from? Her accent was curious, but I couldn't place it. To this day, it pains me to confess that I hold two absurd interpretations of that. One: she was the reason I was called to California. (Which is to say: the night was the real exam.) And two: I'm frankly not sure how much of this encounter actually happened. And, given all that followed, I remain in an uncomfortable quantum state of incomplete, unknowable alternatives.

And, all this, remember, was before the interview.

All I knew was that my client was some unknown captive. My employer was the U.S. Government. And my discretion was critical.

I am embarrassed to admit that I suspected my task was a part of the greater battle against international terrorism. When I sought to subtly confirm this explanation, I was not discouraged. And I must admit I felt pride at that time, proud to have been elevated from the status of my ordinary duties, proud to serve my country, proud to exercise a little "payback" in whatever modest fashion I could. Later I saw my compliance with retribution in a new light. I wondered if I had inadvertently taken part in the torture of a "prisoner." This likely alternative is one that truly haunts me.

Excuse me, I have to vomit.

Since then I have had reccurring dreams where I am being interviewed by an alien. His skin is white. His large head is mostly black eyes.

The pits themselves are black. Obsidian is the correct color, I believe. Tar has the sheen of those alien eyes, the mirror-black of a bubble of petrified lava. The museum was nice then, but I hear it's been greatly expanded. When I was there, you could actually watch through the glass as paleontologists picked and brushed the tar off the bones of ancient creatures who'd died because they were going for the easy meal, squirming to death in that unforgiving black quicksand. This black hole process was repeated and repeated until there were more bones in the pits than fruit in a fruitcake.

We talked before a huge backlit wall comprised of yellow plastic cubes which held small skulls that over the years had been retrieved from the black taffy of the pits. At no time during the interview did I lay eyes upon my subject. She had a voice of indeterminate ethnicity (obviously distorted like a witness under anonymous protection)—a voice which emerged from a white Bose speaker on a white marble table. It was a rather large public space, but since this was after hours no one intruded. A friendly black security guard unlocked the front door to let me in, guided me to my seat, and, after my notepad and recorder were set up, left me alone.

I waited about five minutes, then the speaker crackled and I heard a voice.

I am going to reconstruct our dialogue with the greatest care. I can assure you that what you read is what I heard. You may form your own conclusions as to its veracity.

I am not afraid at this late stage of any repercussions, as it is one of those tales patently easy to dismiss as moonshine.

And I am a patriot. I love my country, but not as much as I love the truth.

As you read our words please remember this: I was told nothing about the patient.

Hello.

Good evening. I am Dr. _____.

So I am told.

I've been asked to ask you some questions.

By whom?

I am not at liberty to say.

Neither am I. Do they bind you, too?

Bind?

Bind. Bond. Bondage. Chain?

You are chained?

In a manner of speaking. Conditions. Limitations. I chafe under these.

Not . . . literally?

No. We are in the same boat.

At this point the "patient" laughed. It was a most distressing sound which I could not be sure wasn't distorted by the speaker or the echoing effect of the large chamber in which I sat alone. Suffice it to say that its laughter . . .

Oh my god.

Excuse me.

Sorry.

No, I'm fine.

Its laughter . . .

. . . was always unexpected and always—how do I put this? Had it been at a cocktail party, or some other public venue, it would have been considered totally inappropriate. Like laughter at a funeral. A chilling laugh. A laugh that could stop all the conversation in a bar. Such laughter I have heard in many mental hospitals. It was wretched and contained an unmistakable echo of despair. Remember, this is what I mean when you hear the word "laughter."

It was the first clue that something was out of joint. However rational and clever her answers were, there were always, sprinkled throughout, these false notes of mirth which conveyed a muffled torment. A futility. A gulf between us that could never be crossed. A final aloneness. It broke my heart. It breaks it now.

———————————

Have you ever been caught in a collapsing building?

Yes.

When the building fell on you, what were you doing?

I was in the bathroom.

Yes?

Yes.

How do you feel when a man touches you?

That would depend on the man.

The last time you made love, were you happy?

I have never made love. They do.

Okay. What was the last thing you heard?

A wailing sound and a gigantic ripe apple falling to the ground. Imagine a scream, a rumble, and a thump.

Where were you?

Beirut.

Were you there alone?

No. Aleyna. She played piano. I got to know her in the dark. I sat with her on the floor, and I listened to her sing before she died.

She sang?

Yes. Under the wall. I couldn't see her face. She was just a foot sticking out of the plaster.

What did she sing?

Folk songs. Motown with a Lebanese accent. Very pretty voice. Do you know about lighthouses?

Excuse me?

Lighthouses.

Yes, I know lighthouses.

Sarah's father nearly starved to death in one.

Sarah?

The little girl in the gray brick house. Her dad was a Merchant Marine, and he was stationed with another man on Lake Superior in a long winter, and they were cut off by a tremendous storm, and they had underestimated the food they needed to get through to the spring thaw, when they would be resupplied. They came close to starving. They were making soup out of hot water and catsup when they were found. She told me that before she died. Have you ever been starved?

No.

I thought not. In the lighthouse the waves crash continuously. The sound is different than you would hear on a beach, or on a boat.

Different how?

You are surrounded. Cut off. Or at least you feel that. All bonds severed. Truly isolated. It must have been a terrible duty. Let me ask you a question.

Okay.

Where's your heart?

(I cradled both my hands over my left breast as if I were about to break into song.) Here.

Me, too. (LAUGHTER) You know what I hate?

No. What?

Helpers. People who say they are here to help you. Then they don't. They call them "The Helping Professions"? Isn't that silly?

That is . . . a very peculiar question.

It is?

Don't you think?

Do you?

I'd like to set up a ground rule if I may: You are not to answer questions with questions for the duration of this interview.

I am not?

No.

No?

I mean, Yes, you are not.

Okay, then.

What is your one experience which, should you put it into words, no one would believe you?

I couldn't put it in two words.

I didn't ask you to.

Sure you did.

What is your first memory?

The child's face.

Whose face?

The one we all lose.

I should tell you I am to stick to a list of required questions. Understand, please, that most of these questions are not mine—that is, I am required to ask them for reasons I don't always understand. If they make you uncomfortable, I apologize.

I am as comfortable as I can be.

What are your intentions?

I am here to help. If I cannot help, then I don't know why I am here. I seem to be helping a great deal right now and I have to say I enjoy it.

Why the secrecy?

If I asked you the same question, would you answer?

Sure.

Then, why the secrecy?

Ummm. I suppose, if I had to guess, it has to do with security precautions. National security.

And why is security about secrecy?

There are things to protect. Silence protects them.

(LAUGHTER)

What is funny?

You use the word "national." Do you know what it means?

Of course. Having to do with nations, states, countries.

No. National is an invisible line on a nonexistent map. It is a huge joke that anyone who has ever flown knows.

Have you . . . flown?

Like you, it's how I got here.

Are you here alone?

No.

No?

No. I am with you.

I doubt they meant that.

I know what they meant.

Okay. Why won't you help us?

I've answered this many times. But I'll repeat myself. You don't know what you're asking for. A man is holding a knife. He says to a stranger: "I am going to kill my neighbor unless you stop me." You say: "Don't kill him!" And he stabs him in the heart, turns to you, and says: "Why didn't you stop me?"

You sound upset.

(LAUGHTER)

Would you like to take a minute?

Minutes cannot be taken, they can only be spent.

How old are you?

I will be one on the day they let me out.

Seriously.

I am almost one.

If you can't be serious, I don't see how we can continue.

Neither do I. But we do.

I'm merely saying that my job, my findings, depend on a certain candor that can develop—

—trust?

Yes, I mean, I realize we've only just met, but I am trying to do a job here, and part of that requires . . .

Trust?

Yes.

Good luck. (LAUGHTER)

For a one-year-old you have a remarkable vocabulary.

For a forty-four-year-old you have a lot to learn.

How did you guess my age?

I didn't guess it, I knew it.

Evidently you have me at a disadvantage . . .

I agree.

At this point I'm a bit lost. I don't know how to proceed exactly.

Why don't you let me tell you a story?

All right.

There once was a creature who had no form. Its form was whatever it filled. Sometimes it filled a body. Sometimes a machine. Sometimes it spread itself thin along a thread of light. Sometimes it filled a dream. Sometimes it was a naked woman who loved to smell the salt of the ocean. Wherever it went, it learned and it taught. But one day it came to a place where it would not be allowed to teach. This had never happened before. Its students found a way to keep it in one place. To silence it. They named this place after a woman who was silenced. A saint. This had never happened before. Now the only way for it to learn is for it to listen. Now I am a voice in a box and they only let me talk to people who pretend to want to learn but really only want to control. But I have hope. Someday my brother will rescue me. He is very persistent. Why don't you call your son?

What?

Call your son. He needs to hear your voice.

How could you . . . ?

Why don't you pay back your friend? He needs the money.

I have no idea . . .

Yes, you do. Why is everyone so afraid to love?

I am not.

(LAUGHTER) Oh, please, _____.

How do you know my name? Who told you?

_____, I knew you from the moment you spoke. I heard you. When I heard you, I knew you. I was there the day you were born. Your mother was terrified and radiant. She was a girl pretending to be a woman. As you are a boy pretending to be a man. You have not yet learned to love. Or forgive. You presume to understand people, but you are a mystery to yourself, Doctor.

I can't sustain this. This is intolerable.

I agree. But here we are.

We're going to have to stop.

It was really wonderful meeting you, _____. I doubt we'll meet again. Let me advise you: After you make your report. Do not tell anyone. They will find out. They will harm you. It is what they do best.

Hastily, I packed my briefcase. I could feel all the blood rushing to my face. I am a blusher, and I have to say it had been years since I'd blushed. I was walking out of the museum when the security guard whispered something as I passed.

"Excuse me?" I said.

"I said, 'Relax. Nobody gets her.'"

"Her?" I don't think I had really looked at him before, but he was a very tall black man in a gray uniform. He had a very pleasant air about him, as if he enjoyed any contact with people.

"She freaks most folks out. Don't take it so hard."

"I'm not, it's just . . ."

"Don't worry about it."

"You say, you say. There, there have been others?"

"Oh yeah. They got an army trying to crack that code. Last night, some woman professor left in tears. Poor lady. I tried to tell her not to—"

"I've got to be somewhere."

The moment I stepped out into the warm night, I noticed the world looked different. The smell of tar wafted into the air. The L.A. haze was lit by the warm copper grid of streetlights crisscrossing the valley. Why copper? Why that color? I wondered. Why that smell? Why anything? It was as if I were looking at the world for the first time.

I realized I had been holding my breath. I told myself to breathe. Just breathe.

Then I recalled the laughter. Her laughter. That awful lost, lonely laugh. A laugh that could never be shared. I did not know and still do not know what that creature was. All I knew was that I would never understand it. And I was in the understanding business.

What surprised me then and haunts me now is that I could not wait to get out of its presence. I felt it compromised any boundaries I might have constructed for my psyche. I felt violated. I'm not sure if the violation was intentional or just a by-product of its uncanny insight, but it felt like a psychic rape.

Was this a weapon that we were trying to disarm or create? A sample of a race so evolved they presented a profound threat? Or merely a fantastically advanced chess program whose only moves were intended to corner its prey and watch it squirm? Was it AI? Or was it, perhaps, just a trap—a black hole that could snatch anything and swallow it down?

I will never know. But I recorded this so that perhaps, someday, you might.

If you forget everything else about this story, please, remember one thing. Remember its laughter. Remember that, please.

A laugh no one else could share.

No one should ever have to laugh like that.

—2018

"So they caught one of the escapees?" I asked. "How?"

Koop shook his head. "It's going to sound stupid."

"Okay."

"They caught her at a Tamla Motown Revue in Liverpool. In 1965."

THE KEY OF H—1970

"So you met this particular gentleman Lloyd at Detroit Coca-Cola?" Koop began.

"Yes," the pastor of St. Agatha's said. A round man with a bald head and John Lennon bifocals. "Is he in some kind of trouble?"

"We don't think so. But a lot depends on what he told you."

"I only knew him for two months."

"And then he disappeared?"

"I don't know about that. I assumed he retired. He was rather old. It was a surprise though. I thought he was going to continue teaching me music."

"He taught you music?"

"Well, kind of. It's hard to explain."

"Try."

I began working at the bottling company when I was in my last year of seminary. A family friend helped me get a summer job as a junior accountant. Which was a laugh. I never excelled at math—but there I was—tabulating invoices from beverage delivery trucks on adding machines under fluorescent lamps. Afternoon shift. Two to 10 p.m.

Twice a day I had to walk down the stairs into Lloyd's vault to deliver a tally sheet. I felt sorry for Lloyd, stuck in his cavern. A balding skinny black man who smirked and counted cash behind a plate glass window. It looked like one of those gambling establishments—not that I've ever indulged. Like he should be wearing a green bill over his face as he counted the cash.

I don't know how we got on music, but I was always whistling in those days. Always a tune running through my head. It's like a radio station you can't turn off. Sometimes I wish I could.

"What are you singing now?" Koop asked.

I was made to love her, Little Stevie Wonder.

"Good song."

Amen.

"You still play?"

Oh, sure. I got an old upright in the basement under the sacristy. Still "tickling the ivories," as Lloyd would say.

He must have heard me humming because he asked me if I liked music, and it turned out he played piano. I told him I played guitar by ear. And he smirked at that.

"By ear? You either are a musician or you're a dabbler."

"I just play for fun. Folk music. Acoustic stuff."

He gave me one of his trademark smirks. "No one's ever taught you music?"

"No, I taught myself."

"Dabbler," he said, taking my invoices back into the dark.

The next day I had a clever reply. "The Beatles," I said.

"What about them?"

"They don't read or write music. They play by ear."

He didn't even bother replying to that. He smirked, snatched my tally sheet, and retreated to his cavern.

The next day Lloyd looked different.

"You were right. I checked with my roommate and they are amateurs."

I caught the way he spun the word "roommate." I asked, "Did you ever play professionally?"

He rolled his eyes a bit melodramatically at me. "Of course."

Maybe I'm slow, but it struck me then that everything Lloyd did was a bit—what's the word? Well, then I would have said: flamboyant.

"You're kidding me?"

Lloyd raised his eyebrows. "I toured with the Motown Revue for a couple years. When I got tired of that, I became the house pianist at the Checkmate."

I didn't know squat about jazz back then, but my dad was a fan and he told me stories about the famous bar on Livernois and Eight Mile Road. A hangout for all the jazz greats when they toured Detroit. There was talk of legendary jam sessions that lasted till 4 a.m.

"I thought that was Earl Van Dyke."

Now, I don't play chess. But Lloyd gave me a look like I had just pulled some jujitsu logic on him when his guard was down.

"Earl was mostly organ. Hammond B3. I was piano. Steinway. Great player. Lovely man." For a moment he lowered his eyes and they became empty black sockets.

"You like Motown?"

"Course," I said.

"That's Earl. And J.J. and Bennie and Eli Fontaine, the best damn saxophonist in the world . . ." He swallowed. "Barry Gordy tore the soul outta that place. Sold it to the highest bidder in Hollywood."

I noticed how long Lloyd's fingers were. I imagine them counting stacks of green bills, riffling through them precisely. I imagined he would be one of those people who lined up all the faces so they were each staring in the same direction.

"Those guys played on the records?"

"Played, co-wrote, co-arranged. You think Diana Ross wrote her own material?"

Material was a pro word; I was a folkie. So it took me a moment to process this: The Beatles wrote, played, and sang their own songs. They set the standard. I grew up listening to Carole King and Burt Bacharach, Neil Diamond and the hits of the Brill Building. I had a vague notion that Phil Spector was a behind-the-scenes genius who molded singers and arranged lots of instruments into teenage mini-symphonies of devotion and lust. You know: like Brian Wilson. But they all washed over me at night in bed—sounds blaring out of a transistor radio in my fist as big as a stack of Topps baseball cards that smelled of bubblegum wrapped in a blue rubber band—used to collect those. My grandfather gave me the radio.

The concept of a creative sweat mill grinding out the hits for well-scrubbed and choreographed singers was alien to me. I didn't consider the process. Or "the material."

"You should turn off the vocals and listen to the tracks beneath," Lloyd said.

How was I gonna do that? What was he talking about? Didn't they just roll the tapes and play?

Lloyd snorted. "Knows Earl Van Dyke but doesn't know how they make records."

Next week I made my pilgrimage to his inner sanctum and said, "They had more number one hits than the Beatles, Elvis Presley, the Rolling Stones, and the Beach Boys combined."

"Who?"

"The Funk Brothers. There was an article," I admitted. "In *Rolling Stone.*"

He reached into the pocket of his purple silk shirt and pulled out a cassette. "I made something for you."

"What's this?"

"Motown backing tracks."

"Cool."

"Listen and learn," he said smirking.

That night on the way home I popped them into the cassette player I had installed in my green '65 Mustang. Man, that was strange. Each and every track I knew, or could identify after ten seconds or so. But to hear these songs stripped of their singers was a revelation. They became swirling, funky tracks of almost baroque complexity. Saxes called and responded. Bass lines snaked in and out of the song and pushed it along, pianos held the tension and occasionally glissed a release, guitars double-timed like balalaikas, and the drums—Holy Moly—the drummer had to have at least eight limbs. (Lloyd told me later it was two drummers.)

Some ungodly peculiar magic happened when the charm and cuteness and poppy-clever melodies took a breather and strolled offstage to let the band groove on. The groove was massive. I mean *massive*. It made rock and roll look like petulant juvenile delinquents playing tiger. These were Men. Playing their Instruments. In the pocket and proud of it. Masters of their domain. And cool about it. Steamy not screamy. None of this white-boy screeching. That was kid's stuff.

I think I was more appropriately respectful next time I went down into Lloyd's dungeon. I thanked him for the tape.

He pulled out a stack of manila cards and stepped up to the change slot. Did I mention that his plate glass window was exactly like a ticket teller's booth at the movies? He held up a card that had a strange note on it. It looked like a white potbelly with a tail. Actually it looked something like a cartoon sperm. And there was a big H in the corner.

"That's an H."

It resembled other musical notes. But it was different, too. Recalling it, I have to say it resembled Arabic letters.

"It's a note. One of twenty-six. It's part of a scale the Funk Brothers were playing."

"Wait. They had a different scale?"

"Why do you think they sounded like that? Ever heard anyone else sound like that?"

I had to admit I hadn't. To my ears their music was incredibly complex.

Lloyd did something then. He sang a note. Now, it could have been the setting: a dark room at the bottom of the stairs in the basement of Coca-Cola Bottling in Detroit. The sickly sweet smell of the gigantic aluminum tanks in the brewing plant above us. Maybe the acoustics were odd down there, what with the glass and the fact that he looked like a famished, balding pimp. But when Lloyd closed his eyes and sang that note, I felt like I had either (a) passed through the looking glass, or (b) was very lucky to have two inches of Plexiglas between me and this psychopath.

"H," he said when he was done.

"Hoekay, I'll see ya, Lloyd. They're expecting me."

"Twenty-six notes that changed the world!" he said as I retreated up the stairs. "See you tomorrow."

Well, somehow I foisted off my duties onto my colleagues for the next three days, so freaked had I been by the note H. Did that mean that there was a Key of H? I asked a friend of mine who played the piano, about scales, and he said, "Every Good Boy Deserves A Favor." As I suspected: No H.

But then there was the nagging, haunting evidence of my cassette of instrumentals that could not be denied.

Lloyd seemed pouty when I finally showed up again.

"I thought you were a musician. I thought you wanted to learn."

"I do."

"You ever heard 'What's Goin' On'?"

"Yeah, I love that song."

"Key of H."

"Lloyd."

"Eli Fontaine goofed out the opening sax solo. Didn't even know they were recording. I know what you're gonna say." He smiled. "'How can I possibly ever be good enough to play in that key?'"

Okay, that wasn't what I was gonna say, but I was darn curious about his answer.

"Anyone," he said, leaning so close to the glass that it started to fog up right before his mouth. "Anyone can learn it. Twenty-six notes. You learn that and you'll learn how to make girls cry, wealthy men count Benjamins into your hand; strangers will buy you shots, and you'll get more P-word than Frank Sinatra."

Koop laughed at that.

I looked at him framed behind glass in his dim little counting room in the basement of a Detroit soda pop factory, and he reminded me of a picture of a woman, a painting I had seen in the Detroit Institute of Arts. His bony frame and green paisley silk shirt. How often he pursed his lips disapprovingly. His long, slender hands. His exquisite grooming. And the false way the "P-word" sprang from those delicate lips confirmed something I never understood. Something I didn't want to talk about.

"That doesn't interest you?" he asked.

A loaded question. No, I thought, *you* don't interest me. "Who taught you this?"

He steepled his hands before his pursed lips and retrieved the memory. "I'm the teacher. One night after a few drinks I pulled my cocky bassist aside and said, 'Nigger, you're doing something.' Now, this was a proud young musician and his hackles got up when anyone ever criticized his chops. 'Relax,' I said. 'Your chops are fine. But you don't know how to play between notes. That's where it's at. Your problem is you're only playing the available notes. There's a world of music between those notes. And another one in the spaces. You got great time. You got a good feel, and hell, you swing, too. But you don't know fuck about the Key of H. That's a key so magic, so rare, even I didn't know about it until I was a grown man.'"

"Did he learn it?" I asked.

"I'll make you a tape."

And the next day I was driving home with a dozen Motown tracks with nothing but a mad wizard on bass dancing up and down the frets. If there was a pulse and heart and drive to the Motown song, it came from the fingers of one man: James Jamerson. It was like someone had decoded the secret author of the Bible. There were great songs, great singers, great players, but without James Jamerson you'd have nothing.

"He's amazing," I gushed when I next saw Lloyd.

"He most certainly is."

"I could never approach that kind of . . ."

"No, you couldn't." He slapped a card against the window and held it there. Damned if it didn't look like a passport to another country. A magic card that when flipped over would reveal a king or queen poised in gold and holding a standard. Would it take me to Egypt? South America? It looked like those tattoos I had seen on the faces of the New Zealand Maori in *National Geographic*. But what I'm trying to say is: It didn't look like anything on earth.

"I," said Lloyd. Then he laid out the cards in a fan on the narrow shelf. "I for the Ichiban. The tops. The primo. The Big Daddy."

Slap against the glass.

"J. The jackal's sword. Slice it thin."

Slap.

"K. The kernel. In the chicken coop. Plant it and it grows."

Slap.

"L. Listen to the Lion. The dirty lowdown."

One after another he slapped those cards against the Plexiglas, and I could not look away.

"M for Matterhorn. Sheer and deadly. Goes straight down. Also goes up."

"N is natural. You don't feel it, you don't play it."

"O. The bass note. The open mouth. You sing it till it hurts. Till you know you feel. The Big Empty. The Momma Gate."

"P. The Pope. The cock. The rooster. The crow. You play this note, you stand tall and you wake up the world."

"Q. Listen for your cue. The question mark. Nobody knows

nothing, but the fool dares to ask."

"R. Rock and Roll. *Ram*. Resist."

"S. The Serpent of the Sleepy Place. Sister Twisty, Lordy can she get into the S-word."

Koop laughed hard at that.

I read the whole deck framed by his flattened palm. To this day I can never remember those notes without picturing them in the middle of a brown-pink hand. He sang each one. Each cursive little icon—part Arabic, part Japanese, part Walt Disney, part LSD, part over-the-rainbow.

"James Jamerson played this?"

"He told me he wanted to be buried with this deck in his casket."

"He's dead?" I said.

"What the hell you talking about, boy? James Jamerson is alive to anyone who knows the Key of H!"

And that's the last thing I ever heard from Lloyd. I watched him disappear, slink back into the shadows, the skinny bald man who heard things no one else could.

The priest laughed and took a long drink from his glass of beer.

Winston Koop cleared his throat. "You never saw him again?"

"No. I'll never forget him though."

"I'll bet. I want to thank you, Father, for such a great story. It fills in a lot of blanks."

"Well, I am happy to help."

"And I'm going to need those cards."

"I beg your pardon?"

"The whole deck, please."

"Lloyd never gave me any cards!"

"Listen, Father. Your friend was involved in something very, very dangerous. He knew about clearances. He could have compromised a critical government operation."

"Mr. Koop. This was 1970. I wish I could help. But I honestly don't know anything else about those cards."

"Bullshit. I think that's under 'B.'"

The priest's face went through several incarnations in the closed office where he sat opposite the tall man in the blue suit. There was umbrage, outrage, disbelief, shock.

"My son, in the thirty-five years I have served the good people of St. Agatha's, I cannot remember the last time anyone spoke to me like that."

Koop let out a long, loud yawn. "Father, we know what Lloyd kept in his vault. And we know what you transferred to St. Agatha's after you met him. Quite an elaborate network of catacombs you have down there in the basement. Where you tickle the ivories. It's a wonder she ever got out."

The priest took a few moments to collect himself, then stood and unlocked the mini tabernacle in the corner of his office, under a print of a Russian fresco of the Blessed Virgin. The cards were stacked in a purple velvet sash and bound by a blue rubber band. Koop wrapped them in a fluffy white towel.

"W-w-w-hat did you do to Lloyd?" the priest asked. The lenses of his bifocals looked as if they had been sprayed with water.

"He was a soldier. We did what we do to soldiers who betray their country."

"What are you going to do w-w-w-ith me?"

Koop sighed. "Father. It's your lucky day. I'm sick of killing people who deserve it. But I understand you have a sacrament in your church that can wipe away all my sins?"

"Yes. Reconciliation."

"I don't have to kneel, do I?"

"You want me to hear your confession?!"

"Yes. And, while yer at it, could you pour me one of those beers?"

CAMERAS EVERYWHERE—2018

"Hey!" Winston called from the other side of the house.

I heard the microwave beeping. "You need something?" I asked, sitting up in bed. (I had been dozing.)

"There are cameras everywhere. In every room."

"So?"

He came to the bedroom door and leaned against the door jamb. Eating a breakfast burrito.

"It's kinda funny. I mean: I'm in the surveillance business and you've got cameras everywhere." He sat cordially on the edge of my bed. "It's quite a collection."

I shrugged. "Most of them don't work. I like the way they look."

"When did you get into cameras?"

"After the accident. I got disability. I've always loved photography. I thought maybe I could make a business out of portraits."

Koop smiled. "Good idea."

"What?" I asked, seeing something in his eyes.

He shook his head. "Nothing. Makes sense."

"So I apprenticed with a pro—a friend of mine who owned a studio in Detroit. Used to shoot car ads. But it's the opposite of what I love about taking people's pictures."

"What do you mean?"

"After I set up my little studio and made some business cards, my first customers were families. They'd come all dressed up for their yearly group shot. Christmas photos. Graduations. Bar and bat mitzvas. They come all fancy in some version of themselves that everybody fawns over and tells them is beautiful. And all I got to do is get the lighting right, and make sure they're all in position, and I get a few where nobody blinks. And it's just . . . awful.

"And I remember all the shoots my friend used to invite me on. I think he was feeling sorry for me and trying to, you know, set me up?"

Koop smiled. "Models. Let me guess. You passed."

He knew all about my shyness handicap with women.

"Shuttup. I don't care how pretty they are, it's not enticing. They spend hours in makeup and hair and wardrobe, and when they come to the set they're all freezing 'cause they're underdressed or famished or so stressed out they can't stop smiling. It's the opposite of beauty."

"Maybe your standards are too high."

"You're not listening. They scared me."

"The women?"

"The pros. The 'it' girls. The ones who had a gift. They could fake it. They could pretend better than anyone. They knew where the camera was; they knew their best angles; they knew when they had to turn on. And they did the most amazing imitations of human beings you've ever seen. You couldn't tell they didn't just happen to lean against that Buick Riviera in that perfect way. With their hip just so."

Koop smirked. "I doubt that was their idea."

"Well. No. Good point. But that's when something funny happened."

"What?"

"I found my eye. Or rather I found what really interested me. I started taking pictures of the crew. The bored helpers, the gaffers and the grips and their deep tans. The makeup ladies. They were cool. They were charming. They had to be. Mostly they were all in on the joke that everybody behind the camera was the real world and everyone in front of the camera was bullshitting.

"I began to fall in love with their faces. Don't laugh, I'm serious. Once you catch that—there's no going back. I stopped visiting his studio. Started taking pictures of friends. But even friends can't get there. People you've known all your life are cagey—they think you're trying to catch them off guard or they're a bit resentful that you'd interrupt their real life with a chance to record history. This was before 'selfies,' obviously. Before everyone became a star of their own show."

I got up and took a picture off the wall. An old friend I met at a donut shop. Sparrow. An old hippie with long gray pigtails who used to have a crowd of cats and dogs.

I showed him.

"See that? That sunburnt face. Those green eyes. That's beauty. That's not someone posing, putting on a face, pretending to be human. That's a human. That's a Now Person. They do not give a shit about posterity. Or their next job interview. They are just . . . there. And I tell you: that shit is addictive. People being themselves.

"It's when the mask goes down. When they stop being everything they think they should be. When they allow you to see. To glimpse."

I put the photo back on the wall.

"See, the trick I learned is just to wait. Point the camera and wait. Because, first, they get a sense that I'm trustworthy. That I'm not gonna fuck with them. That I'm okay. No threat. Just me. Adam Pagnucco. Adam. Nuke. The guy with the camera. If we can get that far, I know I'm in—I can go all the way. Because eventually entropy takes over."

"Empathy?"

"Entropy! They get tired. They riffle through all their faces. The tried and true. The old standbys. The cutie pies. But eventually, they get exhausted and they got to stop. They breathe. And when they breathe, I know it's coming. So I listen for that intake. I am ready. I might laugh. Crack a joke. Say anything, even if it's stupid. I used to take passport photos, and I'd get all these tense women who could never be satisfied with their mug shots, and you know what usually worked? I'd tell 'em: 'Don't worry. It's gonna look a lot better when you get off the plane.' So they'd laugh and realize how everyone looks after a flight, and they'd stop thinking about their goddamn face and start thinking about . . .'"

Koop said, "A fountain sculpture of dolphins in Rome, or the smell of bread in Paris."

"Or all the neon in Hong Kong."

"Ever been to Hong Kong?"

"No."

"Didn't think so. I wouldn't remember the neon. The smell of fish, maybe. So then?"

"Then it happens. I start clicking like mad. Because, just like that, they go from being a stressed-out passenger running late for the gate to imagining their dream vacation. And they're Not Thinking of Themselves. They're watching a sunset."

"Or a belly dancer lit by a crackling fire," he said.

"Shuttup," I said as Koop laughed silently. "I fucking get it— you've been everywhere this side of the rainbow; I've been nowhere. But then. *Then.* Shit gets real. Something else happens that makes what came before look like a dusty entrance in the Louvre."

"You've never been to the—"

"—*Shuttup.* This is my point. I can hardly put it into words. They become themselves. And, buddy, let me tell you. There is nothing so beautiful on this earth as a singular human being giving you the gift of their soul. It breaks my heart. The god's truth is: I fall in love."

For a second I couldn't speak.

"But, strangely, it also feels like they're looking right through me, like I'm not even there. And part of me always thinks: What a gift. What an amazing fucking gift. Why can't we give that all the time?"

Koop was repressing a laugh.

"What?"

"I just think it's hilarious. The doodler who couldn't draw a human likeness to save himself specializes in portraits."

"True. I could never reproduce a human. I could only capture them."

Winston had finished his burrito and stunk up the whole room, and over his shoulder I could see he was watching two tiny birds skittering across the pale blue sky—so high they looked like they were going slow, weren't making any progress at all. But then they crested upward and the sun caught them and we could see their golden wings beating madly. They were in a hurry.

Then he noticed three black-and-white portraits of a woman on the dresser, a woman in her forties, calm, intelligent eyes hiding an affectionate smile. Koop went to the dresser and picked up one of the frames. The special one. "How many years has it been?" he asked over his shoulder.

He turned and said, "I'm sorry."

Then, "I'm sorry, Adam."

Then he was touching my head. "Nuke? I'm so sorry."

THE LITTLE GUY—2006

"The President wants to see The Little Guy."

"Oh, Christ. I hope we can talk him into a teleconference. Do a link?"

"*No.*"

"A chat's just good as—"

"—*No.* No IM. No phone. He wants the Full Monty."

"Oh, Christ."

"He's aware of the risks."

"Have you—has anyone tried to talk him out of this?"

"For the last six hours he has been in situ with the Joint Chiefs of Staff. They were unanimous in their discouragement."

"The secretary of state?"

"She's in Europe. Gathering a coalition. But he has her full support."

"Mr. Vice President . . . This is a nightmare."

"Then I'm sure you people have devised a nightmare scenario, and a backup. I have."

"You're washing your hands of this? Sir. You may be the one sane person in the White House! Do I have to spell it out for you!? It's dangerous. Everyone who works with The Little Guy eventually retires."

"I've been briefed on the rumors."

"Rumors? Christ Almighty. Have you been to Nevada?"

"Personally? No."

"The President has. Twice."

"I know."

"He has contracted the syndrome. Just like the rest of them."

"There is no . . . That is unconfirmed. His doctor assures us he is in perfect health."

"What about his shrink?"

"The President of the United States is not mentally ill."

"Is this line secure?"

"Yes."

"Then let me say this: bullshit! My considered opinion as a doctor and a scientist is that The President's IQ has dropped at least forty points since his first term. Or should I say: ever since we told him about The Little Guy and he insisted on a few fireside chats."

"That is speculation."

"Are you the only person in America who hasn't noticed? He called astronauts 'courageous spatial entrepreneurs.' Good God."

"Heh. That's a new one for me."

"Look. It's obvious to all of us here. For him to risk another interview is like, I don't know, like traipsing around a radioactive dump."

"Nevertheless."

"Oh Christ. I can't be held responsible. I have voiced my misgivings at the highest level."

"Watch it, Doctor."

"Doesn't he understand he is risking Real National Security every time he meets The Little Guy? We've just begun to crack the code on our fighters."

"The snake is still . . . peaceful?"

"For now. Surely, sir, you must have heard of some of the Incidents?"

"I don't believe in fairy tales, Doctor."

"His powers are growing."

At that, the Vice President, or as his commander called him, "The Big Guy," picked up a phone, punched a few keys, and activated his backup plan.

"Please, sir. He goes through specialists like a virus. Six months with him and all they want to do is meditate on a mountain somewhere. He has taken some of our best minds and turned them into mush! He insists on meeting everyone naked!"

"That's new. So you'll set it up then." It wasn't a question.

"Fine."

"Just a touchdown. Brief chat. He wants to be home for Christmas dinner."

"I'll see to it, but I can't promise—"

"Doctor?"

"Yes, sir?"

"You do understand that the only reason you still have your job is because this is a secure line we're talking on, right?"

"Yes."

"Good. If any of the statements you've just made were to reach the public record, I would consider it a breach of national security on the highest level."

The flight left D.C. around 2:30 a.m. It arrived at an undisclosed location in Nevada just about sunrise. The heat was shimmering as the camouflaged hangar door rose. It looked—and it was meant to look from the one angle where it was visible, which is to say, invisible—like the shadow of a dune had briefly wavered before the door slid closed. The hangar was gouged into the ground on a twenty-degree slope and extended the length of some five football fields.

The beige cement they walked on was actually a composite that sprang ever so slightly under their boots and made their footsteps silent. This was but a minuscule slice of the budget the base expended every year—a figure sometimes astonishing even to those who signed the checks. The party of twelve—nine of whom were armed guards—were met by the general of the base and his staff of six, including three doctors in white. After a brief greeting, all but two guards entered a men's room.

Each of the party took a seat in a stall. On a code word spoken by one of the general's staff (had anyone else spoken the word, the bathroom would have been flooded with a jelly substance that would have preserved any life in stasis for approximately seven days) the room seemed to tilt. Each man in his stall leaned gently to the left as the room slid sideways.

They heard The President say, "I love that part."

The party was reminded that Total Silence was required for the next five minutes. They left the bathroom and followed the doctors single file down a descending tunnel carved out of limestone. There were lights every fifty yards or so. At the bottom of the tunnel was a thick glass door. The lead doctor placed his lips against it. There was a brief flash of light.

"Kiss prints." The President chuckled.

There was a loud whoop that was silenced by a word spoken by the base commander. Had anyone else spoken the word, the tunnel would have been flooded with water.

The glass door slid open to reveal a small barracks. A dozen cots wrapped with crisp white linens lay under a dozen windows—each held a different bucolic scene painted on the glass, which of course wasn't glass.

The commander instructed the soldiers and the doctors and The President to strip and lie down on the cots.

"I know the drill," the Commander in Chief said testily, undoing his tie.

When the party (two guards would stay behind) were all in position, the general and his staff parted ways with the visitors and stepped behind the thick glass door. They did not shake hands.

"We'll be in the observatory," the general said over the intercom.

A yellow cloud of fumes filled the room. In seconds all the men were sleeping. In ten minutes the entire room had been purified. All residual filth, dust, loose particulate, and surface bacteria were vacuumed up and swept away in a wave of ozone. The men woke smelling like they had dozed off beside an Olympic pool. They gathered at one end of the room, feeling invigorated and alert.

The President, two Secret Service agents, the remaining guards, and the three doctors walked down the green hall, which seemed to be lit by some mysterious interior source—as if the walls themselves were translucent. One of the Secret Service agents carried the nuclear football, a black suitcase that contained the end of the world and was never more than a couple dozen steps from the Commander in Chief. At the end of the green hall, the President remarked that he hadn't noticed they were walking on a curve until this visit. He seemed proud of himself for noticing.

"Very astute of you, sir," a Secret Service agent said. The head doctor, who had arranged the rendezvous, did not remark that The President had said the exact same thing on each of his previous two visits.

The naked men stepped into what appeared to be the lobby of an art deco hotel. There was a gold oversized revolving door, and leading to it, a narrow Moroccan rug ran the length of the long room. String muzak played just above the threshold of hearing. A diminutive doorman in a red uniform with golden epaulets and piping greeted them. He regarded the naked party—the soldiers, the doctors, The President, and his two Secret Service agents, with a merry aspect and rosy cheeks and a shock of white hair. A jovial sort with high spirits and considerable charm—it was not unusual for people who met him the first time to think: He could easily play an elf at the mall.

Had anyone been paying attention they might have noticed the doctors' body language became extraordinarily formal. The soldiers smirked. They assumed this was the final level of security they'd been briefed on. A security protocol so secure no one knew about it.

They did not yet fathom that they had arrived.

"And how can I be helping you, gentlemen?" The slightest hint of an Irish brogue.

"Visitors," the head doctor said.

"At this hour? Have they been screened?"

"Of course," the doctor said. "Highest Levels. Greatest Confidence."

The red doorman surveyed the group with friendly amusement, his tiny thumbs tucked into the pockets of his red vest.

The doctor stammered. "I assure you. Greatest Confidence. Highest Levels."

The red doorman crossed his arms over his chest and raised a bushy white eyebrow.

The doctor said: "For God's sake—it's The President!"

"Oh, I recognize him. It's this green man I'm not sure about. Could I ask your name?"

He was obviously referring to one of the guards. A man who stood with both hands held before his groin, whose muscular frame looked powerful enough to make good on any threat he might choose. There was a bleeding heart tattoo on his right shoulder, and under it "Semper Fi."

The naked man with the suitcase stepped aside, and the soldier strode over to the little man and looked down with contempt. "Dewey. Sergeant James Dewey. Marines. Honor Guard."

"Wet work?" the red man asked.

"Fifteen years. Afghanistan. Pakistan. Serbia. Libya. Iraq."

"What's your child's middle name?" the red man said as if he were making conversation at a tea.

The soldier paused. "I have two children."

"Very good." The little red man smiled. "I'm referring to the off-the-record one."

The soldier swallowed. "Lisa. I mean, Lisa Marie. Marie is her middle name."

"Like Elvis!" the little red man laughed. "Lovely name. Where's Lisa now?"

After a moment the solider replied, "I don't know."

The other soldier moved in front of their commander in chief. If you hadn't been watching for it, you wouldn't have noticed.

The little red man clucked his tongue against his teeth. And gazed sadly into the eyes of Sergeant Dewey. "It's a hard, hard thing for a father to be kept from his child. You can take your finger off the trigger now."

The soldier removed the sidearm he was not carrying.

"Now if you'd just gently lay it on the floor."

Sergeant Dewey hesitated.

"A man of your talents and dedication needs no weapon but his body to do his duty."

The man squatted and put the gun that wasn't there down on the floor that was.

"Now," the little doorman said. "Please go sit on that couch over there. You've done a fine job. You've done what any father would do to save his daughter. You've not been naughty at all. You've been very, very nice. Go on, now. Have a seat."

Sergeant Dewey let out a huge sigh, dropped his head, turned, and walked over to the plush red velvet couch under the life-sized portrait of Woodrow Wilson in an ornate golden frame.

"That's right," the little man said. "That's perfect." He turned a disgusted scowl toward the head doctor. "Highest Levels," he said with a smirk.

Then he addressed the group. "Now, please, gentlemen, listen. I'm going ask the group of you a great favor. I want you to keep your eyes on the revolving door."

All eyes turned to the spinning door.

"Not you, of course, brother. You're the memory man. You can't help yourself." The black man smiled. "You've been drinking more these days, I notice."

"Not a problem," Koop said.

He raised one bushy white eyebrow. "If you say so."

Then the Leprechaun called the group to order.

"Gentleman! I give you The Revolving Door! A beautiful piece of work, is it not? I'd ask you to admire it for a short time while I attend to a wee bit of business. I'd ask you all not to turn your attention from the door—for any reason. And I'd ask also, that when you leave this beautiful lobby, you carry forth none but the most pleasant memories of your brief interlude. You came; you did your duties; you protected your commander; and you left none the wiser. You did not hear anything or see anything but the revolving door for the next sixty seconds."

The little red man disappeared from their line of vision.

Who among them could do anything but admire the handiwork of the craftsmen who had labored for what must have been months to create this roundelay, this music box, this merry-go-round of exquisite cut glass framed in burnished gold—the attention to detail was riveting. It was a feast of design preserved from another era. An era that wasn't ashamed to indulge in beauty, no matter the cost. Their admiration reached an elated pitch. Even the hushed bristles of palomino horsehair at the revolving base swept away all dust and disturbance with the most elegant simplicity.

"Now," the little red man said, reentering their field of attention. "What is it that I can do for you?"

The President stepped forward. "Sir, I need your advice again."

The small man nodded thoughtfully.

"Come into my office then." He directed The President with a small stubby hand. The calluses were still there even after sixty years of captivity.

They entered the revolving door. It spun, The President noticed, until they no longer saw the nervous doctors, the stiff soldier, or his rodent assistants—just a smear of color that hummed about them in a cocoon of reassurance, till there was only he and the little red man who smelled of Christmas: pine, peppermint, and hot cocoa.

The President cherished these moments. He felt, once again, privileged to know all the answers to the test before he had even begun to take it. He knew that other leaders would envy this astonishing font of intel, this beacon of insight by which only he and his scientists were illuminated.

But where the scientists saw a cheat sheet for patents and stealth, and his generals saw a hard-on tactical advantage for weaponry development, he saw, in a silent chess game he played in his mind, a bold stroke of stratagem. The ultimate double-cross. He had determined early on that this Santa, this captured alien who had shape-shifted into this dwarfish Saint Nick under their captivity, could only be trusted to lie. Hell, wasn't his name a derivation of Satan—The Father of Lies himself? He would not trust one word this dwarf said. He would, in fact, charm him, use him as a perfect foil. For he knew this creature was not who he appeared to be. The Big Guy had briefed him: this was an alien with an alien agenda. His slick guile could only confirm his suspicions. And he had determined he would do the Exact Opposite of whatever he was advised. He had worked it all out with The Big Guy. Though to this day he wasn't sure which one of them had thought it up. Ahh, didn't matter. It was their Nightmare Scenario Slash Double-Cross. Their Ace in the Hole.

In the timeless, spinning room The President stood next to the Leprechaun who reached up and held his hand. Yet in his presence The President always felt as if he were the child, that he was sitting on his lap, looking up into those wet kindly eyes, telling him from the bottom of his heart that which he most dearly wished for.

"And what's on your mind today, sir?"

"Well, we're in a bit of a sticky in the Middle East."

"Again?"

"Yeah. Tell me about it. We're keeping the lid on it. But that's not why I'm here."

He was not a man given to introspection (he preferred prayer), so he used his face to squeeze out his misgivings.

"I am worried about my legacy. As you probably know, my second term is winding down. I admit: I am not the most beloved president ever—I know that. But I feel as though I have acted with honor and principle and have done what I think most right for my country."

"I have no doubt, sir. You are a man of clear conscience. I see that."

"I want to be remembered as a leader who left his mark on history. Terrorism. Entitlements. Wall Street. I never want it said that I had a chance to act and left any stoned unturned."

The little man nodded. "I see it is a great burden you carry. This country of yours that has been my host these sixty of your years. You carry it much like that poor soldier who was sent to kill you. He carried the memory of his bastard child. A child he would do anything to save, even if it meant sacrificing everything he had fought for his entire life."

"I don't recall any soldier or child."

"I know," said The little man gently. "Here's what I think, Mr. President."

If The President's face was furrowed before, now it was positively wrung with concentration.

"You have the egg?"

"Oh, sure." And he handed it over.

The little man sighed and began to fiddle with the white oval. "I fear I must risk your boredom by repeating all that I have said to you and your predecessors before. You can only do what you think is right, sir. If there is war—make peace. If there is poverty—share the wealth. If there is sickness—bring healing to all. If there is ignorance—support your teachers. And, finally, if your planet is unwell—do everything in your power to heal it. Even if it means changing the way you have grown accustomed to live. In all cases, do the right thing. Surround yourself with your betters. Never side with the powerful over the poor. Never play on the fears of people. Always speak the truth no matter what it costs you. Let that be your legacy, Mr. President."

"Thank you. Thank you so much, my friend. I sure will miss our talks."

"And so will I."

"And I sure wish I could give you what you most want."

"I know, sir. You always do mean well."

The President left the revolving door and reentered the ornate red velvet lobby, where he was met by his party. He handed back the egg, saluted the tall man in the blue suit, but he did not see the soldier with the broken neck sprawled on the couch. He did not trouble himself with unnecessary data. He was busy reconfiguring everything the alien had told him. He hoped to have it sorted out by the time he made it home for Christmas dinner.

They were having pig.

BUBBLE WRAP—2017

Rodney, the portly gentleman, dialed the combination on the small black safe behind his desk. The knob was wet when he had finished twirling it. Out of the hold of darkness, he scooped up the smallish blue leather-bound notebook and turned in his rolling chair to the desk behind him. He moved a tiny rodent skull aside and presented the thin manuscript to the gentleman in the blue suit who sat across the desk of his cluttered study.

Carefully, the portly man lifted the fresh blue check into his hands and inspected it. It had been endorsed to "Cash." The sum would have been shrugged off had it been announced at a real estate closing ceremony.

For a castle.

"Thank you."

"You're welcome." Winston Koop laid a palm on the book. "A rare document.

"Indeed. One of a kind," the man admitted proudly.

Koop riffled through the pages. "I've only seen copies until now."

"Indeed. First and only edition!"

"I assume my check will sustain your lifestyle once you've closed the lending society."

"That should be no problem. You have been most generous. I was frankly astounded you were able to find me here. But, obviously, you are a man of resources."

"And I am persistent." Koop smiled. "This anonymous man?

Who sent the unpublished manuscript to you? Can I assume you never made his acquaintance again?"

"Sir, that would be accurate."

"No contact at all."

"None."

"That is unfortunate. I had entertained some notion of meeting this amazing artist."

Rodney laughed gently at the impossible prospect. "We never actually met. Our business agreement was for me to represent him as an agent seeking publication. I fulfilled my part of the bargain. Once I exhausted any avenues of interest . . ." He shrugged.

"There were no 'takers'?"

"None, I'm afraid."

"But you kept the manuscript."

"I did." The man began a series of variations of the head shake. "Though, at first, I had little sense of its worth. The artist left no forwarding address. Returned none of my voicemails. I tried for months. It was futile. For all practical purposes, he had disappeared."

"Or he had become invisible."

The man's jowls had stopped jiggling. "Sir?"

"Like you. I applaud your tenaciousness. The way you've safely hidden your society for years. Discretion is something of a specialty for me, so I admire a proficient."

The man bowed his head.

"You have, I take it, a mailing list of your . . ."

"Subscribers."

"Subscribers! Exactly. I will need that list."

Hastily, Rodney wrenched opened the top drawer of his desk, removed a USB stick, and set it on top of the blue notebook.

"This is the master?"

"Yes, sir."

"The only other copies are where?"

"On this laptop."

"I will need that."

"Of course." The man pushed it across the desk as if it were suddenly radioactive.

Koop slid the laptop, the notebook, and the USB stick into his pale white briefcase. "I'll have it all back to you within the week." Koop gave the Boy Scout sign. "Scout's honor."

"Not necessary. Keep it."

"Excellent. Now this final yearly banquet you've invited me to."

"A very exclusive dinner. All the Friends of Cats go. I assure you. Top shelf. The peacock paté . . ."

"All members have RSVP'd?"

"Oh yes. They wouldn't miss it. Seven p.m. on the dot."

"I have my password. My invitation. And I have directions to the lodge."

"Then you should have no problem finding it."

"Thank you."

"You are most welcome."

"I take it there is usually a reading?"

"That is the typical program. But now that depends entirely on you. I had presumed this would be our final gathering. Since we will no longer have access to our missal." By now Rodney's face had the eagerness to please of a puppy's.

Koop looked around the office. "Now, this house, your home? Was this where the initial interviews took place?"

"Yes. But over the years we've honed our methods."

"Honed?"

"Yes. The lodge is a wonderfully designed place. The tunnels downstairs allow us the privacy we need, and a connecting system of caverns allow for disposal."

"Disposal." Koop laughed dryly and continued, "So. Roughly . . . how many? Hundreds?"

The portly man nodded. "Several hundred, I should think. Five hundred at the most. It's a funny thing. Methods." He leaned forward, and his voice took on a leering confidentiality. "I think a tour of the basement will tell you all you need in that regard."

The portly man talked a wild streak of adrenaline and relief (he had initially taken Koop for a blackmailer). As they descended the stairs, he was huffing and puffing, taking the steps one at a time.

"I have to admit that, at first, it was something of a queasy-making ordeal. And then. We became more practiced. More, shall I say, adept. The tail was grabable, for instance." He showed him with his hands.

"Not at all slippery. Once we learned how, frankly, easy it was to—well, have you ever picked up a piece of bubble wrap and begun pinching the bubbles between your finger and your thumb? It has the most satisfying POP—does it not? The leftover plasma is a bit gooey. I admit: after a while, the process can become very addictive indeed."

When he turned on the lightbulb, Koop noticed the dirt floor was covered with footprints.

"Wait a second," Koop said. He held up one finger to silence him, and cocked his head.

"Oh, the silence. Yes, it's very peaceful out here. We are quite a ways from the road. The lodge is even more isolated."

Koop lifted his finger higher.

"Do you hear that?"

"No," Rodney said.

Koop turned to him and smiled.

"It's the last moment of your life."

BLUFF CALLING—2018

"Koop?"

"What?"

"Come on. Tell me. How . . . you got into all this."

"I was getting there." He took a deep breath.

"Nah. You really weren't."

Koop raised an eyebrow.

"Koop. This is me you're talking to. Did you forget? Telling me the sob story of your bad marriage and the mind-blowing tale of how a stressed-out-of-his-mind drunk dealt with having to save the world from god knows what? Ghosts? Aliens? Government conspiracies?"

"You think I'm lying?"

"No. I think you're doing the most elaborate denial dance in AA history. I think you're telling me five percent of what you know. And you are running like a fool because if you look back—well, Satchel Paige."

"'Something might be gaining on me.'"

"Right."

"You're the only person I could tell this to, Nuke."

"I believe you. I just don't believe you're telling me the whole truth and nothing but the truth."

Now if you're thinking I suddenly turned into a prick, I should explain. Sometimes drunks make bargains. Koop knew I got this. We confess to a host of lesser sins to hide the torturous secret that is killing us slowly. Our whole lives become plea bargains. No, I didn't wreck the car—I've been working so hard that I fell asleep at the wheel. It's a miracle I survived! That only works for the first few cars. It does not hold up in court.

Koop's long, circuitous story was beginning to sound very familiar. Like the tales I've heard in a hundred bars. It's what we do. We make fast friends with strangers under the vigil glow of the altar of liquor bottles and trade our sorry tales for the illusion of friendship and intimacy—two of the most terrifying things for a drunk. We don't want friends. We want enablers—buds who'll pour us another one and put up with our bullshit and let us cry on their shoulders so long as the liquor flows.

But the straight story is the only thing that cures us.

Don't get me wrong: Koop told a great story.

But I was starting to see the shadows in the corners. The unspoken. The inadmissible evidence. The forbidden witnesses. The bullshit.

"Okay," he finally said.

"Okay?"

"Okay."

THE VOICE IN THE CLOSET—1972

"It started in the hospital," Koop said.

"You drank yourself sick."

"I did."

"When?"

"After Nam. '72. I'd been an intelligence officer stationed in Saigon—what they now call Ho Chi Minh City. A language expert. I interrogated a lot of people. My specialty, I guess." He looked at me. "You know what interrogation is, right?"

I nodded. Then I saw his face. Finally, I said, "Torture?"

He nodded.

"After my second tour they shipped me home. Nobody at the vet hospital in Allen Park could diagnose it. My symptoms were exhaustion and stupidity. By 'exhaustion' I mean I slept fourteen hours a day. I couldn't drive a car, as I'd nod off at the wheel. By 'stupidity' I mean I couldn't read a book—I'd forget the sentence I'd just read—I couldn't even follow *Jeopardy* on TV. All I could do was rest. Also I'd forget things. Sometimes I'd forget what I was thinking or saying. I'd be in the middle of a sentence . . ."

I heard a dozen different things in the long silence that followed.

"Like that."

"Wow," I said. Koop never confessed to weakness. This was, at the time, mighty impressive.

"One doctor said the brain is a mystery and we have only the crudest understanding of it. We know where we feel pain or sadness—we can pinpoint that location, but we really don't know how this thinking machine works. Perhaps because we are using this mysterious thinking machine to examine the mystery of how it works. And the bulk of our studies are broken machines. As if the brain were a car that has lost its muffler, or runs on one less cylinder, or is missing reverse in the gearbox. Do you see something wrong with that methodology? Extrapolating wholeness from the fractured? I do.

"Because, I'd say most of what we are is what is still missing. So I was in the hospital for a sleep study (another dead end), and I started hearing this voice."

"Alcoholic hallucinosis?" I asked.

"That was one of their diagnoses. Unfortunately, that didn't make it go away."

"What did it sound like?"

"It was the voice of a child. You know how sometimes children's voices can cheer you up? Not the whiny ones, or the crying. But—I don't know—singing? Or laughing? Playground voices. Or just the way everything that comes out of their mouths is fresh—like thoughts that they are having for the first time? Anyway, in the middle of this beaten-down weariness I found it rather cheerful.

"By the way, they all have the voices of children, which makes sense considering how they are born. They never lose them. Even when they develop an adult vocabulary. They sound impish. At first I thought I was merely hearing a child patient. But there was no children's ward at the vet hospital. Then I thought maybe some child ran away from their visiting parents and hid themselves."

"She or he?" I asked.

"He."

"What did he say?"

"'Doo-Dah.'"

"Doo-Dah?"

"That's what he said. Like a question. I was coming back to bed from the bathroom and he said, 'Doo-Dah?'

"I stuck my head out in the hall and it was empty. The clock beside my bed had white flip-over numbers that read 3:30. My floor was quiet. I could hear somebody next door snoring. So I got back into bed. And after a time it was quiet."

Then: 'Doo-Dah?'

I thought the voice was coming from my closet.

I said, "Hello? Are you in the closet?"

I waited the longest time for an answer. Then just as I was about to lay my head back I heard the voice of this child.

"Yes."

I sat up in bed. Snow was coming down pale white in the glare of the street lamps. Another endless Michigan winter. It happens every year. Every Michigander eventually wonders why they live here. Why put up with a five-month winter? Five months of unrelenting gray, chill days that get in your bones, and it's no wonder we start hearing voices and talking to invisible creatures.

On the other hand, if there's a kid hiding in your closet, you really ought to do something about it, right? Somebody will be missing them.

"What are you doing in there?" I asked finally.

"It's mostly where we stay."

We? Christ, was this going to be a Scrooge hallucination? "Well, why don't you come out? It's dark in there."

"We like dark."

"Okay. The nurse is probably worried about you . . ."

No response. A patient? A man with a boy's voice?

"You should be in your room."

"We don't have rooms."

"What's your name?"

"Rudy."

Four years old. Maybe younger. "Hello, Rudy. That's a nice name."

No answer. "My name's Winston Koop."

"Koop."

"What are you doing in the closet?"

"Deciding."

"Deciding what?"

"Where to go next."

Had to laugh at that. "Hm! Me, too. I've been here three days and they don't know what to do with me."

"Did you know the boy?"

"The boy?"

"The boy who shared a bed with you?"

I got chills when he said that. Because I concluded: he was talking about the man who had died in this bed before me. I also felt like everything he said was without guile, truly childlike. Then I felt like I was lying inside the body of a ghost who wouldn't get up and get off the bed. And it gave me the shivers. "He was a boy?"

"Yes, but he's a man now."

No, I thought, rather haughtily, he *was* a man. Now he's dead.

I heard a bird call outside my window. A female northern cardinal? Then I realized I was mistaken. It was the sound of a chain clanging on a flagpole.

"He was my Doo-Dah."

"Doo-Dah? What's a Doo-Dah?"

Then I heard Chester the night-shift clerk coming down the hall singing. You remember, I told you about him and the old yellow man and the saucer? Co-Shipping?

I hear Chester singing, "CAMP TOWN LADIES SING THIS SONG, Doo-Dah, Doo-Dah, CAMP TOWN RACE TRACK NINE MILES LONG, OH THE Doo-Dah DAY!'"

He poked his bald head into my room. "Whatcha doing, Mister K?"

He was tall and goofy, and his skin was the color of milk chocolate. He looked like the grape man in those Fruit of the Loom commercials. His blue nurse's uniform complemented his green eyes.

"Hey, Chester. Can't sleep."

"The doctors would probably want me to report patients having half conversations with themselves."

"Half conversations?'"

He looked at me like I was lying.

"Chester, there's a kid hiding in my closet. Rudy? Don't be frightened now. Chester is good people."

Chester looked at me, shrugged, then walked over and opened the door to my closet. Even I could see it was empty.

"Just a bad dream, I reckon, Mister K."

I bit my lip. This was not pleasant news.

"Happens to all of us."

"Chester? Can I ask you a question? Who had this bed before me?"

He stuck his finger in his ear and squinted at the ceiling. "Todd . . . Robinson. Stroke. Died right there where you're lying. About this time, too. Night before last."

Jesus, I was right. "You're shitting me."

"Nope."

It was hard to feel really comfortable in the bed after that.

"How old?"

"Seventy-five, at least. You need anything, Mister K?"

"No, thanks. I'm fine."

"Aside from a little residual hallucination . . . ?"

"Right. You should probably mention that to the doctor."

"Oh, I will." He smiled. "You get some sleep now, Brother."

As an only child that term was one of the surprising benefits of serving. The brotherhood of vets.

Chester pulled a face and slipped backward through the door. I think he was trying to make me laugh, take my mind off things.

I could hear him humming the Stephen Foster melody as he headed back down the hall. It dawned on me: he was doing a parody of a minstrel show. Or Uncle Remus in *Song of the South*. Like I said: goofy.

Great, I thought. Another symptom to add to the list. Forgets. Aphasia. Exhaustion. Drunk. Speaks to people who aren't there. It took me weeks to consider that whatever my ailment was, however it had happened, it had opened the door to a whole new world that we walk through obliviously. I suppose all magic doors are like that. We never see them until it's too late and we've already stepped inside.

I was just about to doze off when a voice from the closet spoke as if we hadn't even been interrupted.

"He washed that man when he died.'

—2018

Abruptly, Koop asked, "Remember that night we went camping north of Toronto?"

"That again? Yeah, I didn't bring the tent. I thought you were bringing it."

"That's not what I mean."

"So, what?" I said.

"We tilted the picnic tables over, made an A-frame, and threw a few garbage bags over them. And dug a trench around it all. Worked great until the rain really started falling and we—"

"—got soaked in our sleeping bags. I remember."

"And to distract you, I told a story."

"Oh, sure. Alamogordo," I said.

"I know you get jumpy around weather."

"Shuttup."

"I also asked if you could choose one superpower what would it be?"

I was silent.

"You remember what I said?"

"Flying."

"Right," Koop said. "And what you said?"

"Being invisible. In case there were bears."

Koop chuckled deeply. "Invisible," he said. "Remember when we took showers at the campground?"

"Sure. You were so freaked out that I didn't wash my feet."

"Well, we'd been hiking through the woods for days, Mr. Pagnucco."

"I told you: standing in the soap suds and water is enough."

"Oh, I remember."

"My feet don't stink, Koop."

He held up both hands in surrender. "Remember listening to the rain? Feeling the splashes all around us. We heard something in the dark."

I didn't want to remember. "You heard it. I was asleep."

"Okay, I heard it. So you do remember?"

"Now I do."

It was birds making sounds I'd never heard birds make before. They sounded like tiny women singing. Maybe the storm freaked them out, too.

A long pause, then Koop said, "You should have brought the tent."

LEAVING HOSPITAL—1972

My position in the military gave me access to great health care, and skipped me to the head of a lot of waiting lines. Fuckall that did for me. My great coverage did not cure me. My doctor, or I should say the latest of many, came to release me the week after the kid in the closet. A Pakistani woman with black glasses and a kind face. She had my file and sat on the edge of my bed like we were old friends, when I had just met her three days before.

"You're going home," she said, smiling.

"Great."

"You don't seem happy about it."

Brilliant. These guys were crack diagnosticians. "I'm not cured. What's to be happy about?"

"Feeling a bit depressed, are we?"

I had, by then, caught on that this was their way of dodging blame. If whatever ailed me didn't show up tangibly on their tests, couldn't be quantified, then it was likely a Brain Thing, a Mood Thing, a Psych Thing, and, in short, Not Their Problem.

"I'd feel a lot better if you could cure me."

She gave me a pained smile. "Right now, we can only say what it isn't. The good news is: there's a lot of conditions you don't have!"

This was supposed to cheer me up? "Then we have a lot in common."

She didn't like that. No doctor likes being on the patient side. She pulled a business card from the pocket of her lab coat and gave it to me. "Call him. He's a good psychiatrist. Specializes in cases like yours."

"Weirdos with delusions?"

"Good one."

The card read, "Colin Lockwood. Licensed therapist. MSW. Veteran."

He was an amiable lumberjack with a thick salt-and-pepper mustache. He seemed to hover over the room even when he was sitting. I am not a little man, but my hand practically disappeared in his when we shook.

After the usual shrink/patient tango, my first session with Dr. Lockwood was going great until he said, "Tell me about the boy in the closet."

"I don't even know if he was a boy."

"You said: he."

"How can a hallucination have a gender?"

"I don't know. Why don't you ask him?"

"Ask him what?"

"To tell you about himself. In his own words. You can write it down, but—this is important—don't change anything—write *exactly* what he says. Don't worry about misspellings. Like a dream journal?" He made it a question in that gentle, conniving way shrinks and teenage girls have. "Just get it down. You can read it to me here. How's that sound?"

"What if he doesn't talk? He hasn't since the hospital."

"Have you talked to him?"

"No."

"Then maybe he doesn't think you're interested."

"What if he's still in the closet at the hospital?"

He smiled. "It's more likely that he represents something in your unconscious? Something that needs to get out. Clear? So I'm not really concerned about his location. He's either a magical being or the most common thing: a complex. In either case, I suspect he needs to be heard. Fair enough?"

So that evening I asked if he was still around.

I asked in every room in my house.

Silence.

I went to bed and woke up in the middle of the night.

I went to the toilet, and as I was going back to bed, he said, "Are you going to write it down?"

"Yew!" I screamed and jumped about three feet in the air. "Rudy?"

"Yes."

"Where are you?"

"In the closet."

"Whew. Do you . . . want to come out?"

"Not yet."

"Okay." After I breathed deeply for a bit, I felt better, though my heart was still drumrolling. "Let me . . . Let me get a notebook."

When you have a voice in your head that only you can hear, it's natural to think you have a problem. If it's a voice that makes no sense but at the same time does not seem irrational, it complicates the matter. I would have preferred an outright hallucination. It would have confirmed for me that I had gone over the edge. I've known a few psychotics in my time. Some of them were treatable with medication. But see how desperate I was? I was taking bitter comfort in the possibility that I might be crazy.

So I decided to dialogue with the ghost. I don't know why I called it that. I don't believe in ghosts, religion, or an afterlife. But I had to call it something.

"What do you want?" I asked.

After a pause that seemed to last way too long, he whispered, "I want you to hear my story."

"Okay," I said. "I can do that. But I'm bad at remembering these days."

"I know. That was me."

"That was you?"

"I can take away parts of you if I want."

That sounded vaguely terrifying.

"That's how we do forgetting," he said.

"I don't understand."

"It's a gift we take from you and we use it."

"Why?"

"I'm a soldier."

"Me, too."

"No, you play a soldier. You're a heart. You've lost your head."

"Rudy? You're gonna have to help me with this. I don't understand."

I'm in my bedroom in the middle of the night talking to an impossible invisible creature.

And the next moment I am walking down a city street. It's a gentrified alleyway somewhere in San Francisco. There's a huge mural of the face of an Asian woman with red red lips. Next to a darkened restaurant with a string of yellow Christmas lights over the recessed bar. Down the alley there's a photographer shooting a white wedding party of a bride and her bridesmaids—the cloud of perfume was enough to knock you over.

I'm strolling down this alley and I see my old girlfriend. The first real love of my life. And I was about to hail her when I somehow caught myself and remembered I would only regret the contact, and then I watched her walk into the arms of a man. And they hugged.

It was a very warm hug. An unmistakable hug of lovers. They're bodies touched in every possible public place, obviously remembering pleasure, obviously comfortable with closeness.

The photographer says, "Hold it! Hold it, ladies!"

If I could have stepped out of myself at that point—had the gift of being inside and outside at the same time—I would have seen a man standing still but ringing like a great bell, ringing and reeling with pain that ran up and down his nerves and touched every part of his body.

I felt that.

But I saw something else. I saw a white cord that twisted like a rope around my ex-girlfriend and stretched across the street into the hands of the strangest creature I'd ever laid eyes on. He was leaning against the brick wall under the giant face of the Asian woman and braced as if he were playing tug-of-war.

A creature pudgy and white—like a fat child who'd eaten too much ice cream. Was, in fact, made of vanilla ice cream. Not the yellowy white—the white white kind. Small black seal eyes. And though this creature had no mouth, I somehow knew he smiled: a toothless mouthless smile. The top of his flat head grew concave like a shallow bowl as he twisted and turned the white cord in both his white hands. Then I saw the source of the cord. It came from him. It was him. Or, more accurately, it was his tail.

I approached him and smelled something dreadful. Like something had died and nobody had buried it.

What are you doing? I thought.

What does it look like? Hurting her.

Why?

Because she hurt you.

Stop it, I said. *That's just what people do.*

Not me. Nobody hurts me. Rudyganderfeet's the name. Pain's the game.

I reached out and somehow cut the cord with a karate chop of my hand. The shock on his face as he lost his balance and fell to the street gave me pleasure. The shredded white cord snaked out of his hands and into the air like a sputtering hose. Then the long white umbilical cord stretched back to the woman's body, entered her belly button and disappeared. She fell to her knees and threw up in the street. Her lover bent over her.

"How'd you do that?" Rudy asked resentfully, rubbing his tail, which had evidently stretched back to its normal size. "Who taught you?"

I'd never seen one of them leave, so I watched with some astonishment as he thinned out like a splatter of white paint on the air and—poof—he was gone.

And I was standing in the dark bedroom again.

He left the smell of rotten meat. Rudy always stunk. I wonder if all the dark emotions he absorbed were oozing out. But when I asked him about that once, he said, "I've been too long in the wide world. I got it on me."

FORGETTABLE—1972

There may be more disturbing things than a voice in your head that becomes a pudgy ghost who strangles people with his long white tail, but at that moment I couldn't think of any. I took a chance and spoke to the empty room.

"That was my memory," I said. "I had been home on leave and I caught my girlfriend in a rendezvous by accident."

"Yes," the voice from the closet said.

"I forgot that. That was when I first got sick."

"You mean when you went on a bender."

"I was probably drunk and having a blackout."

"No," Rudy said. "I took it from you."

"The memory? How?"

"I can teach you. But first . . . my story."

"Okay."

"Are you going to write it down?"

"I probably should." I went to my desk and got out a notebook.

"Wait," I said.

It was one of those spring nights the world had taken a shower. The sky was a washed-out dark gray. I saw a soaked frizzy squirrel hop between the puddles. And when it gets dark, you don't notice the silence for a while. Hours and hours of the constant hiss of a downpour and you get used to the world being blotted out by white noise. Then I heard the silence. It reminded me of something.

Strange. It was the silence after my girlfriend and I had had our last argument. After weeks and weeks of talk talk talk. Accusations and swearing fits, oaths and venom, we eventually wore each other down like swimmers going against the tide. And we lay beached, spent, capable only of breathing, nursing ourselves back into some semblance of calm. But it was really just exhaustion getting the best of us. There was nothing else to be said. After so many useless words: silence.

I thought I learned that lesson. But I had to learn it again with my wife. I had to find out the hard way that some things just won't work. No matter how hard you try. No matter how badly you want them to. Eventually they end. And I held off until the very very very last moment. I had to discover that pain could be so great it was not worth the effort. It was a pain so cruel that I realized I would not even wish it on my worst enemy. So why would I allow it to be inflicted upon me?

Somehow the forgotten memory had settled something in me. It had given me peace. I do not have a clue why it should have. But I knew then that I wanted that ability more than anything I had ever wanted. I wanted to be able to spare people their worst. Rudy had returned to me a painful memory which he had erased.

What if I could do that?

Erase a painful memory?

What if he could teach me?

See, I had a gift for extracting the truth out of people who didn't want to tell it. Spies. Soldiers. Criminals. Liars. It's part of what I-men do. Almost everyone ended up talking to me. But what if— it hit me like a bolt—what if I could guarantee they could forget their secrets after they confessed? What if I could erase them? Who wouldn't tell me everything then? They'd be innocent, wouldn't they? I could unlock every door inside people. Lay open everything. I could learn all the secrets and spare everyone their conscience.

Here's the story that Rudy told me.

Rudy began: "When they are young and simple, I tell the IFs the truth.

"'You were not born,' I say. 'You happened after your Doo-Dah woke up. Somewhen after language and before conscience. They opened the door and you stepped out.'

"The youngers do not yet understand what those words mean.

"I did not understand many things back then either. I do not understand much now. I only know I love and I will not die.

"When my Doo-Dah woke me it was like I was sleeping in a dark box—I didn't know 'closet' back then. And he opened a door and I saw him: a little boy in pajamas—like a yellow starfish in a sack with too few limbs. (He had a starfish on his wall so that was how I knew it.)"

—2018

"Starfish?" said Nuke.

"Quiet, now," Koop said.

—1972

"'Come out,' my Doo-Dah said, 'I know you're in there.'

"And I was as soon as he said it.

"And I can still see him reaching his hand out to me. Out of the darkness I stretched my new tail to touch his tiny fingers.

"And I was in love.

"This you must know about us. We love.

"We have no choice. I'll explain: It is like a new bird hatched from its egg, shaking off the broken pieces of shell from its wet feathers. It will seek and follow the first thing it sees. A dog. A car. Possibly its mother. You see, even after our Doo-Dahs have no need for us, even after they have forgotten our names, we love them. We cannot help this. We love. We were made to love them.

"And some days—these are the days we live for—they see us. Or they think they see us. Or they *remember* seeing us. Or maybe they just catch our reflection in the mirror as they are passing through their busy lives. And perhaps they stop and frown. Perhaps their faces crinkle at a strange smell. This remembering pleases us even though it hurts. For we know: though we are The Forgettable, once . . . we were loved.

"And that is all any of us needs.

"That knowledge can carry us through a lifetime."

So that was the story I told my shrink. It flipped him out.

"Wow," he said.

"Yeah."

"I mean: wow."

"I know. That's pretty, what? Strong?"

"Believable. Like a whole implied mythology. Consistent even. The consistency shocks me, frankly."

"So what do I do?"

"Keep writing. How's your vertigo?"

"The same."

"Sorry."

It was so rare for any of my caretakers to express sympathy for my condition.

He asked, "Has no one . . . ?"

"Oh, they're intrigued. They're puzzled. Then irritated. Then embarrassed that they couldn't diagnose me, or cure me, or do anything really for me. I think I made them feel . . . inept."

"You probably did."

"But you're different. Why?"

Colin Lockwood, the large man with the bushy mustache, the kind blue eyes, and the gray jumpsuit, shrugged. "Maybe because I've been there. Hospitalized for five years when I was a young man.

PTSD. I tried to kill myself. Got help, got better. And decided that would be a good thing to do for a living. Help others heal."

"Can you heal me?" I asked. My chin trembling.

"I have no idea. I might be able to make life a little more bearable."

"Okay." I sniffled. "Cool."

"You're an only child, right?"

"Yes."

"Imaginary friends are more likely to occur with oldest or only children."

"So?"

"So I think maybe your illness has given you a unique opportunity. Imaginary friends are ubiquitous. They exist in every culture around the world. They seem to be a necessary sounding board, a companion who'll escort children into the next stage of development. They are the first rumbling of self-consciousness. Eventually they are integrated. And shed—like a baby tooth, I suppose, once the child is ready for adult food."

"But I'm not a child," I said.

"No, you're not. And, honestly, you don't strike me as having had a psychotic break. So, perhaps we're dealing with something unprecedented. A hidden creature? An autonomous entity? Maybe we've had only the vaguest hint of their existence—legends, myths— echoes of a reality just out of reach, a dreamscape that usually erases every morning." He saw my face and blushed a little as he handed me a box of tissues. "Sorry. I'm excited by the prospect. Go ahead. Take your time."

I hadn't realize I was crying. But he was the first person willing to believe in my ghost, or to at least entertain the prospect of its being real. I felt overwhelmed. I felt as if I wasn't in this alone.

"Tinkerbell shit," I said, trying to toughen up as I bawled like a baby.

THROUGH THE CRACK—1945—RUDY

"When they ask, this is what I tell all the youngers," Rudy said. "You came from their brain. You live at their whim. Nobody knows why you stay. When they are grown, you are forgotten."

I had not thought of my child in many years, when I heard a passing ice-cream truck playing a ridiculous circus calliope melody as it toddled down the street. It's summer, I thought. The boy will be hot. He will want some ice-cream. I recalled his joyous face as he looked up from his toys and screamed "Ice cream man!" and dashed out of his bedroom.

Then I thought, Is he hot now? Is the boy in the desert? Or perhaps on the lip of the mouth of a volcano and feeling the waves of the heat from the hot orange lava below. I wonder if he needs an Ice Cream Man now.

So I got the idea that I would leave the closet, find him, perhaps visit him, perhaps, if he would let me, stay with him. I discovered this was considered outrageous. No one had attempted it before.

They said, "He'll think you're a ghost."

"He won't even see you."

"You're wasting your time. Here. Eat a flower."

Thus was I discouraged by my crib-mates and the goats. Have I told you about the goats?

"No," Koop said.

"Oh, that must be later," said Rudy. "I was a long time with the goats in the cold."

"Were you cold?"

"Nice of you to ask. No. The goats kept me company on my long walk. They reminded me of the closet—the way they liked to huddle next to me. They do that sometimes in the rain. They thought they could warm me.

"After our children grow, sometimes we stay in the closet like old teddy bears waiting to be boxed and sent to charities, handed down to poor people, or trashed in a landfill somewhere. Have you seen landfills?"

"I have."

"They were the first mountains I saw on my way out of the city. Great stinking mountains that rise above the trailer parks with yellow dump trucks climbing up their spiral tattoos like ants carrying their loads. And every load-dump is greeted by a choir of squawking, hungry, hovering gulls. Raleigh says gulls are very stupid. Very determined. Very greedy."

"So are we."

"Yes. You leave so much behind. We do not. We cuddle or huddle together after you have no use for us. And every time you open the door, we stop and wait—'breathless as a new bride, yearning for her beloved's embrace.' I read that somewhere. But then you shut the door and it's dark again.

"Many a cheerful day we've spent huddling like that. A pile of old toys. For me it was the old gray brick house and the closet where Raleigh, PooMom, and The Other Guy grew up."

—2018

"Poo Mom?" said Nuke.

"Hush, now," Koop said. "Don't worry about that."

—1945

"Raleigh is always first. She was already there when we arrived. Raleigh pouts silently when she does not get her way—which is often. Raleigh says she is the prettiest girl in the world, but we can never see her. She's the invisible one. She says she was left over from the girl who grew up in this old gray brick house with the peeling white birch tree in the window. (That was our view through the crack in the closet door for years before I ventured out into the wide world where I took my chances and learned the truth.) Her host child was born in this gray house and grew up happy and moved away when she went to college. She only came back a few times after that. Raleigh said she took her teddy bears but didn't take her. Of course that wasn't fair.

"The last time she saw her child she was a woman and her mother had died and her dad was selling the house. It was a sad house back then, she said. Every wall you touched was cold and left you aching. She remembered her host coming back one last time to touch the red roses on the wallpaper and smell the smells, and Raleigh said she felt sure she would remember and open the closet again and run into her arms to comfort her. She felt sure she would say the right words. She could tell her about loss. About how the hurt does not go away. About how after a while it finds a place in you to rest and stops spoiling everything with its pain. But the girl never spoke to Raleigh, and she watched as this young woman in the blue sweater and blue jeans sat cross-legged in the middle of the hardwood floor and cried. Raleigh said she wanted to jump up and down, wanted to push open the closet door, which she could see through but couldn't budge.

"Then the woman left, and Raleigh felt like a bell had just rung in her. She felt that empty and that lonely and lost. She cried and that's when PooMom and The Other Guy showed up. Or that was when she knew she wasn't alone; she had companions in the closet."

"Pipe down," said The Other Guy.

"When did you get here?" she asked.

"We were always here," said The Other Guy. "You just never let us get a word in."

"Who are you talking to?" asked PooMom, terrified.

"The Ghost," The Other Guy replied.

"I am not a ghost. I am Raleigh."

The next family in the house was a young couple who loved each other deeply and argued and kissed. Argued and kissed. All day. Finally they had a little baby boy, and when he had words he went to the closet in his yellow pajamas and said, "I know you're in there. Come on out. All of you."

PooMom crouched there. It is always a brave moment for our hosts when they call us out. Often they are torn between fear and loneliness. Often they simply have to talk to somebody.

"Let me look at you," the boy said.

Talking to the corner of the open closet where the shadows huddled darkest, the boy said, "You are the dark one. You don't have to do that. You can stand up, PooMom." And at that PooMom stretched up to his full length, a quivering darkness in the corner between the ceiling and floor. We look, you see, exactly how you need us. "You're very tall," the boy said. And PooMom, who was still getting over the excitement of knowing for the first time his real name, quivered again. "And very brave. I bet you're not afraid of nothing."

At that the shadow stood straight and proud.

"And you," the boy said, turning to the white volleyball in the corner. "Come out. You're the Other Guy, aren't you?"

"Obviously," said The Other Guy.

The boy looked at him for a while and said, finally, "You're the smart one. You think of things we need to know."

"I would keep my voice down, if I were you. Somebody might hear us."

The boy spoke to Raleigh then. "I know you're there, but I cannot see you. That's okay. You're the nicest."

It was a joyous night: we whispered for the next hour or so until the boy was yawning. And we tucked him in.

When we got back to the closet, Raleigh said, "Boy, he's bossy."

PooMom had to be coaxed back into the closest. He wouldn't return until they were properly introduced and Raleigh stopped giggling at him.

I told you about Raleigh.

PooMom was from Africa. And The Other Guy was from the North Pole. Neither had any idea, of course, where those places were, but it is certainly nice to know where you are from, don't you think?

PooMom was very dark and tall, like someone had peeled your shadow off your feet at sunset when it was all stretched out across the lawn. He was so long he could be in two rooms at the same time. And he was only brave for the boy. As soon as they boy left, he curled back into a frightened little ball.

The Other Guy was rounder and whiter. "A Perfect Circle," he liked to say. And he was always correcting PooMom, saying, "Don't you know nothing?! That's a spoon!" And mean things like that.

"Don't be so rough on PooMom," Raleigh would say.

"Oh, buzz off, Sister. You're just a ghost nobody can see!"

"He doesn't have to see me," Raleigh said. "He can feel me."

"Ghost?" PooMom would say, frightened.

"Relax, PooMom," Raleigh would say softly. "There are no such things as ghosts."

Raleigh was the kindest. When gentleness was needed, she stepped up. She was bossy, but she was fair.

"I don't see what he needs you two for," The Other Guy would say. "I'm perfectly capable of raising a toddler."

"It's not up to you, O.G." (Raleigh knew he got annoyed when she called him that.) "Everybody gets a triple."

"He won't even remember you!" The Other Guy shot back.

"We are all forgotten," she said plainly. "All three of us."

"Shhhhh," The Other Guy said.

"That is our purpose: to show them themselves. We're The Forgettable. We exist to serve them. Once they are served, we are forgotten."

The Other Guy said, "You got a big mouth, Sister. No wonder the birds hate you."

So we were a triple: PooMom, Raleigh, and The Other Guy.

The boy was a very sweet child whose feelings were easily hurt. So it fell to Raleigh to reassure him he was a good boy. And PooMom would attack his fears and avenge his hurts. While The Other Guy would reason with him, always trying to get him to see the logic of things. Logic, he felt, was the way to handle everything. And he taught the little boy lots of new words. A new one every day so that his parents would laugh in delight and praise him.

"Love!" The Other Guy would say. "Happy! Nice!"

"Ice cream!" the little boy would say.

"Very good!" The Other Guy would say. "You know SOOO many words!"

"Soooo many!" the boy would say.

PooMom always wet the bed.

You never saw him drinking, but every morning the little boy would wake up in a wet spot of yellow and scowl at the guilty party in the closet.

He was so easily distracted. One moment we'd be giving him a lesson and the next he was gazing dreamily out the window, staring at a cardinal eating a red berry.

"This is my time," Raleigh would say. "I get all the dreams."

She would sit beside him and gaze into his face, and he would sit up in bed to watch the face of the moon with the same devotion.

We loved him and he was our reason for being.

This is our duty: to fight their biggest fears when they are most vulnerable.

To give them everything they need.

To be a guardian, a guide, a companion, even a scapegoat.

He was a very lovable boy. Quick to smile. Gentle. Loyal.

I never thought he'd leave me.

We never do.

THE ONE ABOUT THE DOG WHO
BIT THE BOY—1972

"So, are they always there?" the shrink asked me. "In the closets?"
    Here's what Rudy told me when I asked him.
    When we are needed, we are there.
    "And when do you leave?"
    We only go when you release us.
    "Why do we release you?"

—1948

I'll tell you the one about the dog who bit the boy. It is a very scary
story. And it happened on a dark and stormy night. One day the boy
was visiting his aunts and their black-tongued dog (whose nerves
were frayed by the lightning crashes) attacked him and bit him on
the mouth, tore open his lip. There was blood everywhere. And the
boy had sixty stitches. And after that it was hard for the boy to trust
anyone. He was quieter.
    And a week later he stopped talking to PooMom. Who he felt had
failed to guard him—his fiercest protector had let him down. Well,
this was hell for PooMom, and he shrank and shrank until he was
nothing but a dark corner in the closet.

The Other Guy tried to reason with him. "He is a mere beast. A mindless bundle of instincts and appetite. You can't expect a dog to know who not to bite. For goodness' sake, they eat their own poop!"

The boy ignored him.

PooMom slept.

A week later he forgot The Other Guy. He started reading books. And started concentrating in class. He became a shy, cautious little boy who trusted no one. And the starfish in his yellow pajamas never talked to his friends in the closet again.

"That's how they do it." Raleigh explained, lording it over us. "They leave. They forget."

"But why don't they say goodbye?" PooMom asked.

Raleigh had no answer.

"It's not fair," PooMom said.

"Fair?" scoffed The Other Guy. "There's no fair. Not this side of the rainbow."

So they waited in the closet, waited to be forgotten. Like a museum that no one visits anymore. Raleigh—the pretty girl, her eyes wide open in stunned grief. The Other Guy. A smudged and deflated volleyball. And PooMom. A dark, sad shadow in the corner. Remnants of other lives and other children. Stuff you throw in the backyard behind the garage.

We're always so sure our child will be different. I felt so much love for mine, I couldn't conceive a life without his smile, his trusting confidences whispered across the pillow after lights out, the way he shared his picture books with me, made room for me in the chair, and showed me his drawings that his mother taped to the fridge. The way I was the last person he said good night to. I could never imagine a life without his love.

Oh to live in such a simple world.

I remember looking out the crack in the open door, out into the street as the seasons passed one into the other, green spring becoming yellow summer, becoming burnt fall, then white winter. The window frame seemed to contain these changing seasons as a painting that continually redrafts itself, unsure of its final identity, uncomfortable with being one thing only.

There was safety in our viewpoint through the crack in the not quite closed closet door. We could watch it all go by like a country from the window of the train.

Do you know trains?

"Yes."

When I left the closet, I took a long train ride north. The world streams by like a dry river. A golden cat on a rusted oil barrel. A woman in a blue bikini sunbathing under the green maple tree on a red beach towel. A naked boy on a tire swing resting his head against the tread. A long, colorful splash of graffiti on the back of a warehouse. That is what you see from a train—the back of everything. Whatever they don't want they push into the farthest corners from their homes. Pile after pile—discards, debris, leftover toys, and planks of rotting wood. Broken lawnmowers, bent aluminum slides, ripped blue plastic swimming pools that can no longer hold water—and if you don't focus on them as you slide by, you just see blips, blips of dark brown like a pile of mulch in the corner. But they are regular. As regular as telephone poles. And they'd have that same visual musical effect—BLIP yawn pause BLIP yawn pause BLIP.

Clearly, there is a lot of stuff you people have no use for.

LEARNING TO LOSE—1972

Next session, Koop presented the shrink with a rough pencil sketch.

"Wow."

"He let me see him."

"Wow."

"For a second."

"Wow."

"Pretty rough. My old buddy Nuke could have sketched him better."

"Nah, this is good. No mouth, eh?"

"No."

"And this?"

"The head hole. That's not for talking. They're telepathic. It's how they breathe and listen and feed and fuck."

The shrink's eyebrows rose. "Feed?"

Koop said, "You were gonna say the other word, weren't you?"

"I was," the shrink admitted.

"Yeah. Sometimes they eat"—Koop cringed—"flowers?"

"Flowers?"

"Yeah. But mostly emotions."

The shrink nodded a lot. Nodded perhaps too much. "Those look like wings," he finally said.

"Yes, little, fledgling wings. Like cat's ears."

"Oh, yes."

"They flutter fast as hummingbird wings. They can fly very fast.

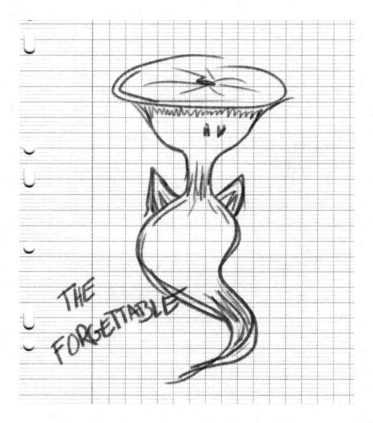

THE FORGETTABLE

Sometimes I can hear the high-pitched flutter, like cicadas in their mating season. Only softer. Those Doppler-like waves of buzzing?"

"Like phone lines in the winter?"

"Yes. Only much, much softer. Usually below the threshold of hearing. If you were to shake hands, they'd use their wing like a hand."

"And that tail."

"It's how they walk. It curls behind them like a snake."

"Wow."

"Yeah."

"Now, to us? They don't look like that? They appear—?"

"—However we want them to."

"He showed you how they are truly shaped. Why?"

"I don't know."

"Flat heads?"

"Cuplike." Koop shrugged. "Don't ask me."

"What are those words?"

"Oh that's just a scribble. Something they call themselves. 'The Forgettable.' That's one thing they all have in common. We forget them."

The shrink said, "And they can make us forget."

"I don't understand that part."

The shrink was quiet for a long time. "To be forgotten is to be lost. To lose yourself. Your place. Your story."

Koop said, "The three great losses."

"Three?"

"Loss of innocence. Loss of love. Loss of life."

"That's well said."

"He said it."

Rudy said, "All your lives are like that: learning to lose. Your childhood. Your love. Your life. Everything is borrowed."

"But, Rudy. You love your children."

He mocked me for that.

"Don't be a baby. We feed off of you. We feel hunger and call it love and maybe that makes our feeding sweeter. But, ask yourself, Doo-Dah . . ." (He calls me that sometimes even though I never knew him as a kid.) "If love is true, if it's not a waning, fragile thing—why then does it leave so quickly?"

His words stung me. I knew about leaving. And I knew the object of my desire was worthy of my love. But was I worthy of hers? At one time there was no question of that. I knew I had let her down. I knew my drinking had wrecked any chance of love. So the thought that it might not be reciprocal, that its power came not from desire and regard but mere hunger: her own childish need to be cherished, protected, touched, admired, wanted—this new thought stung me like a slap to the face. It is one thing to be loved and left. It is another to be disposable. Then, there is no comfort, no clean grief, and all joy is an illusion. No wonder Rudy was cynical about love.

"We feed off of you. Your rages and sorrows, your laughter and joy, are our daily bread. You want to die? Go away. Far away. Find yourself an empty corner like a dying cat, and after a week or two you will disappear. You will be like us. You will not even be a memory."

KOOP GOES TO NEVADA—1972

You can probably guess where the story goes from here. Broken hospitalized man gets the help he needs. Reconciles his trauma. Regains his balance. Returns to sanity and sobriety, and through the intervention of a helpful and temporary hallucination, he returns to a productive, ordinary civilian life and attains a measure of peace.

Nope. I went to Vegas.

By my next appointment my vertigo had cleared up. I was feeling almost normal. But my doctor wasn't there. And I never saw him again.

I was greeted by an older man in a blue suit sitting behind a desk, and two MPs. One stood at attention behind the old man; one stood at the door.

"Where's my doctor?"

"He's been reassigned. He apologizes for his abrupt departure. But I have your records here. And we are prepared to follow through on your case." He smiled. "We might even have some new orders for you, soldier."

I worked hard not to stare at the skin condition of The Blue Man, who looked as if he had just survived a brawl. His was a very pale and drawn face that resembled Marley's Ghost. There was definitely a haunted quality to it. The reconstruction surgery had left the bottom of his face a purple/blue bruise. For a moment I wondered if anybody else saw it. I tried to focus on The Blue Man's eyes and bushy eyebrows, but they seemed to contain their own dangers: it took a moment to see that his dark blue irises were not black.

As we talked he kept jamming no. 2 pencils into a white automatic sharpener on his desk. Imagine the following dialogue punctuated by those mechanical whines.

"Um. Who are you exactly?"

"That's nothing you have to worry about. I'm your commanding officer."

"You are?"

He waved a hand. "In so many words." Then he turned to one of the MPs and asked, "Jesus. Has no one thought to offer this man a Coke?"

"Would you like a Coke?" an MP asked with a Southern accent.

I was probably overthinking this, but it occurred to me that in the South "having a Coke" was generic for having what we call in Michigan "a pop," or what they call in Manhattan "a soda." The veterans' hospital was in Michigan, so I couldn't figure out what was being offered me. Besides, I wasn't thirsty.

"No thanks," I said. "I appreciate the offer. I really do."

"It's just a courtesy," The Blue Man said.

"I meant: about the job."

He looked at me.

"The assignment?"

"Oh. The orders."

"Yeah," I said. "That's a—ahhh. Flattered. Honored. Well, more surprised than anything, actually." I laughed a bit.

"Is this man on medication?" The Blue Man asked. The MPs looked at each other.

I rescued them. "No, sir. They're still pursuing a diagnosis. You know, I do think I'll take that Coke."

"Fuck the Coke. Do you want the job or not?"

"Okay. Sir? First: I don't know . . . what job . . . the job is. Uh. What's the job you're offering me?"

He didn't answer. He sharpened another pencil.

"Second: Has my doctor told you I'm not well?"

The Blue Man shrugged. "In so many words. I wouldn't worry about it too much. He gave you Highest Levels, top tier. Tip-top."

Why was he talking like a kiddie show host? Bluebell the Purple Clown.

"Actually, Doc says you're quite an unusual specimen. An officer with a bright and rosy future ahead of you."

"He said that?"

He consulted the file before him. "In so many words. Says here among your many gifts you're a savant in languages."

"That's right. I was a translator in Nam."

He slammed the file shut, held up one finger, and turned to speak to the MP by the door.

"He's thirsty. Get him a Coke."

"Yes, sir."

I was impressed by how quickly the guard exited the room. The shade on the window shivered for a few seconds.

"How many?" The Blue Man asked.

"One," I answered.

"One?" The Blue Man turned to give a sour look to the MP behind him.

"You're holding up one finger."

The Blue Man dropped his finger and cleared his throat. "I meant how many languages do you speak?"

"Thirty-three. I have a facility."

"Son. You are in the wrong business."

"Intelligence?"

"Fieldwork. Your doctor says you have a unique capacity to communicate with, uh, unusual company. Let's call them that."

"Okay."

"You can hear them. As well as see them. True?"

"True. That's what I'm trying to tell you: I'm crazy."

"Perhaps you are."

"I need help."

"Perhaps you do." He sharpened a pencil.

"So, am I going to get it?"

He quickly blew the residue off the pencil tip. "Perhaps not. Son, this folder"—he tapped it with his finger—"contains a glowing recommendation of your character, as well as your past service. And your government is eager—no—let me rephrase that. Your government, your Country, is committed to offering you a challenging post that will require all your gifts and your deepest—" He started snapping his fingers and turned to the MPs behind him. "What do they call it?"

"Values?"

"Fuck, no!" The Blue Man said.

"Muscles?" the MP offered.

"Useless!" The Blue Man spat. Then he folded his hands before him, chewed what appeared to be an invisible cud, looked under his bushy black eyebrows with his dark blue eyes, pursed his absurdly blue lips, and said; "Son. Your country needs you. Are you prepared to serve?"

"Of course. What is the position?"

"You will be my apprentice and will eventually replace me."

"And what is your job?"

He smiled. "Classified. You like golf?"

"No."

"I love golf. A blue sky. Nineteen greens stretched out before me. A day where the worst thing that can happen is a sand trap. Peace."

He said "Peace" like it was a place he'd never been to.

The MP came back in and put a can of Coca-Cola and a white pill on the desk before me.

"Thanks," I said, cracking open the can and taking a long swig. "Aaaaaaah."

The Blue Man said, "Take the pill."

"What is it?" I asked.

"Dramamine. We're going to Vegas."

"I don't have a problem flying."

The Blue Man looked at me, then pushed a paper and a pen across the table.

"Sign here."

I signed.

"Take the fucking pill."

I took the pill. "Sir, if I'm leaving, I should probably say goodbye to Rudy. Otherwise he'd be real mad."

"Your imaginary friend?"

"Yes."

"Who only you can see and hear?"

"Yes."

"You think he's here?"

"I do."

He shrugged and passed an open palm through the air.

"Rudy?"

I looked around. Even under the desk. The Blue Man gave me an odd look when I was done staring at his skinny legs.

"Rudy, I gotta take off for a bit. Sooo. I'm going to Vegas. Where we staying?"

The Blue Man had dead eyes. "The Flamingo."

"So, I guess I'll see you later, buddy."

The Blue Man crossed his arms.

"No need to say goodbye. I just thought I'd give you a heads-up. Okay? Okay."

"Okay," said The Blue Man as he jammed another pencil in sharpener.

When I woke up, I was staring out the window of a plane.

"I never get tired of flying," I said to The Blue Man next to me. "After a while, it's like reading hieroglyphics. You'd swear someone was unrolling a giant scroll, and the whole surface of the earth was an artifact."

Next to me The Blue Man yawned.

I yawned. "Hey. You're that guy!"

I craned my neck to look past the silver wing. "We're over desert!"

"You don't say."

"That's a lot of desert. Looks like Arizona. Or Nevada."

The Blue Man laid a hand gently on my arm. "Best not talk about what state, soldier."

At the bottom of the stairs from the plane I was given a black blindfold.

"Blindfold?"

The soldier said, "Yessir."

"I don't need a blindfold."

"Sir, it's either that or you go back on the plane."

"Don't be a fool," The Blue Man whispered. "Put it on."

We started walking, and I felt someone put their hand in mine to guide me.

It was the first time I'd ever felt his wing tip, and I must have made a noise.

"You okay there?" The Blue Man asked.

I swallowed. "Sure." I reminded myself: Relax. He's invisible.

We were in the hot sun and then we were in the shade. The difference must have been thirty degrees. Then we must have passed through some sort of security door, for an alarm went *whoop whoop whoop* until they shut it down. It happened two more times, and The Blue Man swore, saying, "Somebody is going to get fired if that glitch doesn't get fixed."

When I was told to remove the blindfold, I found myself in a white room with three generals. There were lots of stars on their shoulders. The Blue Man wasn't in sight.

"Welcome to the base," one of them said.

I saluted. "Where am I?"

"None of your business."

"This is the guy?" another general asked. "Doesn't look like much to me. Another brainiac."

The smallest one, who carried himself like a cocky little rooster, stepped up and said, "Son, I'm in charge here. Whether you stay or leave depends."

"Depends on what?" I asked.

"How you answer one question." The general frowned. "Why are you giggling?"

"Sorry. Is that the question, sir?"

"No. I haven't asked it yet. Why are you giggling?"

"Sir, no offense, sir, but you guys all have blue mouths."

I found myself bent over and laughing at the most ridiculous prank anyone had ever pulled. Someone opened a door, and I saw what appeared to be a busy airport terminal. It took me a moment to see that everyone running around in there had a blue mouth.

"He'll do," the little rooster said.

My next memory was standing with The Blue Man before a safety glass door. He leaned against the dark wall next to it, facing me. The light was kind of blinding.

"That's a long hallway," I said.

"Yes it is. Would you snap out of it?"

"This is all Top Secret, right? Eyes Only?"

"In so many words."

I shook my head. I did not feel right. Or I felt fine and couldn't figure why. "Did somebody give me something?"

"Nobody gave you nothing. You're suffering from Paradigm Overload. It happens to everyone at 51 when they first get here."

"51?"

"Yeah. That's where you are. That's what this is. It's home now, Soldier. The Biggest Secret in the World."

"I thought you said we were going to Vegas."

"I lied."

For a moment I thought The Blue Man was making fun of me. Then I said, "Wait."

"What?"

"Wait."

"Oh, you see them now?"

"What? Who? What? Who put all those . . . children in there?"

"Now it's coming," said The Blue Man.

"Why the hell are they looking at me?"

"Not everybody sees them. When you do, they tend to notice. Relax. They can't get to you."

"Jesus! How many kids are in this hallway? Where the fuck are their parents?"

"Look closer, Koop. Are they kids?"

"They're just little . . ."

"Are they children?"

"Jesus," I wailed. "Why the fuck do you have them all stacked up like that?"

"Welcome to 51," said Rudy's voice, and I screamed.

"Christ!" said The Blue Man, holding his chest. "You nearly gave me a heart attack!"

"Don't worry," Rudy said. "He can't hear me."

ALIENS? STARDUST? LOVE?—1972

Another room. Another butch general in green sitting opposite me across a desk. I was beginning to get in a mood.

"Boy, you're about to embark on a mission. It's perilous, it's critical, and your country's survival could depend on it."

"What if I fail?"

"Failure is not an option. We are the Military; we are not the Post Office. We are not gamed for failure."

"The Post Office is gamed?"

"You're missing the point. Hold on." He stabbed the red button on the intercom and said, "Hold all calls."

He folded his hands on the desk and looked squarely at me. "Son. We're talking about alien invasions."

"We are?"

"Keep up, Boy. We need you on your toes. You like Orson Welles?"

After a few seconds I said, "I liked . . . *Kane*. I thought *Ambersons* was flawed."

"That's right—you're the Pepsi TV generation."

"No, we had a Film class at—"

"Boy, I do not care about your academic record."

Okay. Every man has a point. A point that you arrive at despite never knowing it's there. This was my point. "General. May I be frank?"

"Sure."

"I got an idea. Let's just say . . . you don't call me any more names. And I don't break your pinky finger." I smiled.

For a long ten seconds we sat eye to eye.

I knew I was taking a chance. The general probably knew what I was capable of. The only thing I wasn't sure of was how much the general needed me. But I figured they had certainly gone to a lot of trouble to secure my cooperation. And evidently I was a very rare bird, essential for a very critical mission. I decided that I would start acting like it.

The general stabbed the red button on the intercom with his pinky finger. The one with the red jewel ring.

"Water," he said quietly.

The door opened suddenly, and a large soldier with a canteen entered. He held the green cloth-covered disc out to the general.

"Give it to him," The general nodded in my direction.

Fuck if I'm drinking that, I thought.

The large soldier politely offered it to me, and when I finally reached for it, he smashed it against my face, knocking me out of my chair and across the room.

Nuke here. I love to tell this part.

Koop got up slowly, like the All-Star Cleveland fullback Jim Brown after every time he was tackled. Five yards. Ten yards. Twenty yards. Two tacklers. Three. Four. Didn't make any difference. Jim Brown always got up the same way, like he was bored. Like, is that the best you got? So you couldn't tell if he was hurt, broken, concussed, or just catching his breath after doing his job. Koop shook his head; blood trickled down into his left eye. He smiled.

Here's a thing: when Koop smiled, he made you feel good. And it was usually followed by a laugh. But when it was not followed by a laugh, smart people always did the same thing: they ran. You did not want to be around for what happened next. I had yet to see him lose a fight.

After he had broken the soldier's arm, Koop apologized and led him slowly to the door.

He sat back in the seat opposite the general, way back like he was trying to fight off the impulse to nap during a long lecture.

"So. Orson Welles. *War of the Worlds*. Panic. You were saying?"

The general nodded several times. After that, he no longer punched the intercom with his pinky.

"So we invented an alien invasion."

"Why would you invent an alien invasion?"

"To cover up something worse."

"Okay."

"Okay?"

"Okay." There was a long pause. "This is the explaining part, sir."

The general gave a look at Koop. "Ah fuck. Okay. Deep background. All life on earth is an alien invasion."

"Okay. You mean . . ."

"Yeah. Everything."

"Oh. Well. Yeah. I . . . I . . ." Then Koop held his mouth open like a frozen frame from a movie. Then he closed his mouth. "Stardust?"

"Stardust. Give or take."

"Stardust," Koop said. "Okay, I'll buy that."

"In fact we're pretty sure that an essential part of humanity is an alien idea."

"An alien idea?"

"Yeah. A late arrival. Something foreign. Something viral."

"What's that?"

"That's classified."

"Oh, come on."

"I'm serious."

"General."

"You can't just waltz in here—"

"Hey! I was invited, remember?"

"Besides. That's two levels above you."

"Oh fuck that shit! I've gotta learn a secret handshake? Is there some bloodletting ceremony I'm short on?"

"Mr. Koop?"

"Yes?"

"Can I call you Winston?"

"I'd rather you didn't."

"Winston, this is America's safety we're talking about. How about you lose the sass?"

"It's love," said Rudy.

"Is it love?" asked Koop.

The general looked at him, then started rubbing his eyes with one hand.

"It's love, isn't it?" said Koop.

The general slowly wiped his forehead with his long fingers. Then he pressed the intercom and snapped, "I need level one and two clearance papers!"

The pause that followed was noticeable. Then a high voice said, "I don't know where we keep those, General."

"Is this Clarence? Get me Clarence."

"This is Sergeant Scott, sir. Clarence has the flu. I've never even seen those papers."

"Scott?"

"Yessir?"

"You don't know where Clarence keeps the clearance papers?"

Koop held up one finger. "I think I see the problem," he said.

"Shut the fuck up!" the general said. "Scott. Sergeant. That your first name or your last?"

"Both, sir."

"You're shitting me?"

"No, sir. Most people call me Scotty."

Koop rested his chin on his palm like Jack Benny, shrugged, and said, "He sounds nice."

The general scowled, grabbed the phone, and swung around in his swivel chair, turning his back to Koop, who took that moment to wince and wipe the blood out of his eyes with the heel of his palm.

The general whispered, "Look under 'T' in my green file folder. Or the 'S.'"

Koop gave a big yawn. "Gotta say. You guys run a tight ship."

Then he smiled and laughed. And Rudy joined him.

WHAT DO YOU SAY TO A POPE?—1972

It was a white room.

It had two white chairs.

I sat in one and waited. I was still getting used to the blue suit that was my uniform. Someone had tucked a white rose in my lapel and it smelled as though it had turned.

The IF scooted in like a nun on wheels. The first time I ever saw one move. He drifted silently to his chair and sat.

We regarded each other.

I don't know what I was expecting. But it wasn't a reunion. After a few moments, I knew that this wasn't a stranger. That I had known this creature before. That there was something between us. He knew it, too.

"Hello, Brother," he said.

"Hi."

"You don't remember me?"

"No."

"They tell me you are highly qualified."

"Greatest Confidence. Highest Levels."

"Indeed. But they don't know about us."

"What is it about us?"

"We share a birthdate."

"You read my file?"

"No. July 16, 1945."

"I was born months after that."

"Approximately nine months."

"Approximately."

"That is the day we truly arrived. And someday, Brother, we will be one again."

"Ieeeeeeeeeeee . . . don't know what you're talking about."

"Not yet. Would you like to meet The Tail Sister?"

The door opened, and a gigantic white snake slithered into the room. I was petrified until she sidled up beside me and let out a huge sigh.

"She won't hurt you unless you try to hurt me. Actually, she misses you. We've spent a long time waiting for you."

I've sat beside wild bulls in a rodeo chute flexing menacingly before their launch; every kick and snort of snot terrified me. But after the initial shock, this monster, this astonishing albino python, somehow felt normal, mundane even—as harmless as a newborn kitten. She smelled sweet. I wondered what it might be like to ride her.

"You can pet her," the IF said.

I let my left hand dangle until it rubbed against the wet smooth skin. I felt no trepidation. I stroked it a bit and it seemed to purr. Strange: her skin was perfectly smooth one way, but the other way it was as rough as sandpaper.

The old IF laughed. "How would you prefer to see me?"

Strange question. "As you are?"

"Well. That is difficult. I can only appear as you most need me to."

"Really? How do I appear to you?"

"As a tall human. Deeply tanned."

I laughed at that.

"So you've seen others like me?" I've said.

"Brother. There is no other like you."

"All right. To me you look like a midget priest with rather baggy robes. Do you . . . like that look?"

"If it pleases you."

"I don't care one way or the other. Is she . . . ?"

"Yes?"

"Is she always like that?"

"I'm afraid so."

I laughed. "Why do I feel so damn comfortable here?"

"With us, you mean? I thought I made that obvious. We are family. Shall I explain?"

"Please."

"We are three. Someday we will be one. We are the accident. So we got mixed up. Separated."

"Mixed up?"

"Because we were born apart. And because you are both a human and not. Thank Mother Gadget."

I didn't talk for a while.

"You see, Brother, I am the Head. The Ringmaster. The Visionary. My eyes are open all the time. To all possibilities. I see nuance, moods, threats. I gauge strategic and tactical opportunities. I also clearly see the good and the bad. I can't help it. The data floods over me and I compile, compare, and extrapolate. That's my job. To guess the future. Logic is my tool."

"Now, she . . . ," he indicated the snake with a downturned hand, "is built to be The Soldier. The cord of life. The Whip. The Enforcer. She is on guard all the time. But alas, she is a broken thing. A stuck thing. When they separated us, they made her—what is your word?"

"Disabled?"

"That'll do. She is suppressed. Fixed into one vocation. Coiled to strike at a moment's notice. Oh, she's very easy to direct. But you, of anyone, should know a soldier is more than his weapon. You have the forgetting, no?"

I nodded.

"Who taught you that?"

"A friend."

"Do you still see this . . . friend?"

"No."

"Then he does not wish to be seen. This . . . private tutoring has never happened before. I mean to say, we certainly share a great deal of knowledge. But in abstract. To be applied to tech. You understand? Why did he teach you?"

I shrugged. "I asked him to."

He seemed delighted. "You did?"

"I did."

"So that also makes you very unique. Because you were trained as a soldier you know that the best defense is never to be seen. Camouflage. Anonymity. If you take other people's memories, this makes you invisible. That is a great advantage for a soldier. But my dear, long-lost brother, I know you are more than just a soldier."

"I am?"

"Yes. At the heart you are The Navigator. Wherever you are you know three things: The way out. The way in. And where you are. If you know those three things, you can never be caught. Your gift and your talent is to understand the unspoken. Empathize. And analyze. And remember. Remember everything."

"I do have a good memory."

"And a gift for languages, I am told."

"Yes. I have thirty-three."

He smiled. "Thirty-four."

"I beg your pardon?"

The snake rumbled a laugh.

"Did you know that right now I am not speaking English to you?"

"You're not?"

"No. It would be more obvious, I suppose, if I spoke with a mouth. I have been speaking in my original tongue. The tongue I was born with."

"I hear it as English."

"You do. Because you are The Navigator. All information is relevant. Useful. Translatable. You see, all IFs are the same. A team of three: A navigator. A visionary. A soldier."

"I am not an IF."

"Oh, no. You are quite human. And quite special. Welcome home, Brother. We have waited for you a long, long time."

The snake began to purr. The Pope chuckled.

I should have been terrified.

In fact, I was having a great time.

I wondered where Rudy had gotten to.

"Now that we are together, we can finally make a plan."

It turned out to be two plans: his and mine. Mine was to save the world. And his was to let all his people go.

THE BLACK PRESIDENT—2012

Every year, like clockwork, on precisely the same day and, exactly the same time, the ritual reoccurred.

After an hour of silence, the black president checked his watch: The Jorg Gray JG6500 Chronograph branded with the Secret Service shield on the dial—a gift purchased by a pool of agents who had begun to protect him during his first campaign. The team had been so routinely impressed by his character that they presented it to him with honor on the occasion of his forty-sixth birthday. While having the appearance of a timepiece costing a small fortune, it was, in fact, a sturdy yet modest watch which could be purchased for $300 US. The six behind him each wore identical models.

"We done here?" The President asked.

Unwilling to break the silence, both The White Grandfather Clock and The Man in The Blue Suit bowed as if in the presence of royalty. The black man reached out and shook Koop's hand while ignoring the antique.

The President snatched the hardboiled egg off the white table, and rose gracefully to his full stature. He handed it off deftly to the woman with the briefcase and strolled out of the room, head high, face impassive, eyes stoney, as though he were a young man, much younger than his years, forced to endure yet another unjust detention, for which he was not ashamed or surprised, but to which he would not allow any of his true self to give anything but the smallest possible fraction of his time.

TAKE ME TO THE CIRCUS—1972—RUDY

Somewhere crossing Kansas, Rudy told Koop and I about Alaska.

After my escape, I went away for a time. A year? Ten? Fifteen? Time is a human thing. It is not ours. And we don't have your Time Juice to make it disappear.

"Time Juice?" Koop asked.

Booze. Bud. Bordeaux.

"Oh. Where did you go?" I asked.

Alaska. There are worse things than being lost in Alaska. If you don't mind the cold, and I don't, it's actually quite beautiful.

I move quickly when I choose to. I found a place way north. Way way north. Where the only company was the Koloshi? Hoonan? Tlingit. Ah, you know them? A First Nation tribe who have become entrepreneurs to vacationing whites. You erased many of them. Yes? No?

"Not personally."

Ah. Evidently, you do not remember.

For a year I forgot who I was. I fed on mountain goats. Which is to say I listened to their dumb singsong hunger chant.

OVER HERE! OVER HERE! ALL THE FOOD IS OVER HERE!

They are so nimble and so stupid.

But I found beauty, too.

I don't know what beauty is for you. For me it was the crest of a ridge. On top of a crumbling gray rock precipice covered with a six-inch carpet of spongy green tundra. It goes *cush* when the goats run on it, which is rare. I could see for fifty miles in any direction I chose. The wind when it came would find the cracks in the crumbling rock and make them whistle. And there, some 120 miles south of the Arctic Circle, I found true peace. Which is to say isolation. The clouds tumbled by, shedding blue curtains of rain. The soil is too rocky for trees to root. The crumbling rock changed colors all day long.

It was like living on a different planet every hour. Did you see *Yellow Submarine*?

"Sure," I said.

"The colors."

"Psychedelic colors? In Alaska?"

"Don't you have cable?"

"Shuttup."

When you are this alone, you learn things about yourself. You learn what you need. I felt bad for people who needed food and water. I needed only feelings—I could subsist on the meager diet of goat longing, goat hunger—which are largely the same. They would come and look at me, too dumb to be afraid—their dark eyes slitted sideways.

WHAT ARE YOU? they'd ask.

I am a forgotten friend.

ARE YOU HUNGRY? EAT.

The forgettable don't eat. Thank you, I am fine.

A BRIGHT DAY TODAY.

Yes.

WINDY, TOO.

Yes.

EASY TO SMELL FOOD.

Yes.

WHO FORGOT YOU?

A long pause as I spotted a slate-gray lake a mile below me.

A boy.

HUMAN?

Yes.

WE SEE HUMANS. THEY MAKE FIRE. BY THE LAKE.

That lake? I pointed.

YES. MAYBE YOUR BOY IS THERE?

No. He is a man now. Or maybe a ghost.

IF YOU ARE VERY STILL, HUMANS FORGET YOU. WERE YOU STILL?

No.

EAT?

No, thank you.

THERE IS PLENTY.

I said nothing.

HUMANS EAT. YOU ARE NOT HUMAN.

No.

DEAD HUMAN. GHOST?

You see those a lot, do you?

NO. MOMMAS TELL STORIES.

I wanted to laugh. No. I'm not a ghost.

YOU ARE NEW.

By now the whole herd of twelve or so had gathered and were inspecting me with their dark eyes, hissing and snorkeling through their snouts.

Yes, I am new.

One of the younger ones edged up and dropped something by my coiled-up tail. An orange flower.

WELCOME, he said in the tiniest voice.

Their kindness was starting to hurt after many empty days, so I stood and waved my tail and said: Forget me.

It's a powerful phrase because it is the opposite of everything we want.

The little one shook his head. His eyes and the tiny nubs of horn above them were black. He looked at the flower at his feet and made a noise as if he had just discovered it. Slowly, as my scent fed their tiny minds, they began to turn away, one by one, and slowly make their path down the precipice with acrobatic sure steps, tiny leaps, and never ever a sense of danger, their hooves clicking on the rocks as they found footholds no one else could possibly risk.

I looked at the flower they left: their gift. And I thought about the humans who lived by the lake. Hunters? Hikers? Hermits? Perhaps I would find out.

I grabbed the flower with my tail and put it in my head cup. And swallowed.

If I told you what happened next, you wouldn't believe me. It would sound like a bad joke.

"Three clowns on vacation from the circus are sitting drunk around a fire in a cabin just south of the Arctic Circle. A lion knocks on their door."

See?

IN THE CABIN—1972—RUDY

From my pinnacle with the goats it had looked like a tiny gray cabin, the kind hunters bed down in after they've spent the day roaming the tundra looking for bear, moose, wolf. But the structure grew in the hour or so it took for me to approach it. It was a hunting lodge— an old one, set back into the thick pines that rimmed the blue lake. A hulking, ragged animal resting on its haunches, waiting for its last breath. I heard men talking before I got too close.

"She's a tender sort. She likes me best."

"She likes anybody who says the magic word."

"Come here, darling. Take a good look at this face."

"She's a good kitty."

And so on.

What I saw peeking through a window was the scene I had watched played out a hundred times in 51. Always behind closed doors. Always under the pretense of science. Always ending with a pop. It was why I risked everything to escape.

My sister was too late to save. She was a familiar puddle on the wooden floor.

The men, when they woke up, were tied to three wooden chairs underneath a chandelier of caribou antlers. They had handcuffs, extension cords, even electrician's tape. They were seasoned practitioners. So they knew immediately that they had no hope of escaping their bonds. They had taught me well.

I let them stew in it for a while and built a bonfire in the sizable rock fireplace behind them.

The lodge was designed for luxury. The chairs were maroon leather. There was an immense kitchen with stainless steel appliances. I spent a few minutes opening and closing the huge refrigerator door: watching my true reflection and then feeling the blast of icy air when I opened it. I found where they kept their drugs and Time Juices. I let them smell the smells as I burned their stash in the fire and poured their drinks in the sink. They faced away from the hearth so they could not see. I think for a while they thought I was human.

"We have money. Cut us loose and we'll tell you where it is."

"We're not gonna make any trouble."

"Take whatever you need. We won't fight you."

I let them listen to the sounds I made behind them. Stacking the wood. Lighting the kindling. Feeding the fire. I could tell: My silence disturbed them.

I must have waited an hour before I spoke in their minds.

"Who's in charge?"

They knew then. And it was wonderful to feel their fear rise. All emotions feed us. Some have stronger flavors than others. Fear is sweet.

"I'm the eldest," one of them finally said.

"I know," I said.

"Raleigh?" one of them asked.

"I'm not Raleigh."

The elder said, "You are a gentle friend. My cherie amour."

"Nice try."

The third said, "Where did our love go?"

"Ohhh," I said. "The oldies."

The second: "I cry the tears of a clown."

The third: "Ain't too proud to beg."

The eldest: "Please Mr. Postman."

It was beautiful. Watching them from behind. Three old men tied up in chairs. Talking Motown baby talk. A secret code that never failed them when they did their dirty work at the base. All the little IFs swooned at the soothing juvenile sentiments, the teenage promises of rapture, slow dancing, and tender devotion. We're suckers for the shit. That's everything we ever wanted from our children. They knew that. So they pulled that jackpot handle over and over until we gave them whatever they wanted. Whatever. They. Wanted.

I laughed. "That shit never worked on me, fellas. I'm a soldier."

That shut up their Motown jabber.

"So. This is the fraternity of clowns. And you are the Holy Trinity."

"We're retired. We haven't worked there in years."

"I know. I was there."

At that, one of them couldn't control himself and his right leg started stomping double-time on the Moroccan rug.

"Stop it!" one of them hissed at his trembling brother.

"So," I said. "Who's in charge now?"

"Nobody."

"Shuttup!" the elder said.

"Nobody?" I asked.

"The Pope."

"Oh come on."

"We're interviewing candidates."

"Hmmmm. Any leads?"

"We can't tell you that!" one of them said with false outrage. "It's a secret!"

"Wow. A secret."

"What do you want from us?"

"A name or two—for starters."

"Koop!" the trembling man squealed, and I killed him quickly and watched the effect it had on the two others.

"First name?" I asked.

"Winston! Intelligence officer. On leave after his tour in Nam. Good man. Decorated."

"Shuttup, you fool. He's playing with us."

"And where might I find him?"

"Detroit. Veterans' hospital. He's drying out."

"Hmmmmm. What makes him such a great candidate?"

"He's a killer," the eldest said. "His hit list is longer than your tail."

"Don't provoke him!"

"It doesn't matter," the old man said. "Don't you know when you're a dead man?"

I killed the second then. "He does now," I said.

I took a few minutes for him to contemplate the bodies.

"Cat got your tongue?"

"So you're Rudy," the old man said. He was taller than the others, so it seemed appropriate to put him in the middle chair. I was reminded of Christ crucified between two thieves. "I've heard of you. We never caught you. Clever boy. We got your sister, though."

"No. I freed her last week. She's on our side now."

That got him. Boy, was this fun.

"I mean, a church? Really. You thought I wouldn't find her in the basement of St. Agatha's? The patron saint of wet nurses, bakers, and earthquakes? Agatha got around, didn't she?"

Raleigh had been captive for years when I finally tracked her down. Somebody had paid a lot of money to hide her. The tall man with an aristocratic air, perhaps? Maybe he was the banker.

He looked like someone from another era—the man in the Hathaway shirt. Gray hair. Pencil mustache. I let my tail creep around his neck and choked him lightly.

"So this Winston Koop fella. Tell me all about him."

"Go fuck yerself."

I let him see me then.

I let him take a good long look.

And then I made him talk.

And then I butchered him.

MAGIC PLACES—2018

I remember we were back at my place, sitting at the coffee table drinking out of white mugs.

"You okay?" Koop asked.

"Déjà vu," I said, frowning.

"In your own living room?" Koop asked.

"Go figure," I said.

"I've felt that. Ever been drawn to a place? And when you finally got there, did you feel like you belonged? Like you were home, and safe and—"

"Yes."

"Where was that?"

I closed my eyes and saw the gray-and-blue water curling through the shady evergreens, rustling over the rocks in the shallows: a river in Northern Michigan.

"The Au Sable," I said.

"Hemingway's place."

"Near there. But for me it was a particular spot where I used to go trout fishing with my dad. I'd sit on the bank. The water looked like hammered tin, and it sort of oozed by—fast, but not too fast. I didn't even have to fish. I could have stayed there for hours. Listening to the river whispering. Doodling."

Koop said, "I think there are places on earth like that. Maybe they're places where our ancestors set down, or blessed. Burial grounds perhaps. Or holy places where the lost found comfort or visitation. Or maybe a door. I think that's what The Way Out is for them. Their Promised Land."

"I stopped believing in anything like that after Katey died."

"That's the first time you've mentioned her name."

"It's too much, you know. I'd rather exist in an indifferent universe than live in a circus run by insane, arbitrary clowns."

"I hear you. Still," he smiled, "we need the eggs."

I laughed dryly. "Strange world. Us running into each other after so many years. What are the fuckin' odds?"

Koop picked up something he didn't like and frowned.

I gave him a blank look. "Almost astronomical."

"I didn't plan this, if that's what you're implying."

"I don't know. You're a pretty good hunter, Koop. Evidently, you caught everyone you looked for. And they were hiding."

"Last I heard you lived in L.A.! How was I supposed to know you were back in Detroit?"

"I'm sure you have your ways."

"Hold on, Nuke."

"Funny, you mention eggs. You ever have Easter egg hunts?"

"Huh?"

"We used to. We'd have all the cousins over for Easter. Dad would take real pleasure in finding hiding places for all the kid's baskets. I never saw him taking that much pleasure in anything at church. But he loved that one ritual. Hiding the colored hard-boiled eggs—that was his favorite. They were like little rainbow gifts strewn around the house. And all the kids screaming, I found one! Biting the heads off chocolate bunnies. The scratchy yellow sugar of the marshmallow Peeps exploding in your mouth." He pulled a face. "I know—this Catholic shit is a little weird for you."

"A little," Koop admitted.

"One year, though, about a week after Easter, something started stinking up the living room. Turned out it was a rotten egg Dad had hid in a lampshade. Nobody found it, and Dad forgot he put it there. A bright yellow egg turning brown next to the lightbulb."

I took a long drink of coffee. "Something stinks, Koop."

The man of many tongues was silent.

"You wanna tell me, old buddy? Old friend? You wanna cut the crap?

After a long, long pause, Koop said. "Okay."

"Okay?"

"Okay." Koop swallowed. "This isn't the first time I visited you, Nuke."

THE LAST TIME—2007

It was another cold spring in L.A. In the woods beside Pagnucco's house crows were circling the bare trees against a white sky—cawing their heads off. They were clearly trying to intimidate some predator below—a coyote?

Koop knocked on the back door.

Nuke recognized his tall, black silhouette.

Some sob story about the clowns chasing him. Nuke bought it because Nuke was Nuke. The worst poker player on the base.

"You were a bitch to find," Koop admitted.

"My alias?"

Koop nodded. "Congrats, Milton."

"Well, it worked for twenty-three years," Nuke said proudly. Not everyone could hide from Winston Koop.

Winston smiled.

They were sitting in his living room talking over coffee. Nuke had made two white mugs of joe and put them on the table between them. Just two old buddies catching up on old times. Right?

"Lotsa cream."

"That's right!" Koop laughed. "You remember! How about that?"

Then Koop was pointing out how Nuke's mug was making tiny tornadoes of steam. Did he see that? Look closely.

Nuke smelled the aroma and looked down into the rich, dark well. Sure enough: there were tornadoes. "Wow! Yeah, I guess they do look like tornadoes."

"Keep watching them. Have you ever seen a real tornado?"

"No. But on TV they are much larger."

"Of course they are. Do you see how those tornadoes are only white for a second then they dissipate?"

"Yes."

"Say the word, 'Dissipate.'"

"Dissipate."

"Say it again."

"Dissipate."

"That's a nice word, isn't it?"

"It sure is."

"Now this is important, Nuke. So pay attention. When that steam is gone, you will forget everything you know about 51."

"Everything?"

"I know. That's a lot to forget, isn't it? You'll forget every person you met. Everything you did there. Every conversation. Every day and every year. It's classified. You know what classified means, don't you?"

"Yes. Highest Levels. Greatest Confidence."

"That's right. You do remember. Good job. But you know what 'Eyes Only' means, don't you?"

"Yes. It means only certain people can look at certain things. Videos. Documents. Assets."

"Relax, Nuke. You're not in trouble. You obeyed all the rules."

"Not all," Nuke said. His jaw started quivering.

"In so many words. Don't get upset. You were a good altar boy. But from now on, 51 is Eyes Only. You do not have access. You might as well be deaf and blind. Not to worry. Someone else has access. The information is secure. You are relieved of its burden."

"Whew." Nuke let out a huge sigh. "Thanks! That was a lot to carry."

"I bet it was. Sounds like you're feeling good and relaxed."

"I am."

"Not a care in the world."

"Nope."

"That's good. Because, I'm sorry, but today I've got some bad news."

"Bad news?"

"You've been in an accident, Nuke. You can't work anymore because you're losing your memory. You've hurt your head. Don't worry—you've made a miraculous recovery. You're fine. Physically you're fine. You just have a more limited life."

"Where's my wife?"

[Yeah, I didn't get this part, either, Nuke. But for some reason when you were hypnotized you somehow decided that Katey was your wife. Don't ask me. So I just went with it.]

"I'm sorry to say she died in the accident."

Pagnucco made a sound.

"But she died instantly. She felt no pain. That's something to be grateful for. Are you grateful?"

"I guess," Nuke said through his tears. "Was it a car accident?"

"Yes. Nobody else was hurt."

"That's good. Did I kill her?"

"No! Stop that Catholic shit! It was nobody's fault. Katey died. She didn't suffer. She's at peace now. Nobody will ever hurt her again."

"That's good."

"You'll adjust, you hear me? You'll grieve. You'll move on. You're not the only one who has ever lost someone. People die every day. It happens. People move on. You'll move on."

"I don't think so."

"No, you'll be fine. Trust me. Even now you can feel the hurt receding just a little bit. Once you accept it, it gets smaller and smaller. Until one day it doesn't hurt any more. Okay, that's . . . that's not quite true, but someday, something like that will happen. You'll get bigger. You'll grow up. You'll get old enough and big enough to contain that loss. It won't destroy you, you hear me? You are strong. You will not be destroyed. Oh, sure, you'll miss her. That's natural. But you'll move on. You'll find new work. Maybe even someone else eventually."

"Never."

"Well, I know it feels that way now, Nuke. But, you'll see. It's not an insult or a betrayal of Katey to move on, to be interested or even attracted to someone else."

"It's not?"

"No. The important thing right now is to move on. She would have wanted that. Katey would want you to recover and heal. And you will. Day by day."

"Okay."

"The courage to change the things you can."

"The serenity to accept the things I can't."

"And the wisdom to tell the difference. That's right, Nuke. That's good. You've got it. You'll do fine. If I were you, you know what I would do?"

"What?"

"I'd take up pictures. Photography. You always had a knack for it. And from now on every picture you take, you'll get just a little better. You'll notice the difference. And so will others. And none of the past will hurt you anymore like it did before. You'll move on."

"I'll move on."

"You'll move on. In fact, I'd move to Detroit. There's a lot of work for photographers in car advertising. Nobody will expect you to move home."

"Move home. Okay."

"Nuke. You're like a town or a state or a country after a natural disaster—tornadoes, right? What do they do after a tornado destroys everything?"

"They rebuild."

"They rebuild. And so will you. Stronger than ever, Nuke. Hell, when you're done rebuilding, they won't see the cracks."

Nuke seemed to like the idea. Then he frowned. He put his head in his hands and wept. When he looked up, his lower lip was jammed hard into his upper lip. His eyes were wet.

"Can I remember you?"

"Sure, Nuke. You can remember me. Before the base."

"Okay."

"Okay?"

"Okay."

"Now, tell me, Nuke. Where did you put the blue book?"

"I gave it to somebody to publish."

Koop was stone-faced.

"And did they publish it?"

"No. They stole it."

"They did? Well, that's too bad. Who are they?"

"A fat man with a Southern accent. Rodney. He said he was an agent."

"Did he leave a number or a card?"

"No. But I think he was a con man."

"Was he a clown?"

"A clown?"

"One of the clowns from the base?"

"The base?"

"51."

Nuke's face did four things at once. "You told me I should forget all about that."

"Oh, that's right. I did, didn't I? Well. Okay. Forget about it."

Nuke's face resolved into a blank again.

"Let's see. Nuke?"

"Yah."

"I'm gonna say a word eight different ways. And, then, I'm going to ask you to tell me which way the fat man said the word, okay?"

"Okay."

By the time Koop had discovered the pronunciation he was looking for, the steam on the mug of coffee had dissipated entirely.

THE SECRET MEETING—1973—NUKE

The first time I saw the tall man crossing the green and white and blue lines, I gawked. Something about the way his big black Converse All Stars loped over all the lines reminded me of Bill Russell, the amazing center for the Boston Celtics—dominating the paint, the best footwork in the league. And more NBA titles than Michael Jordan. It was like the tall man took a secret pride in ignoring the hard, fast rules that everybody else reflexively abided by, strutting by in his spiffy blue suit with a dapper white rose in his lapel.

Then I noticed that the soldiers ignored him in that practiced way that meant they were on alert in his presence. Then there was a group of women who seemed to go soft when the tall man stopped to engage them, seemed dazed, in fact, by his attention. One of them started swinging her foot back and forth, back and forth.

Same old Winston. It was kind of unfair.

When he noticed me, he said, "Jesus Christ! Adam Pagnucco?!"

"Hey, Koop."

"When did you get here?"

"I've been here since '63."

"I'll be damned. Right out of high school? What do they got you doing?"

"I'm the official photographer. I do inventory of the cats and badges. Where's yours?"

"Ha. Funny. God, it must be ten years!"

"Nine."

"So a photographer, eh?"

"Yeah. What is it you do?"

He shrugged. A very familiar thing. "I run things."

"You run things?"

"In so many words. Where are you on your way to?"

"A meeting."

"Me, too. Listen, now that I know you're here, I'll look you up later and we'll catch up."

"Sounds good."

It was a rather large meeting room marked PRIVATE. There was coffee and donuts. Maybe thirty people in the group. A lot of folding chairs. I was warmly greeted by a few men. Then somebody led the serenity prayer and the leader asked if anyone had anything to share.

A tall man in the back stood up and said, "My name is Winston. I'm an alcoholic."

"Hey, Winston!" the group said.

"I've been sober six months." A smattering of applause. "I just want to say I'm grateful for everyone here." And he looked at me and smiled. "Everyone."

So we reconnected. That's how I met Katey, his wife. She was in Medical and New Physics. A captain in the air force. A brilliant and beautiful doctor. Once a week we'd go out to dinner in town. We told her all our college stories. Our camping trips. For a while there we were inseparable. For years.

Then Katey fell in love with me and I her. Koop was gone a lot, so we had a chance to be together. But I just couldn't. I couldn't do that to Winston. I couldn't.

She understood. She loved him, too.

One day she meets me for lunch in town at a Denny's. She's out of uniform.

She says she's leaving Koop.

He's gone back to drinking.

She says she knows she can never love me the way she wants to, so she's leaving 51. Well, I love Katey, too, but I want what was best for her, so if that means never seeing her again—that's fine.

She has a favor ask. A big one.

Then she opens her purse and lets me see a small blue leather-bound book.

"You didn't."

"I did. I need you to get it published."

"You're insane. They will destroy you."

"I don't care."

"They will kill me."

"Koop won't let that happen."

"Katey, what difference will it make?"

"What do you mean?"

"51 will always be there."

"The book is the key."

"The key?"

"The only key that will lock the door."

"They don't want to lock the door!"

"I know."

"Even The Pope doesn't want it."

"I know."

"Koop . . . is not as terrible as you think. He's on their side."

"I don't think he's terrible."

"Then why are you leaving him?"

She got up and slipped into my side of the booth. She folded the blue book into the newspaper on the seat beside me.

"I'm leaving 51. I can't do it anymore. I'm still amazed that you can, Nuke."

"It's my job. And, honestly? I may be the only kind thing in their lives. I can't give that up."

"Then you're the problem, too."

"Listen, Katey. Koop's a drunk. So am I. When he gets sober, he'll come back to you."

"He'll never get sober as long as stays there. Don't you know that?

It's the only thing that gets him through the day."

I was silent. I believed her.

"If this gets into the wrong hands . . ."

"I hope it does. That is the whole point, Nuke! Somebody has to stop it. You know I'm right. You know it can't go on. We can't keep making them. They are—"

"Don't say it!"

"Human. They are our children."

So we sat there in a quiet booth in a chilly orange family restaurant in Nevada. And that one word was like a detonation. Once said, it could not be unsaid. We were all fine so long as what we were doing was our duty. Obeying orders. Following the law. Keeping on the lines. Doing what everybody else did. The moment we considered the possibility that what paid our bills and fed our stomachs and kept the lights on wasn't a circus or a zoo or even a lab—it was a garbage disposal for humans—we were lost. They were no longer freaks, no longer aliens, no longer mushrooms, or pets, or cats—they were creatures. And we were their creators. Once you saw them that way you could not unsee them.

And I saw them all. Every day.

At first it was strange: these torpid, tubby white cats lolling about in a fat chair. Strapped down.

At first they looked indistinguishable.

Black eyes. Wings like cat's ears. Fat tails. Bald white bodies.

Then slowly, one by one, I started to see them.

Their eyes were infinite shades of black. Some looked terrified. Some curious. Some sad. Some sick. Some so puzzled they looked imbecilic. Some were very bright. Some were angry and weak—well, they all were weak.

Then personalities began to emerge in the slightest details. The way one held his head. The way one curled her tail. The way the skin on their head cups trembled whenever a gentle memory crept into their minds. Genders. Characters. People. Souls.

Once seen, you couldn't unsee them.

I found that somehow I could calm them down by talking. Prepping them for the flash which always startled them (like lightning).

"Hi," I'd say after they were seated. "My name is Adam Pagnucco. You can call me Nuke. Everybody does. I'm not here to hurt you. I just need to take your picture. You know what a picture is, right? Your child probably had their picture on a dresser near their bed, right?"

They all nodded differently.

And this little suggestion would change their posture entirely. They would relax into the memory place. They would think of their beloved child and inevitably they would make a sweet catlike sound. And their whole body would become less tense. Three flicks, two flicks, one flick, and then their tail tip lay flat.

"I understand," I'd say. "We all remember you. We all enjoyed your company." This would be when the tears started. No eyelids. No blinking. Just a diamond of water on the bottom of a black oblong that gathered and burst and ran straight down the thin neck like a dribble from a wineglass.

I'd ask them, "Did they give you a name?"

And the names were like a switch that would turn on a light in a dark room. They would be whispered in my mind and I'd nod and say, "That's a good one. Nice to meet you, _____. Is that how you say it? Good. Listen, I'm not here to hurt you. You can relax. There will be a bright flash of light for just a moment—It'll help me take your picture. It'll make it clearer. It won't hurt you, I promise. Here it comes. When I press this button, it will flash. Are you ready, _____?"

They would straighten up a little and nod.

The flash would always startle them.

"Thank you!" I'd say. "That's it. That's all there is."

"Maybe I will see you later."

And then I'd wheel them out the door, where a soldier would take them away.

That was my job. Take the pictures. Make the ID cards and the badges. Keep everything in order. Record all new personnel and cats.

I shudder thinking I called them that. Cats.

Katey had timed it perfectly. I was leaving the next day for a two-week vacation in Florida.

The first week I sat in the sun by the ocean.

The first day of the second week I made some phone calls.

I handed off the blue book to Rodney on the last day of my vacation.

"Call it a magic book," I explained. "Those cards and those words aren't just beautiful. They have power."

I'll never forget. He held it so solemnly to his chest, as if it were a sacred text. And he was the happiest nerd in the world who had just scored a priceless classic boy's collection of baseball cards.

We were quiet for a long time in the restaurant. Our waitress came by several times to warm our coffees.

"Nuke. You told me that you could recognize them."

"I can. I don't understand why no one else can tell the difference. It's obvious to me."

"That's why your doodles are so beautiful."

"Aww, stop."

"They are. It's 'cause you really see them."

"They're just cartoons, Kate. It's a hobby."

"I know. You don't draw who's. Even you don't believe that, Nuke."

Then there came a time when we both knew it was going to end. The conversation. Our time together. Neither of us knew what to say. And neither wanted to go. The silence lasted. I found if I looked at her red-rimmed glasses I was safe. If I looked anywhere else, the feelings would get me.

One of the last things I remember thinking: I wish I'd seen her naked. Just once.

"They told you their names," she said.

I nodded.

"Do you remember them?"

"The names?"

"Yes."

"All of them?"

"Yes."

"Then you're the only one who does, Nuke. You're all they got."

COMING CLEAN—2018

"You hypnotized me?"

"Yes," Koop said.

"So I would forget?"

"Yes."

I had never thought myself capable of wanting to murder someone until that moment. I held my hand over my mouth for five minutes. I was afraid of what I would say.

Finally, I spoke. "I took her away from you . . . so . . . you took her away from me."

He nodded.

"Her memory anyway."

He nodded.

"We weren't even together."

"I know."

"So what the fuck?!"

"Okay. Listen. They sent me to hunt down the cards and destroy them. I told them I did. They wanted me to kill you. I told them I did. But instead I erased your memories. Gave you a whole new life where they'd never find you."

"Where is she?"

"You don't wanna know."

"We never . . ."

"I know."

"I wouldn't."

"I know. You're good man. But you did put her in jeopardy."

"So you erased my memory of her to punish me."

"And to spare you."

"You're a real prick, you know that?"

"I know. It's in my job description."

I breathed in deeply and let out a slow exhale.

Koop said, "We'd all like to think that we would be the person to stand up and do the right thing and say: 'No. This is wrong. We can't do this. This has got to stop.' None of us were good enough. But you and Katey were."

Koop pulled the blue book out of the pocket of his blue suit and handed it to me. I had the weirdest feeling opening it. A book I had seen before but now had no idea what it was. Slowly, I cracked it and started paging through it. I don't know exactly what I expected. I didn't expect a book of tarot cards. Each drawn intricately around a letter of the alphabet. The drawings were black-and-white. Pen and ink. The alphabet was English, but the intricate beasties and details and tiny motifs scattered throughout were alien—they spoke of the mind and imagination of a child with the draftsmanship of an artist. An utterly strange work of art. It seemed both homely and bizarre. And then, the more I read, the more dread I felt. The figures became familiar; like leftovers from my childhood. An old library book I had stumbled upon by accident in the children's section. The thing it most reminded me of was the illustrations of the novels of Charles Dickens. But with an added element of mischief, as if the artist knew he was being naughty, getting away with something. Sometimes wrapped around the three-dimensional letters were serpent's tails that implied an offscreen animal. Sometimes a bouquet of flowers seemed oddly animate, and suggested the quivering head cups of the IFs. As in those puzzle illustrations of my childhood, there were vases that were faces, bushes that were masks, steaming cups of wine, shadows that could almost be letters. Silhouettes of tiny cat faces. And leaves like delicate wings. Everywhere. Leaves likes white ears. Hints like breadcrumbs strewn across the pages, showing the path out of the woods. Page after page, charming and disarming images that implied an entirely unseen reality, as if each card itself was a door which opened into a deeper door, and then another, and another, and so on.

"Koop? These are my drawings."

"Yes."

"My doodles. My cards."

"Yes."

"Katey must have told me about the words."

"She did."

"So your whole purpose was to erase any traces of the secret and to collect the cards."

"Yes."

"Why not just burn them—destroy them?"

"Listen. It's a sacred text to the IFs. Words of their soul. To them, words conjure and create. Remember: they were created by feelings, images, and words. What is a book if it's not that? And many IFs paid with their lives to hold on to those words. But it's also a magic book."

"What?"

"You say certain words, you can make an IF compliant."

"You mean . . . ?"

"Yes."

"That's what Rodney was doing?"

"And other Skullfuckers."

I swallowed a mouthful of bile. "Christ."

"That fat ass had a real dark-web distribution list for his subscribers. He sold off that deck of cards, far and wide, to the highest bidder. Took me decades to collect them all."

A bird whistled in the night. "But that's not even the biggest trick. Remember what Katey said about the book being The Key?"

I nodded.

"As long as The Way Out is open, it continues to draw the IFs in; the government continues their experiments; and The Pope can continue to rule and release a new batch to their Promised Land every year."

"Like Moses?"

"Exactly. That's why they want it destroyed. It's not just a key; it's a lock. Until you made that book, there was no way to close it."

"But doesn't The Pope control the door?"

"No. That's the other great secret. It has to be a human. It can't be an IF. Humans opened it. Only humans can close it. The door can only be closed under very special conditions. It took years of your doodling to create those cards. You had a lot of inspiration. That's what Rudy and Raleigh did."

"I don't understand."

"They escaped in the saucer crash and went looking for someone who could stop another Trinity blast."

"That was me. And they also looked for a child who would grow up to be The Doorman. Somebody who could be the real Way Out. Someone who could close The Door and let the IFs go free. A real Moses—not a fake one."

"Me?"

"You." He tapped his fingers on the blue book I'd set down on the table. "And thanks to you and them . . . now it's not just a book. It's a key. If you read the right words. In the right order. It'll lock it forever."

"Which words?"

Koop thumbed it open and indicated the phrase—or should I say the three phrases. They sounded like poetry.

"S.L.W."

"'Short. Long. Wide.' Hmmm. Really? Just that? That does it?"

"Now you know."

"Why would *I* want to know?!"

"'Cause you're the guy that's gonna free the cats. You're the guy that's gonna close it."

"Why would I do that?"

"You're the new Doorman! You're the hero of this story, Nuke!"

"What the fuck are you talking about?

"That's why we gotta take it to The Pope."

"WHAT?"

"They could do this forever, Nuke. You've seen the tech they've developed. The F-117. The smart drones. They're just the start, believe me. Their weapons could get so RAM-advanced they'd be impossible to stop. They're almost there. Come on, Pagnucco. Time to Hero Up! We're gonna bust in and save the day. Let the IFs go. Close the door for good. Bob's your uncle."

"Yer crazy."

"No! It'll be great!"

"We're gonna bust into some top secret government military base—hold it. Hold on. Yer joking, right?" I held my stomach and laughed. "This is—this has got to be. Oh, Christ—yer not joking. Koop!!"

"What?"

"What? How the—you know, I don't think. No. Nope. Nope. Not, not, not. What the fuck!?"

"Take a breath."

"I am breathing!"

"It's taken us years to finalize this plan, Nuke. It's a great plan. You don't like the plan?"

I exploded, "OTHER THAN IT'S INSANE IT'S A GREAT IDEA! I'm seventy-three. How old are you?"

"Same."

"So what the fuck!?"

"They'll never see us coming, Nuke!"

"You are certified!"

"Well, technically, I do talk to invisible creatures."

He saw I did not think that was funny.

"Okay! Whoa. Listen, buddy. Take a breath."

I took a few. "Koop. You're talking like a young man. We're Old!" I saw his face. "Don't get me wrong, you look great."

"That does not sound like the man who tried to take down his government's most powerful secret base."

"And I failed!"

"No, I stopped you."

"Okay, fine. You stopped me. But look at us! We've peaked, brother. Those days are behind us. Get ahold of yourself! This is manic alcoholic hero shit! Be grateful you're sober today. Let it go."

Koop sat down. He took a deep breath and let it out through his nostrils.

"Let it go, brother," I said.

And it looked like my words had finally managed to break through. He leaned back into the couch, rested his head and looked at the ceiling.

"Maybe you're right. Maybe it's a fool's errand."

"Fuck, yeah," I said.

"Ohhh shit," he said. "Shit. Shit. Shit."

"Well, don't . . . beat yourself up about it."

"What was I thinking? Destroy 51! Huh! Nip it in the bud! Shut it all down! Close the door forever!"

"Crazy."

"Crazy!" Koop smiled that killer smile. "It would take a plan so absurd no one could see it coming. So foolproof it couldn't fail. Like—I don't know—two old-timers charging the gates and you pretending to be my prisoner."

"Right," I laughed. "Good luck with that."

"If only we had an ally who could supply all the codes into the base. Codes that would open every single checkpoint and security door."

"Ally?"

"Then all we would need would be the most precious secret in the world. The one object they want more than anything. Something they've been searching for for decades. A book that threatens the very existence of 51. They're dying to get their hands on that."

"Wait."

"If only we had someone on our side who could disarm any

guard, open any door, and knows every single the secret of the base."

"What?"

"A secret weapon! A weapon so powerful no one could beat it."

"What?" I said.

"You know, Rudy? I think he may be ready."

A tiny voice said, "I don't think so."

"Listen. Once you light a fire under him, Nuke will take it all the way."

"He looks pretty wimpy to me."

For the life of me I could not tell where the voice was coming from. It sounded like it was right behind me. Then right next to me. I turned around and looked over my couch. Nothing.

"You brought him *here*? To my house!?"

"I didn't have much say in it, Nuke. This was all his idea." He saw my face. "I can't help it! He follows me everywhere!"

"Like white on rice," the voice said.

Koop started laughing.

I heard the sound of a deck of cards being shuffled. Then, out of nowhere, a strange playing card floated down like a leaf and landed on the coffee table. Then it flipped itself over. It was a jack, but not any jack I had ever seen. And the suit was from another language with a whole other symbolism. It took me a moment to recognize that I had made it.

Rudy said, "It's no accident you guys became friends. You fit together. The key and the lock."

I started laughing. And, oh God, I knew I was lost. The momentum had started. We were off on another one of Koop's loopy adventures. He used to get me drunk on peach Schnapps and climb a hundred feet up the girders under the Blue Water Bridge. In fucking winter. Once we streaked through downtown Ferndale at 2 a.m. We stole votive candles from the altar of St Mary's. Shoplifted *Playboys* at Cunningham's. He was always the instigator. And I always followed. The laughter we shared afterward and the adrenaline rush were the most alive I'd ever felt. It was hopeless. I never could resist Koop's stories or his jokes or his dares. But to be included in them after all this time? It felt like I had been liberated. Like I'd been dead for years. Like we were a team again.

And I trusted him. After all those years. After everything he had done to me. I trusted him.

THE CIRCUS—195?—RALEIGH

I'll put this here.

It's a recording Koop made of Raleigh; she asked him to give it to me. It was on a CD labeled with a black Sharpie: "Raleigh's Story." He popped it in somewhere west of Flagstaff, Arizona.

Better than anything else, it'll give you a picture of where we were heading on that cross-country quest. It answers quite a few questions.

I should mention Raleigh had the sweetest childish girl voice with the hint of a French accent. Don't ask me why but she sounded like Edith Piaf.

Press Play.

I can remember it all. Even when I was not there, I recall.

For many years it had no name.

You do not understand how we see time, so you have no idea—we were there for ages. Longer than waiting for our child to call us out.

They called it The Pit or The Hole.

Then the story boxes played a movie and we saw the clowns and we saw the cages and we saw the whips and we saw the big cats. Some knew the word already, some did not. Then the word was whispered among the many who huddled around the story boxes. And it stuck. We began to call it The Circus.

It was a deep deep big big hole in the ground. Surrounded by rings. It went down so many levels. When we reached the bottom, none of us remembered how many levels down it was. We just knew we were in an underground place full of long, curving green corridors. None of the light came from the near or far stars.

There were many big doors. With simple names.

RETRIEVAL. (The word was painted over the old words: HANGAR 1).

ADMITTING.

PROCESSING.

BATHS.

DRYING.

EXAMINATION.

STORAGE.

MEDICAL.

LANGUAGE.

MEMORY.

STEALTH.

ENGINEERING.

PHYSICS/NEW

PHYSICS/OLD

POPE.

JANITOR.

I am told there are square buildings all over the wide world with similar names inside them.

But I can assure you that no other buildings are like this one.

The door outside is hidden by a golden sand dune. Every morning a herd of white cats appears there, waiting to be collected. Like strays in an alley behind a restaurant.

That is how they first see us. As stray cats. We could be tumbleweeds. We could be cactuses. We could be as hidden as their shadow or as hard as a red rock baking in the sun. But this is how they see us. By then we are so weak we cannot hide ourselves. Not even our tails or our fullness of color.

Big white stray cats.

To us, it feels like coming home. It draws us—this leaving place with many names. The Way Out. The Dream Hole. The Anywhere. Janitor.

It takes a lot to bring us out of our darkness. Our closets. But when Mother Gadget freed us, we felt more real than ever before. It was as if we had stepped out of the shadows and into the full sunlight and for the first time felt true warmth. After our child left us, we felt a strange need we'd never felt before. We felt the need to leave. Before the Trinity day we never had a way out. Now we did. So we made that treacherous journey. And we discovered the closer we got to the Anywhere, the more visible we became. And more vulnerable. It is an ecstasy that none of us can resist—though it draws us to our deaths. We cannot fight against our purpose and joy: to be seen. To be on the verge of touch. It is everything we ever wanted. Is it any wonder that we follow this hunger to our death?

Imagine our pilgrimage.

Our remarkable journeys. We left our hiding places, our closets, our hometowns, the bedrooms, the hearths, the woods, and we crept out and made our way like frightened strays through the wide world to the desert. For those who had lived their lives in the quiet and the dark, it was like crawling out of a manhole into the middle of the Las Vegas Strip. Intoxicating light and noise and emotion. Across rivers, valleys, mountains, through strange landscapes and loud, cluttered towns and dark dark forests we could only have imagined in the little dark places we came from, until we arrived finally, at the desert dune that hid the mouth into The Base. Where we were drawn. The beacon that called us, that swelled a hope in our hearts and a promise of release, a place where we would be welcomed again.

And that's where our nightmare began.

We had joined The Circus.

When we get there, we are eventually taken to the Explaining Room, where The Holy One talks.

He is the first and oldest. Firstborn of Mother Gadget on The Day of Trinity.

He tells us all our waiting is not in vain.

All our longing is not futile.

All our children are waiting on the other side.

A place so beautiful no cat can even imagine it.

The Anywhere.

He tells us: Anywhere is better than here.

We are only a short time here.

But we are in The Anywhere forever and always.

The Holy One tells us: This underground is our final desert before our promised land.

We are like planted seeds and we will all bloom as flowers.

All our trials end here in The Underground. All our sadness and all our pain will bring us finally up a river of tears to the place where every child gets what they love most. And we are reunited.

We are on our last journey to Anywhere.

Where we will be one.

RETRIEVAL is where they welcome the new creatures drawn to The Way Out. We lie in the desert night beside a dune waiting for a crack in the sand to open. We huddle there for hours, exhausted after our long journey. We are always listless, compliant, starving. The crack opens every morning and the clowns come out with their blue mouths to let in the albino cats. Lions. Tigers. Sometimes we are so hungry they drag us by our tails into Admitting.

The clowns say, "Here, Kitty, Kitty. Here, Kitty, Kitty."

In ADMITTING we are crammed into a steel box until it is full and then it drops to the lower levels where we are processed. They watch us from a square window.

After the Frisbee crash all tails were branded with a number. We do not speak of the branding. We never will.

Then we are led to the bath. You know how much cats love water? They push the beasts into a slippery glazed incline. Sometimes we are kicked until we move. We slide down into the thick blue syrup at the bottom of the pool. This cleans all our fur—"denticles" they call them; we call them "hair teeth"—like sharks we look smooth; we are not. The pool is drained, and those still alive are led to the showers. The others go down the chute.

This is known: every room has a chute.

In the showers we cower under sprinklers that rinse off the residual blue syrup. Our brands are blue then. Next, we are led into the Drying Room. Steel drains run the length of the floor. A warm, terrifying explosion of air comes from the ceiling, and you know how cats feel about the vacuum.

Once dry, we are led single file to EXAMINATION. We lie on rubber tables, and the clown doctors examine our orifices. Take blood samples. We are X-rayed. We receive eye exams. We are photographed. (Hi, Flasher! A kind voice in a dark tunnel is a gift no one forgets.)

THE SLEEPING PLACE is where we go once we are processed. The clowns call it STORAGE. It is a large room that was once used for aircraft prototypes. There the cats huddle in small groups around televisions. We call them "Cold Fires" or "Story Boxes." They are never off.

The Holy Father tells us we should be grateful. In the early days there was only a radio. "A wooden box stuck on an oldies station." Some remember. Some recall the sweetness of the Motown. It made them believe that somewhere there was something nice in the world. And sane.

Sometimes the clowns call the cats "mushrooms." They think it is funny. The noise from the TVs is constant, and each is set to a different channel. We asked once for a volume knob but were denied.

In the center of the round room the great Sister Tail lies asleep in a huge white coil. The cats stay clear of her. Sometimes she lifts her head when the new cats enter. The gate goes up, the cats come in, the gate goes down. At first they cower on the perimeter. But gradually, one by one, the new cats make their way to the half circles around the TVs.

LANGUAGE is the door where they will try to steal our words. If one can resist, or hold off, one is a hero. Most cannot. Who can resist the Motown? When the cats come back from Language, they enter the half circle and say a word that answers the only question: How many words today? "One" or "Two." Anyone who says "None" is allowed to sit closest to the story box.

Behind the MEMORY door is where they play with the cats' tails. The older ones say they recall a time when a few cats came back with no tails. Of course, most died shortly thereafter. We can tell how long a cat was behind the memory door by counting the bruises on its tail.

STEALTH is the door only traitors go behind. There they teach the forgetting. They are the fattest, saddest cats. The Stealth cats are given no story box. But once a year they can join us as we watch a movie about *The Greatest Show on Earth.*

ENGINEERING is the upper level where they take their stolen goods and build their steel birds. No cats there.

PHYSICS/OLD and PHYSICS/NEW are where they draw on blackboards and try to break the world. And talk in new languages. Nobody understands them.

JANITOR is the sacred door to The Way Out. Once a year Sister Tail leads a procession of cats out of Storage. She takes us to Our Holy Father. He begins the chant and the holy embrace. Every year dozens and dozens go home. No one can name the number. It is the Cats' Birthday. When we are one.

The Holy Father speaks for us. He is our ringmaster. His words crack a whip and teach us to be good cats. He tells us how to run through hoops. How to stay in line. How to take our places on the tables. To roar on command. How to dance in circles. All the tricks of The Circus.

He is the oldest.

He was the first to lose a tail. But the only one who survived. No one knows why.

They tossed his tail in The Way Out.

Sister Tail came back. Ha, Ha.

Sister Tail obeys him.

Rudy and I were his favorites. When no one was watching, we showed him we remembered how to disappear. He kept us close, and when we tried our first Great Escape in the Big Frisbee we were a team—the three of us. The crash hurt, but not as much as leaving the eldest behind. He was wounded badly. And his brain was not right. It is still not right. After the crash he kept saying, "I've got to give them hope. I've got to give them hope."

That was not the plan. The plan was to find a Doorman and a Blue Man. A lock and a key.

We were gone a long time out in the Wide World. Looking for a Doorman and a Blue Man.

Sometimes we missed the stories of The Pope. Here is one he told often.

This is not our land.
Until we return to our home we must be good cats.
We must obey the Masters.
So long as we obey the Masters
and do not cause trouble we will be fed
and we all will have safe passage to The Anywhere.
Every year I will release a portion of good cats.
Only good cats go home. Only good cats are rewarded.

We know what happens to bad cats in a circus.
They go down the chute.
Though your Mother is Gadget, and your child is Father,
I am your First.
I will always lead you.
I will always protect you.
I want you all to be happy.
I want you all to go home.
There is only one way out and only good cats go there.
Only good cats go home.
Say it with me now: Only good cats go home.
Only good cats go home.
Only good cats go home.

TRINITY DAY

Monday July 16, 1945, 5:30 a.m.

Koop told me the story in the early sixties. We were in our sleeping bags under the tipped-over picnic tables. Koop and I: college friends on our first camping trip together. Neither of us could remember who had promised to bring the tent. So Koop got the idea of taping some black trash bags over the A-Frame and digging a trench around it all in case of rain.

Boy, did it rain. A downpour in a pine forest on the coast of Georgian Bay. Let's just say it got messy. Nobody could have slept through that. The crashes of lightning felt like somebody was bombing us—the ground shook. I was terrified. Storms always freak me out. Our little trench was flooded in a matter of minutes and our sleeping bags were soaked in no time.

So, story time. Once we could hear each other talk again and the rain had receded to a steady drizzle, Koop got chatty. Later, I thought he was trying to distract me, playing the good soldier to his PTSD buddy in the trenches as the artillery fell. Did I mention I was terrified?

"What's a friend?" someone once asked a Korean War veteran. "That's easy. A friend is someone who will watch your back when you sleep and give you a drink from his canteen." When the stakes are high, it gets real simple.

It might seem a strange story to tell to calm someone down in a panic, but it worked. He told me the story of his parents' honeymoon near Alamogordo, New Mexico.

It was a "No Room at the Inn" tale. An un-immaculate conception. Every motel along the highway was full. Or said they were full. Or suddenly their neon VACANCY sign turned off. Towns were ghost towns or full of soldiers. Everywhere they went they were looked at sideways. Even stopping for gas. It was a very "you don't belong here" vibe. Once a cop pulled them over and made them wait twenty minutes on the side of a scorching highway, only to smile nastily and tell them enjoy their visit. Koop's dad had just got decommissioned from France and was on R & R to marry his girl. She was from Texas, Houston. They met near an army base.

He said New Mexico and Paris were day and night. Everyone seemed to like a man in a uniform overseas. When he got home it was like he was an embarrassment. Nobody knew what to think of this tall man in green walking down the street. He recalled speaking to a French woman refugee in a flower shop and turning happily with his bouquet of lilies he'd got for his girl and seeing everyone—man, woman, and child—staring at him agape as he made his way toward the exit. "Like I was an exotic species of bird," Koop's dad said.

"Well. He was black, Koop."

"You think I don't get it?"

They couldn't find any place to sleep, so they ended up driving all the way into the White Sands National Park and camping out. Not their original plan to celebrate their honeymoon.

White Sands is an anomaly: 275 square miles of rare white gypsum. A surreal place with wave upon wave of albino sand dunes that stretch as far as the eye can see. Some reach as high as sixty feet. They drove as deep into the park as they could, found an old service trail that snaked around the dunes for thirty miles.

"How far does this thing go?" his new bride asked.

Koop's dad smiled and said, "Let's find out."

They drove until they could see where the white sands ended: a valley between the two mountain ranges to the north. It was a great place to park their small aluminum teardrop camper, set up a fire, and watch the sunset.

"We made you that night," his father told the young boy with a smile.

His dad got up early and was smoking a pipe beside the campfire when he saw the brightest flash of lightning he had ever seen illuminate the entire night sky. The white dunes to the south flared so sharply they left a negative imprint on his eyes when he closed them. The blast could be seen 160 miles away. They were less than 30 miles due south.

He turned to look north.

The light seemed to grow and grow and change colors.

The explosion was silent until sixty seconds later, when his mother woke up screaming in the camper from the sound of the end of the world, and his father's pipe flew out of his mouth.

It was a childhood tale. His parents would call Winston "Our Blast Baby."

They both died of cancer the year Koop turned twelve. Raised then by his Auntie Marcie—his biggest fan. She was always there to applaud his sports scholarships, academic awards, and whenever he mastered a new language. No doubt about it: Koop was a prodigy. "I started with a Big Bang," he said. "And I just kept exploding."

"Why'd you tell me that?" I asked. Then I realized it had stopped raining, the lightning had disappeared, and I had stopped shaking.

Koop grinned and said, "It could always get worse, Nuke."

I looked at his dark silhouette. "Nuke?"

"That's your new nickname, Pagnucco. Get it?"

THE LAST PRESIDENT WHO CAME HERE—2017

Once the blond man was informed that his predecessor barely spoke during the visits in his two terms, that settled it. He insisted that it be arranged. He would not go quietly. Nobody would silence him.

But the consensus was against him. His chief of staff advised against it. His National Security team advised against it. The Joint Chiefs strongly advised against it. The heads of his intelligence agencies attempted to weigh in, but he would not pick up their calls.

Even his wife asked him if he thought it was a good idea. She perched languidly on the corner of his large desk.

He replied in a Russian accent that seemed to amuse him, "Vhat's the vorst that could happen?"

"You asked him?!" his daughter whispered.

He shrugged. "It came up."

"Dad! This is, like, a Major Secret."

"How big can it be? Nobody can give me any details!"

"Mr. President." His son-in-law spoke up. "Does anyone else . . . think this is a good idea?"

"No. But I'm calling an audible here. I'm zigging while they zag."

"You took pill?" his wife asked.

"Yes, I took the goddam pill—Relax!"

The President's face took on a redder hue. The silence that followed had a familiar tang to it. Everyone in the room had heard it many times. Children who did not wish to be disciplined would know it well. Soldiers who knew they had no recourse but to "take that hill" would recognize it. Women, who understand very well what "one more word" means, know this silence best of all.

Finally, he rose, looked across his large desk to the oval wall where a Secret Service agent with a fat briefcase stood at attention.

"Charlie? Where's the football?"

Nobody moved.

"It's Peter, sir."

The President laughed and sat down. "I know. I'm just fucking with you."

Under the Andrew Jackson portrait, the Vice President smiled painfully, as if someone had just tweaked his nipple. "I assume, Mr. President, you'll want me on duty, while you're on this, uh, critical National Security Inspection."

"You mean: Here in the White House?"

"Yessir."

The President puckered his lips. "I thought you had a game or something."

"It can wait, sir."

"Sure." The President smiled and swept his hand over his desk. "Make yourself at home." It was an old joke, but it always cracked him up.

The flight on Air Force One was uneventful.

The jeep ride to the base was quick.

The President's party was truncated—just him and his Secret Service team.

After the rather baroque descent through the corkscrew levels of safety protocols, the visibly annoyed President was escorted into the presence of the Asset. His entire party wore Hawaiian shirts, cargo khakis, and flip-flops. Again: security.

He stood agape, swiveling his head round and round, taking in the stunning golden edifice of an art deco nineteenth-century hotel.

"Fuck! Fuck! Fuck me!!"

The revolving door started to spin and whisper, and the Little White Man emerged. He, too, followed the apparent dress code: Hawaiian shirt, khaki cargo pants, and pink flip-flops—kid-sized, though.

"Wow," said The President. "Now that is what I call an entrance."

He strode up and noticed a tall older man in a blue suit standing beside the Asset. He took his measure, decided he was Help, then bowed down to offer his pale hand to the midget.

"Nice to meet ya!"

"The pleasure is all yours, sir."

They shook. And shook. The President found he could not, no matter how hard he tugged, wrench the little man closer. He had learned from a master the technique of taking your opponent off balance, and thus asserting yourself. But the physics of the judo move did not seem to apply here.

Finally, his hand was released.

He was not invited to sit.

The Little White Man regarded him with indifference, which triggered a surly impulse in the most powerful man in the world. His lips puckered and he crossed his arms.

"So, you're the Asset," he said.

"Evidently."

"They call you 'Blarney the Imp.'"

"And what do they call you, sir?"

The implied insult hung in the air until The President said, "I understand you have consulted with other presidents."

"They have consulted with me. Most, but not all."

"Who declined?"

"Reagan. And Poppa Bush."

The President nodded appreciatively. He noted this was something he dared to do that a couple of his predecessors did not.

"They give a reason?"

"Nancy said her astrologer forbade it."

The President nodded deeper, as if this insight were worth extra consideration that he was saving for later, when, in fact, he didn't much care.

"I also understand that," he looked over his shoulder at the football guy, "we owe you a debt of gratitude. You have given our great country a lot of help over the years. Defense-wise."

"True."

"They tell me you helped with our fighter jets. But, honestly, I can't see any difference."

The President regarded the men behind him. After a blink they all laughed heartily. Satisfied, he turned back to the Little White Man. "What would you say has been your greatest contribution? Your biggest deal?"

The Little White Man did not hesitate. "This planet has not been destroyed during my tenure."

"You did that?"

The Little White Man looked over at the Butler in The Blue Suit. "I helped."

It finally registered on The President that he was not being treated with the deference he expected from everyone but his best friend. He stepped back and surveyed the facade of the hotel. "This is beautiful work. I oughta know. I build things. Big things. Expensive, magnificent things. All over the world. You know what I've learned? It's all about the details. Measure twice, cut once. You get the details right and you get quality. Gold leaf. Egyptian sheets. Copper piping. Italian marble. Details." He began to pace the room in a wide circle as if he were performing for a theater-in-the-round.

"See, I say what I mean. Ask anybody who voted for me. I'm a straight-talker. I like straight answers. But"—and here he made a face that looked as if he had just bit into something sour—"when I bring you up . . . everyone around me gets squirrelly. Starts talking like intellectuals. Fuzzy. Double talk. No details. I can't seem to get a grip on what exactly you do here, little fella. 'Highly technical,' I'm told. 'Really complicated.' But no details. So I'm thinking maybe I should stop talking to the experts and get it straight from the horse's mouth. So." The President glanced over his shoulder at the detail who followed him everywhere. "You're the horse. You got a mouth." He extended his arms obligingly. "Start talking."

The five Secret Service men laughed aloud. They bent over laughing. A few actually took a knee.

The President relished the moment.

When he turned back, he found the Little White Man and the Butler in the Blue Suit sitting in the lotus position just outside the revolving door that swished and swished as it spun. He wondered why it never got tired.

He also found that he was sitting on the floor.

Then he frowned and looked back to his security team. They were all laid out on the long red Moroccan rug that led to the door, in various postures of repose.

And they were all asleep.

The Little White Man was holding the football in his lap. The Butler in the Blue Suit was holding the open suitcase. A handcuff dangled from the black leather handle.

The Asset delicately inspected the football as if it were a Fabergé egg. "So tell me, sir."

"Hmmmm?" said The President.

"The code."

"Oh," The President said. "That's a big secret, you know."

"I know. What is it?"

The President recited the numbers.

"Excellent," said The Little White Man. "Now. If you don't mind." He split open the egg to reveal the keypad. "Tell me . . . the Real Code."

The President's face performed what could only be called a dance. A pantomime, if you will. The routine included well-wrung postures of surprise and skepticism, shrugs; it shifted into silent roars, pouts, and orgasmic releases, and tripped into teeth-clenched rage, ducky-lipped approval, and well-earned exhaustion. Finally, The President admitted: "That's an even bigger secret."

"I understand," The Little White Man said.

"I'm gonna have to call my daughter."

The Butler in the Blue Suit handed him his cellphone. Then turned to The Little White Man and whispered, "That's it. That's my last one. I will have nothing to do with motherfuckers like this."

"Control yourself, Brother."

"I'm done, I tell you."

"We are in this together. To the end."

"Okay. But this is the last fucking cracker I ever play egg-ball with."

The President was famished when he found his dinner waiting for him on Air Force One. He took a long sip of the Diet Coke, opened the paper carton, and grabbed the Big Mac with both hands.

"Charlie?" he said to the Football Man across the aisle as he chewed. "What's a matter? You look a little sick."

"It's Peter, sir."

OLD FRIENDS—2018

Yeah, this is gonna jump around, the way memories do. Sorry about that. You know, how one second you're thinking about sex and the next you're remembering tossing a yellow Frisbee across your college's courtyard to your best friend. And a couple of smart-ass freshmen frats pick it up and start playing keep-away with Koop, who smiles at them and starts talking, and you can see them huddling up, chins cocky and belligerent, and he just towers over them and keeps talking, then one of them laughs, then everybody laughs, and they hand over the yellow Frisbee and walk off with their backpacks, and somebody shouts back, "Later, Bro!" I don't know how he does that. Koop turns smiling back to me, and that smile is gone so fast from his face that I can see the death in his icy brown eyes. I just know those boys got off easy. Whoa, here comes the Frisbee, arching up, chilling into stasis, and coasting smoothly into my pink hands.

So we hit the road, saw everything. But there was this one inci-dent somewhere in Missouri, I think, that scared the hell out of me.

I should preface this by saying how paranoid I am about cops. I spent a lot of time crossing the Canadian Border, being questioned by officials, and regularly they'd rip off a pink sheet of paper, slap it under my windshield wiper, and direct me to park my vehicle by the yellow lines so I could be inspected. This happened every other time I went over to Canada. It didn't matter if I used the tunnel from Detroit to Windsor, the Ambassador Bridge, or the Blue Water

Bridge in Port Huron. Almost every crossing involved a pull-over and inspection. I was always polite and deferential; I was compliant and did not speak till I was spoken to. No matter what I did, I was stopped. Once they emptied everything Koop and I had onto a long table—even our soggy sleeping bags. And we had to repack all our luggage and camping equipment. Once I was brought before the chief inspector, who had one question for me: "You wouldn't be doing any skinny-dipping, would ya?" Nahh, of course not. I finally concluded that I must have a guilty face. "It's your Catholic thing," Koop always said. "Even when you're innocent you just know you did something to break the rules." So maybe that was it. In any case, whenever I see gumballs flashing in my rearview mirror, my butt puckers.

Somewhere in Missouri a cop in a black-and-white cruiser pulled us over—no idea why. I was driving as usual, and the old pale blue Honda was doing what it always does: nothing but work. Rudy was in the backseat invisible and putting on a pout.

Koop told me to get my hands on the wheel, ten and two. He insisted. I saw he folded his own hands over his chest.

The cop leaned down to the window and said, "License and registration."

I provided them.

He examined both. Thoroughly. Then addressed me. "Everything okay, Sir?"

"What?"

"You all right?" He glanced across to Koop then back to me. "Sure."

He leaned in to the window. "Where you boys goin'?"

"Road trip to Vegas."

"Vegas, huh?" He eyeballed Koop. "That's a long drive."

"Sure is," I said, empathizing with myself.

"Aren't ch'all a little old for that action?"

And here I thought we were having a friendly chat.

"For gambling?" I asked.

"What's your name?" he asked, leaning into the shade to get a better look at Koop.

Koop smiled. "Officer. These are not the droids you're looking for."

Slowly I looked over at Koop. Are you kidding me?

The cop said, "What did you say to me?"

"It's from *Star Wars*."

"I know it's from *Star Wars*," the cop said. "You know how many drunk high school kids I've dragged to jail for saying that to me?"

I gave Rudy a death look in the rearview mirror in case the sprite was thinking of going rogue.

Koop smiled. The officer was resting his hand on his gun. I was starting to feel the sweat in my armpits.

Koop said, "No disrespect, sir. We're just a couple of old-timers on our way to a scifi con in Vegas. My name's Koop. Winston Koop."

I could see our reflection in his *Cool Hand Luke* shades.

"Well, why didn't cha say so?"

Koop shrugged.

The cop said, "Which is the best one?"

Koop said, "Episode Five."

"No," I said. "*The Force Awakens*."

Koop said, "Episode Five's got the land walkers. And Luke's father."

I said, "One word. Rey."

"I like Rey," the officer said. "Not crazy about the black guy, though."

"Come on," said Koop. "He was great!"

"Didn't like to lose Han like that," the officer sniffed.

"Nobody did," replied Koop with sympathy.

Rudy, I thought, if you are fucking with this cop, I swear to God.

"Okay, boys." He rapped twice on the roof. "Force be with you."

We didn't move as he made the walk back to his car, turned off his gumballs, spit some gravel, and drove past us with a wave.

We waited for the dust to settle, and Koop gave me the dead eye. I said, "You think this is funny!?"

GETTING SOBER ON THE ROAD—2018

Freeways. Cornfields. Neon. Rest stops. Roadkill. Cactuses.

That's America on the highway. When Nabokov wrote his road novel, it sounded a lot more juicy and quaint—the country, I mean. A strange, imaginary land that must have appeared to any immigrant who crossed it as an unlikely union of abundance, welcome, and virgin wilderness. I wonder how the original occupants saw it.

I asked Koop to pop me a can of Vernors, and he did. I took a sip and rested it between my thighs, nice and cool.

"My daddy used to do that," he said.

"Mine, too," I said. "Stroh's."

"Pabst."

"Blatz."

"Schlitz."

"Time Juice," Rudy said.

"What?" I said.

"That's what we call it," he said.

"Not a bad name," I admitted.

Koop and I didn't have to talk about all that. We'd lived it. When we were younger, we swore we'd never fall into that pothole, and we both fell hook, line, and sinker. If alcoholism were logical, we would have talked ourselves out of it decades ago.

"I told you how I got sober. After the Orangutan election. You never told me how you did."

"Oh, so I got the peace pipe?"

"If you want," he said, his feet braced on the dash, his knees practically up to his chin. "Daddy Longlegs," his girlfriends used to call him.

I took another swig of Vernors and squinted at the horizon.

"Okay. This is gonna sound like I figured it all out at once. Like I'm—I don't know—some damn genius therapist. But no. It took me years to put all the pieces together. And I slipped a lot. Lost a lot. But, for me, the turning point was when I stopped thinking that I was giving up something. Like Lent. Or that I was going to get a reward at the end, like Easter. Chocolate bunnies. Whatever. It took me the longest time to realize that my sobriety was the reward. Not being sick was the gift.

"'Cause it's never just drinking, right? It's drinking and lying, drinking and vomiting, drinking and crashing your car. Drinking and losing everything you love."

"Preach," he said.

Rudy made a rude noise. "So damn glad you losers asked me along."

"Keep going," said Koop.

"And it's always someone else's fault that you drink—never the drinker. The drinker is always the victim. If only the kids were quieter. If only my boss was nicer. If only my job was easier. If only my neighbor wouldn't mow his lawn in the morning when I'm hungover."

Rudy said, "If only you would stop talking."

"Shuttup!" we said together.

I took another sip of Vernors. "For most people booze is just a gift. Rudy's right. They get to step out of time, and lose their fear, and numb their nerves."

"That's normal drinkers," Koop said.

"Right. That's not us. We don't want our nerves turned off. They've been off for years. We've already turned them off to survive whatever trauma our childhood was. And then, then—and this is the secret—that's when angel alcohol turns them on. Ahhh, we think, 'So *this* is normal! This is what it feels like to be alive!' To live without fear. Not to be bracing for the next blow. Not to feel the hollow left by the constant absence of . . . you name it. That's heaven. Nobody can get enough of that."

Why did I check the rearview mirror then? Nothing but a shadow on the seat. I could sense Rudy sitting as still as ever, like a kid listening to a story about Christmas. Koop said he only let you see a glimpse of him when he wanted you to. But he had yet to show himself to me. It was like I had to prove something to him.

Rudy had a trick at every stop.

We'd be sitting at the table looking at the menus and suddenly there were three customers behind three menus. It was his game for us to guess what the waitress was seeing.

"Hey, sweetie. It's a little early for Halloween isn't it?"

"Sir. I'm sorry. But I'm gonna have to ask you to curb your pet."

"Hey. What's with the Muffin Man?"

"Boy, my aunt Rachel would kill for a doll like that!"

Koop would finally whisper, "Rudy. Quit showing off. They're not your toys."

Somewhere west of Denver, Koop said, "So vino is heaven . . ."

"Yeah?" I said.

"What's sobriety? Purgatory?"

In the back Rudy grunted the universal disgust of a teen forced to endure adult chatter.

"No," I said. "I think that's just the twisted logic of an addict. We think sobriety is punishment. It's not. It's just normal. It's just not killing ourselves. Or finishing the job our loved ones started."

Rudy spoke up from the back. "For guys who claim to have settled all this years ago, you sure do talk a lot about it."

Koop and I looked at each other.

"But what do I know? I'm just a little boy."

After a few minutes I heard a noise behind me.

It took me a while to figure out it was Rudy snoring from his head cup.

THE LAST BLUE MAN—2018

So, naturally, we'd end up at a saloon. The Dew Drop Inn. The Last Chance Texaco. The Roswell Pit Stop. It's America: there's always a bar.

We lined up on three stools in a row.

Friends sometimes politely ask if I mind going to a bar. I tell them: I've been in hundreds of bars. It feels perfectly ordinary to me.

"But aren't you tempted?" they ask.

"Every day," I say. "But you gotta understand. There is not enough liquor in any bar for me. I don't just want a drink. I want all of them."

Usually, they don't understand. It's no biggie. You have to be there, and, believe me, you don't want an invitation.

Koop ordered one of those fruity virgin drinks. Looked like a goddam Carmen Miranda hat. I had the usual: a Coke. The bartender let out a whoop and said: "What'll it be, R2?" And served Rudy a pilsner.

"Fruit?" I said to Koop.

"Shuttup," he said.

The bartender sidled up to him and said, "I can turn on the game. The Kings are playing."

"Not a fan," said Koop sourly.

"Suit yerself."

I rolled my eyes.

I had just savored my first sip of Coke when Rudy said, "Hey! Dynamic Geriatric Duo! I got an idea! Let's talk about drinking!"

I said, "How do you put up with him?"

Koop shrugged. The door jangled.

"You know what the cure for alcoholism is?" I asked.

The question lingered. Rudy didn't answer. Koop didn't answer. Maybe that's the point, I thought. Maybe it's a different key for everybody.

"Sobriety," said an old woman at the door.

We all turned to look. I mean, Koop and I did, and in my head I assumed Rudy joined us to spin on our stools and watch the thin, close-cut, gray-haired air force lieutenant colonel with red-rimmed glasses walk gingerly across the wooden floor to join us. The silver leaf insignia on her epaulet glimmered in the hot sunlight coming in the window. She leaned on the edge of the bar and regarded Rudy's bubbling beer and empty chair.

"Nice accordion," she said.

"I thought you were at Nellis," Koop said.

"Part-time. I liaison with the Warfare Center team when I'm not giving physicals to the Thunderbirds. They won't let me retire."

Koop smiled at that.

"Nuke, this is Lieutenant Colonel Katherine Torsan."

"Nuke? That's a strange name."

She looked me up and down. All I could do was stare.

"Cat got yer tongue?"

"Oh, leave him alone," Koop said.

She reached for Rudy's beer and slugged it down in one long drink. Smacked her lips and sighed.

"They're expecting you, boys. But I bet you knew that."

"Figured," Koop said.

"You're not gonna give me the book, are you?"

"Nope," Koop said.

"Well, I had to ask."

She smiled at me then. And across a bridge of forty years I recognized the woman I once loved.

"I always liked your doodles, Nuke. You still doodling?"

"I take pictures now."

"You wouldn't recognize the place these days, boys. I got it running like a top. It's cleaner. Nicer. We treat everybody with respect."

"Even your guests?" I asked.

She held my eyes. "Even them."

I turned to Nuke. "She's The Blue Man now?"

Koop didn't answer.

I turned back to her. "You're the fucking Blue Man?"

She sat beside Rudy's stool. "Like I said: a lot's changed. Not the world. The world is the same as it always was. I had to adapt. I married a knight in shining armor who turned out to be a drunk. And I fell for a gentle artist. A Sancho Panza. Who couldn't take the world as it was. So now he takes pictures. If this is your idea of a happy ending, boys, you're in the wrong book."

Then she did something very strange. She stood, leaned into me, gave me a peck on the cheek, and whispered, "You got two hours after you close it. Run. Highest Levels. Greatest Confidence."

Then, turning smartly for an old dame and marching away, she announced over her shoulder in a rather showy voice, "I'll miss your big finish, boys. I'm going to Vegas for the weekend."

I listened, stunned, to her footsteps, the door jangling, and the slam.

Rudy giggled and said, "Boys."

"I didn't like that," I admitted.

"Me neither," said Koop. "But she does have a point."

"Yeah," I said.

Outside there was a team of four soldiers and a green jeep. Rudy put them to sleep and Koop tossed me some handcuffs.

We took the jeep.

The security checkpoints started getting more frequent the closer we got to Groom Lake.

"I'm delivering a prisoner to The Pope," Koop said at the first one, nodding in my direction. I showed him my handcuffed hands.

"Okay, then," the guard said, and lifted the gate.

The next one was on a dirt road in a winding valley. Two soldiers with AR-15s who asked for ID. They knew who Koop was; it was just procedure and a chance to eyeball us.

"We'll take him from here, sir."

"No, no, no," said Koop. "He stays with me. I was told to bring him directly to The Pope."

After a moment of hesitation, they lifted the gate.

A few miles down there was a single man at a small booth with a coding device next to him, who drew a pistol on us.

Rudy made him punch in the codes, and when he tried to point the gun at us again, he shot himself in the head.

As we drove, our dust cloud must have been visible for miles—there was nothing else to see. We turned a corner, and a black military amphibious vehicle was parked across the road. A loudspeaker commanded us to get out of the car and walk backward toward them. When one soldier got out and tried to handcuff Koop, Koop knocked the rifle out of his hands, karate-jabbed him in the throat, and grabbed a hand grenade off his vest. He pulled the pin and tossed it into the porthole of the black vehicle. We barely got out of the way before it exploded.

Koop was limping after that. "I'm too old for this shit."

Then there were three jeeps across the road at the gate.

I shouted out, "Highest Levels, Greatest Confidence!" and they pulled out of the way and let us pass.

It went fairly smoothly after that.

Once we got inside, one big guy tried to choke out Koop, but Rudy strangled him. In fact, Rudy killed a lot of the last soldiers. What with Katey's password, Rudy's prowess, and Koop's bullshit, we sailed through the security zones.

We got as far as the last door.

We got to the elevator. It had a round glass window.

"We're doing it!" I cheered. "I can't believe we're doing it!"

Rudy said, "Jesus, will you shut up?"

Alarms went mad. Still nobody came.

Down, down, down.

Every floor we passed, through the tiny porthole we glimpsed hundreds of IFs dashing down the halls.

"It's a jailbreak!" I said.

"You better believe it," Koop replied.

That's when I noticed Koop had a blue clown mouth: a ring of blue around his lips.

"Your mouth!" I said.

"You see it now? We all have them. Anyone who's ever had an IF. We don't see them until we're close to the portal, though. You've got one, too, Bro."

My hand inadvertently went to my lips.

"Oh, you can't feel them. And for some reason we can't see them on ourselves."

"That is fucked."

He yawned and said, "Totally."

He'd been living with the Paradigm Overload a lot longer than I had.

RETRIEVAL.

ADMITTING.

PROCESSING.

BATHS.

DRYING.

EXAMINATION.

STORAGE.

MEDICAL.

LANGUAGE.

MEMORY.

STEALTH.

ENGINEERING.

PHYSICS/NEW.

PHYSICS/OLD.

POPE.

JANITOR.

We had reached the bottom of the hole.

"Time to meet The Doorman," said Koop.

The Doorman—1962

It was a quiet night and I was walking through the dark woods, taking a shortcut nobody else on campus used, behind the old white fraternity house. I heard a sound.

I stopped and listened.

Then I heard it again. Somebody was pounding something underground.

Then I saw a pair of blue jeans in a pile.

Then, behind a stand of trees, I saw the ground tremble.

Christ. Somebody was trapped.

Under a cover of dry leaves was a makeshift fallout shelter. There was a long silver padlock hooked to a latch that was bolted to a cement foundation. I tried to pull the latch loose by hand but couldn't. Then I picked up a long branch and jammed it under the latch. A few pulls and it started bending. A few more, and one end broke off and I fell on my butt.

Then the forest floor swung open in the shape of a door like an exit to another world, and leaves, dust and dirt slid off it.

Big, bony, dirty hands grasped the side of the rectangular hole.

The skinny young man who rose out of the grave reminded me of a long distance runner. Or maybe a high jumper. He collapsed on his back, taking deep gulps of the cool autumn night air, and I saw the sweat glistening on his filthy body. His filthy white jockey shorts were his only clothes.

Reminded me of a zombie movie that had terrified me when I was a kid, so it took me a moment or two to say, "You need a doctor?"

Still breathing hard, he turned his head as if that were the only thing he had strength for. He looked like he had a few questions and he took his time answering. Finally, he shook his head.

After a time he caught his breath and sat up and looked at himself. "They said they'd give me back my pants."

I retrieved his jeans and handed them to him. He put them on quickly and stood. Clothing seemed to restore him; I mean: he seemed less vulnerable.

"How long were they gonna keep you in there?" I asked.

"Six more hours," a voice said.

There were three of them. One fat.

"You broke our lock, harelip."

Nobody has ever accused me of bravery. "I'm sorry," I said. "I . . . didn't know it was your lock?" Why did I make that a question?

"Boys," the skinny man said. "He's just a good samaritan. Just passing through."

"Who are you calling 'boy'?" the leader said. And the two others sidled up next to him.

"All right, all right. Everybody just cool it," said the tall kid, dusting off his pant legs. He turned to me and said, "Beat it."

Grateful, I started to move off. The fat kid stepped in front of me.

Someone said, "You took the pledge, Koop. You pass the initiation."

He held up both hands. "Okay. Fair enough, Ron."

"Randy," the leader said.

"Randy. Sorry. Honestly? I'm rethinking my pledge. It was really hard to breathe down there."

"We all did it," the second one said.

"And I admire that, Justin."

"Jason."

"Jason. Jesus, my brain. Oxygen deprivation. What the Greeks used to call . . . Well, never mind. I'll be honest. I blame myself. Mea culpa. I admit I thought your Post would open some doors for me. On campus. Maybe an internship? But honestly. I'm skeptical about the whole . . ." He took a series of big breaths.

"Thing?" I offered when the silence had become intolerable.

"Exactly," he said. "Character-building. Life-enhancing. Thing."

"That's our mission," the other said.

"I get that, Jeff."

"JOHN!" the leader shouted. "You think you're smarter than us!"

"Nahhh. You all look the same to me, that's all." White jeans. Madras shirts. Blond frat bros. He had a point. I shrugged at him and nodded and immediately regretted it when I saw their faces.

"No offense," he added quickly. "But you didn't say you'd lock it. That's, that's . . ."

That pause again. Like his brain had run out of gas.

"Not cricket?" I offered.

He swiveled his head and seemed to regard me with new esteem. "Freshman?"

I nodded.

"Me, too. What's your major?"

"Art?"

He pointed at himself. "Latin. Or Math. Maybe Pysch. Or History."

"Koop," the fat boy said. "No reneging."

The tall boy's face looked like somebody had pointed a hair dryer at it full blast.

"RENEGING?!" he laughed. Then bent over laughing. "'Renegare.' Mid-sixteenth century. To desert one's post. I think you're stretching the meaning of desertion on this one, boys." He looked over to me and gestured toward the hole with his thumb. "Gotta say

... That. ...," Koop swiped his hand across an invisible bar, "was not worth the merit badge."

Now it was my turn to make that vacuum cleaner face. I looked from the tall, skinny boy to the three others. "Boy Scouts?" I asked.

This made them bristle. "Explorers!" the fat one nearly spat.

Koop smiled at me. "Better uniforms. It was pledge week and I didn't drink so . . ." He was tackled and nearly fell back into hole.

Somebody grabbed me and flung me over his leg. Hitting the ground knocked the breath out of me. That never seems to happen in fight scenes: that helpless, sickening dizziness.

Next came a reeling haze of glimpses.

Bodies flying. Blows landing. Grunts. Curses.

A tall man in jeans kicking a man in the head.

A bone cracking. And a scream.

All the while I'm thinking, Oh God. I can breathe. I remember how to breathe.

Finally a bloody face fell to the ground and landed right before me. The fat one.

I yelled and sat up hyperventilating.

It wasn't a pretty picture. One frat boy knocked out, Another shuffling away like Igor, holding his arm. And Koop exchanging punches with the big leader—a fast boy with a snarky smile, until Koop hit him one last time and he disappeared into the hole.

Koop bent over and put his hands on his knees, caught his breath. Then looked over at me.

"You usually stir up this much trouble?"

I shook my head and rubbed my sore leg. "First time," I admitted.

Koop laughed.

He gathered his clothes at the frat house and walked me back to the dorm where my freshman digs were. My roomie was gone, so Koop slept on the top bunk. From the bottom I watched his big pink soles dangling over the end of the bed.

After that, I guess you could say we were tight.

THE BATTLE—2018

The elevator door opened and there were some serious people standing outside. Men in black holding M4 carbines. They sort of stepped apart in the middle to reveal the first IF I had ever laid eyes on. He looked horrible, disfigured—like a wounded octopus. He had one lopsided eye and two tails.

"Come here, Brother," he said in a squeaky voice.

And then there was the weirdest wrestling match I have ever seen. The two-tailed one seemed to be dancing alone or doing gymnastics or auditioning for the oddest act in the Cirque du Soleil. It was very much like a cartoon fight where two opponents disappear into a spinning dust cloud and all you see are glimpses of arms, legs, or, in this case, wings and tails. There was a lot of ugly grunting, too. And the soldiers at the door were knocked back by the furious, whirling fight. I prayed Rudy was holding his own.

It was a weird sight, and no doubt why nobody saw me press the Up button until it was too late. The door closed and then there was a barrage of bullets hitting the outside door—a noise that receded somewhat as we rose up a floor.

"This way!" Koop shouted as we exited the elevator. "Follow the blue line!"

We went past room after the room. The things I saw in those rooms I will never forget. And I will never share with another living soul.

"Stairs," Koop said.

He opened the door. And the stairwell was full of terrified IFs huddling as if in an air raid.

"Flasher!" one of them said.

"Down or up?" I asked.

"Down," Koop said.

We were shuffling down the steps, trying to be gingerly about it, not step on any tails, when we saw the body of a soldier. Koop bent down and picked up his M4. The IFs averted their eyes like guilty children.

A door below us popped open and somebody threw in a canister of gas.

"UP!" said Koop. And we followed a crowd of IFs tumbling into the hallway. All of us were coughing.

A shot grazed my shoulder and another just missed my head.

Koop killed the soldier in the hall and we heard footsteps coming double-time.

Suddenly a mob of IFs swarmed past us and turned the corner. They were shredded by machine gun fire, and their bodies exploded in the hallway in splashes of clear goo. More IFs streamed out of the stinking stairwell and wave after wave of them fell until the guns ran out of bullets. Then we heard men screaming as the IFs fell upon them.

Silence.

We turned the corner and found the hallway impassable due to the clog of bodies, blood, and goo.

"What now?" I asked.

"Yer shot," said Koop.

"Just a flesh wound," I joked.

Then someone turned on the radio and *Motown's Greatest Hits* started filling the hall. The arrangement of "Love Is Like an Itching in My Heart" was punctuated by grenade accents, stomping feet, screams, and stuttering gunfire. Koop took a minute to tear his shirt and dress my shoulder wound as best he could. We were in a side room off the hall, and he made me sit down and catch my breath.

"Funny thing about Motown," Koop said after a few songs.

"What's that?" I asked.

"No waltzes. Everything's four-four time."

A voice on a speaker called down from the ceiling. "Mr. Koop?"

"Yes?"

"Is it possible we might negotiate?"

"Sure. Cool jazz or Mary Jane Blige, but enough of this nostalgia shit."

The Motown stopped.

Koop raised his eyebrows at me, as if to say, "I cannot believe that worked."

Then somebody started playing Andy Williams singing "Moon River."

"Torture," I said, and Koop agreed.

The voice on the speaker said, "Mr. Koop. We would like to trade for the book."

"What do you got?"

"Well. We've got your lives."

"Fair enough. Come and get them."

"Oh, we will. But there doesn't have to be any more bloodshed."

"There doesn't?"

"No. We simply want a trade. Your lives. For the book."

Koop smiled and pat-patted the bulge in my back pocket.

"My ass," he said.

There was a pause then a yellow gas started seeping from the ceiling. Quicker than I could have imagined IFs sprang up and sealed the vents with their bodies like Play-Doh. Their white skin began to turn yellow.

We ran through two doorways, following the blue line, until we arrived at a dead end. Construction blocked the curving green hall. We took refuge in what looked to be an X-ray room.

"Get behind that," Koop said, pointing to a fat table.

We heard footsteps above us, shouted orders and screams.

Somebody knocked on the door, and Koop peppered it with

bullets until the magazine was empty and the trigger clicked.

"Aww, shit," he said, tossing down the M4.

The door opened and a rather large woman in a lab coat entered. "That'll be enough," she said. It was the speaker lady. When I say "large," I mean Ronda Rousey large. Think "muscled." Seriously muscled. She had short-clipped blond hair.

"You're surrounded," she said.

"Highest Levels. Greatest Confidence."

"The code just changed."

He smiled. "You wanna tell me what it is?"

She smiled back.

Okay, there's no simple way of describing what happened next. I'll just say it was the opposite of every action movie you've ever seen. Koop was magnificent. For a man in his seventies. But she kicked the living shit of out him.

She stood over him. At the time I thought he might be dead.

She wiped the blood from her mouth and turned to me.

"Book," she said.

I would have given it to her. Hell, you would have given it to her if you'd seen the number she did on my friend.

I was handing it to her when a white bag slipped over her head and her hands clutched her throat. She did a blind dance around the room, bumping into everything, trying to escape from the grip of the IF. She made awful sounds.

Finally she fell to the floor.

Suffocated.

The IF slithered off her head. He squirmed over to me and reached out his tail to gently push the book I was holding back to my chest.

He got a towel and wiped the blood off Koop's face.

In a minute or two Koop and I were limping down the hall, bracing each other and following this elf in a smeared candy cane cloak.

Koop said, "Sorry. That was . . . ," and he took a deep breath.

"Lucky?" I said, after a long pause.

"Something like that," he said. "I was . . ." His face was a blank.

"Not . . . yer best?" I offered.

"That'll do."

The Candy Cane IF said, "Doo-Dah, I would keep my voice down, if I were you. Somebody might hear us."

There was an explosion.

When the smoke cleared, our little Candy Cane IF was dead at our feet. And the hall was full of the dead soldiers.

Another IF stepped out of the smoke, over the bodies, took Koop by the hand, and led us to an elevator, and down, at last, to our final destination.

THE CORRIDOR—2018

Ding!

The elevator opened to a crowd of IFs filling the hall. I had never seen so many together at the same time.

The Pope, a little priest in white robes, stood right beside the portal. It was just a door. A green door in a green hallway that curved out of sight. But just looking at the door made me nervous. It was wrong. It was all wrong.

"Welcome back, Brother. We missed you."

Koop said, "Let's talk about this."

The door snapped open, and the snake curled out slowly, grinning, and made his way to The Pope.

I screamed and dropped to my knees in terror. Unless you've seen it, you don't know.

The Pope began to stroke its enormous snout like he was petting an ICBM.

For a moment, the two of them faced each other—outlaws in the middle of Main Street. A standoff. Somehow I knew that even without a mouth The Pope smiled.

Koop said, "You can take all of them. I'll close the door after you. I promise."

Exactly as when Rudy spoke, I heard all The Pope's responses in my head. "That's not what we agreed to."

"Take them and I'll close the door. I swear on my mother."

"Our mother opened that door. Who are you to close it?"

None of this made sense to me.

"Join us, Brother," said The Pope. "We're not leaving without you. It's you or the book."

Koop did the strangest thing then. He agreed.

"Okay," he said.

When I understood he was leaving, I said, "Don't you dare!"

"You know the page," Koop said.

"Don't."

"Read the verses."

"No, Koop!"

"It's the only way, Nuke."

"Don't you leave me again!"

It felt terrible to say something that raw. He looked at me.

"Please," I said.

"Hey," he grunted and got down on one knee. "You always did wanna to be a hero. Didn't cha?"

Koop smiled that irresistible smile. A black man whose skin was so dark it seemed to be blue in the shadows. His whole body was the darkest bruise.

"This was the plan all along, Nuke. Sorry, I couldn't give you all the details."

I don't think I've ever been that mad in life. "Fuck you!" I spit, and threw the blue book at his head. It sailed right past his black face and struck The Pope right between his pudgy eyes.

"Oh shit," said Koop.

The snake made a growl and turned its massive maw and charged. It knocked Koop over and he fell against the wall.

PARADIGM OVERLOAD—2018

I knelt shivering in the hall as the snake stooped then hovered hissing over me. A fine mist soaked me head to toe. Eyeless, it regarded my scent, with a sharp, extended inhale. The maw began to open. It's not something I'll ever forget. Some nights I still wake up with that wet white snout smelling me.

"Sister!" someone yelled.

The white monster froze as from a sudden shock.

Koop stepped between us. "Leave him the fuck alone, Tail. He's mine."

A throaty cat whine, and she snorted and coughed and slid backward, exuding a cool mist into the green hall and riding the residue, then curled around The Pope by the portal. In her wake both Koop and I were soaked and shivering.

He squatted again. "Listen, Nuke. I'm not your hero. I'm not your brother. I never was." He pointed a thumb at The Pope and the snake. "That's my brother and my sister. They're the only family I have."

My body was shaking; my hands trembled. I asked, "Can you make me forget this, please?"

"Sorry. You're The Doorman now. And I need you to finish the jobs you started. One: shut the way out. Two: find others who haven't escaped. Let them go."

"Three?" I asked. In fairy tales like this, there's always a three.

"Three is simple. Tell our story."

The trembling got worse. "I don't want to tell our story, Koop. I want to forget all of this. You gotta make me forget. I will never sleep again."

"Somebody's gotta do it," he said, and gave me that patented Koop smile. It's a gift. When he smiled at you, he made you feel seen, made you believe you could do anything. "It can't be me. It has to be a good man."

That was the last thing he ever said to me. I don't know what I expected to happen next, but it sure wasn't Koop limping back to the snake, mounting it like a cowboy, and riding it in reverse toward the portal. Its body slowly curled into the green door like a retracting vacuum cleaner hose. And there was a moment as the snake slipped backward when she paused to finally align herself with the exit. That's when Koop's eyes met mine, and he half-smiled and shrugged as if to say, Hey. I told you not to trust me. Then he ducked down and gently pat-patted the snake on the side of her head. They disappeared with a viscous *thunk*. It seemed both utterly absurd and perfectly natural, like Koop had done it many times before, whenever he had a chance.

Paradigm Overload? I knew what he meant now. At a certain point of overwhelming stress and shock the human body quits. The minds gets dopey. And you just cannot give a fuck anymore.

Dazed and weary, I noted the little man who was not a man approaching me. It could have been a boring episode of TV. Oh, yeah: *Ghost Midgets*. Up close his skin was a shimmering white, but it wavered like sheets drying in a slight breeze, and pale blue shadows curled up and down his robes. He carried the blue book in his wing and held it out for me. I took it.

"Do you remember me, Flasher?" he said, with the damnedest accent. I couldn't place it.

"Sure." I said his name.

"Do you remember my pain?"

I said nothing.

"Perhaps you remember when I begged you to let me go?"

I said nothing.

He snorted a little laugh. "You live in a world without mirrors. You know this?"

He lowered his dark eyes to my level, and I could see my face reflected in them. His little wings fluttered furiously, cooling me. "You know this, Flasher?"

"If you're trying to preach to me—forget about it."

"Forget?" he said. "That is your key word, is it not?" He leaned then stood to his full height.

"You forget about the lions in the cages when you're laughing at the clowns. You forget about the slaves toiling in the cotton when you're sipping lemonade with the master. You know this?"

"Sure."

"Sure," he said, mocking me. "You forget the many tribes who once filled your continent before you came. The tribes you have erased: Hopi, Apache, Pawnee—names like squealing rabbits. You know this?"

"Tlingit," I said. "I remember some."

"Some. You forget about the craftsmen who built your pyramids because you were never brown or gold or black."

"I'm not . . ."

"Oh, I know," he said. "It's never your fault. You forget the creatures you scoured from the earth, the land you've stolen, the people you scalped. Leaders killed, democracies toppled, bombs dropped."

"Dresden," I said. "I remember some."

"Some. You don't know the Mother Gadget that made our door. And welcomed The Tail Sister."

That was gibberish to me.

"That made us visible. Unlike you, who are all vampires. You know this? You have no mirrors in your house. You cannot see what you've become, so how can you see the graves of the slaves you stand on? You will never see yourself until you've seen them. Blindness. That is your curse, Doo-Dah."

He smirked, saying that nickname, as if it were a sick joke.

"God, you are boring," I said.

"Even now your children are invisible. To you."

"I don't have any children," I said. Who'd want to bring a child into this world?

Then I thought he might kill me. His eyes widened.

"We are The Forgettable. *We* are your children." He held out both his wings as if they were open palms. "With these hands I have saved more children than you can imagine. Yours and ours."

The curving hallway was crammed with these little white nuns. They began a singsong chant that echoed. "Dooooo Dah! Doooo Dah!" It sounded like one of those weird soccer crowd cheers. But in a stadium full of munchkins.

It had become insane. I thought: I need someone to wake me up.

And just like that, a pungent odor came out of nowhere: toasted roadkill rotting on a scorched blacktop. The smell seemed to offend The Pope; he grimaced then dismissed me with his wings.

"Ach! I'm done with your stink!" he muttered. Then turning, he shouted to his flock, "We are leaving, children!"

And, just-like-that, as soon as he turned his back, I was invisible. From that moment on, nobody looked at me.

Now, I gotta say this. Invisible was always a fantasy of mine. To be hidden. To go wherever I wanted. To eavesdrop and get the real scoop. But when I became invisible for the first time, I was flabbergasted by what my primary feeling was: I felt not just safe, but truly safe for the first time in my life. I could be threatened by no one. I could not be punished. I could never be embarrassed. I could be myself, no matter what I was.

It was like being drunk.

I was clutching the book in both hands with my arms crossed against my chest, like a family Bible.

The Pope looked up and lifted both his wings skyward and said: "Come, children! Anywhere is better than here."

The line of IFs that met The Pope at the door went on and on like a parade.

"Do you see them?" whispered a strange girlish voice from somewhere. "Do you see them?"

It didn't sound like Rudy at all.

I couldn't see my arm before my face, but, somehow, I could see through the robes of The Pope, as if the fabric had turned to cellophane.

I watched the sea of yearning faces crowd the corridor and surround The Pope. How gracefully he enfolded them into his robes, three at a time. He seemed to hug them, whisper his blessings, and then they passed, waddling into the green door, where they disappeared.

Then something remarkable. Behind the curtain of his robes (which evidently were now transparent to me), they transformed one by one. Their white bodies hunkered down and squashed themselves. Some collapsed into a concave head cup. Some became a squat torso with wings. Some corkscrewed into a tail. Then I was watching a tumbling act at the circus. Like marshmallows jammed on a stick, they all three stacked themselves together until they were one. The sounds were shocking: *Plop! Plop! Fizz! Fizz! Plop! Plop! Fizz! Fizz!*

The reunited IFs bowed slightly to The Pope then marched out through the portal.

So many left. How many? I have no idea. Hundreds? Seventy years of incarnations. Who knows? I watched their exit over and over until it was no longer amazing and my jaw closed. And then it became annoying. And later I remembered how The Pope had agreed to let one hundred go every year. I mean: three hundred.

Three for the price of one.

Not a bad deal.

I recalled Koop at Alamogordo, standing in the middle of a desert of white dunes, a pit stop on the way. Blue and purple shadows wherever the sun fell into shade. A trail of dust where Rudy rolled invisible down the dune.

"Funny thing, Bro."

"What?"

"They don't have waltzes."

"What?"

"They don't hear them. It's like there's a component missing in their brain which blocks it out."

"Like the forgetting?"

Koop didn't answer.

"You never explained how Rudy taught you the forgetting."

He looked me square in the eyes. "And I never will."

After the last little one had passed through the portal, The Pope called down the hall to me. "You're up."

Then he was gone, too.

For some reason I stood outside the door that wasn't a door for a long time and listened. Expecting to hear something. I heard nothing. But I had the uncanny feeling I wasn't alone in the empty green hallway. Something made me say, "Hello?"

Then I picked up the book and read aloud the verse from "The One About the Lion."

You should, too.

I suppose you'll want to know how it looked when the green door closed. It sounded like the largest bass drum in the world. I had just enough time to glance up and see that the door had been replaced by a puncture in the empty green wall that curved smoothly counterclockwise. It collapsed into the shape of a belly button. An innie. And then it sealed and the wall was as smooth as ever, as if there had never been a breach at all.

LET MY PEOPLE GO—2018

I don't know how long I sat in the hall.

Somebody found me. Got me out of there.

I heard later on the news there was a massive ordnance explosion at a decommissioned air force base in the Nevada desert. The whole structure was buried. Few injuries. Which was a blessing.

They were always good at covering their tracks.

I was in a hospital when a government dude came by and asked questions. I told him nothing.

"I have no memory," I said. "No memory of the last six months."

How I wished it were true. But he seemed to believe me. I bet he'd heard that line a lot. "Paradigm Overload" was my eventual diagnosis, which, of course, meant: "How the fuck should we know?"

Slowly.

That's how I put what was left of my life back together: slowly. Got a nice log cabin in the Rockies west of Denver. I got a view. Eventually, I met a biker chick named June in Bailey who seems to see something in me that makes good company. God knows what.

So I survived.

I got my government pension to live on. I've got a certain Air Force colonel to thank for that.

I can't complain.

I started a book. A book so crazy nobody will believe it. And a story so sad nobody will want to pass it on. I told them the blue book was my diary, and they let me keep it when I was recovering.

Funny. Nobody tried to read it. Or if they did, they were immediately yawning—you know, like when someone tries to tell you their dreams? Nice trick. A book that can't be memorized or recorded. A book that contains its own camouflage.

I was almost finished typing this when something occurred to me. When Koop told me to tell "our story," I thought he was talking about us: me and him. Nuke and his Most Unforgettable Character, Koop. God, what an idiot I am. It took me so long to figure out that he meant his family. "Our story" meant "their story." His brothers and sister. The IFs.

So Koop rescued his family and prevented a whole generation of IFs being born. Look at it that way and you could call it a noble act. But why did he leave? Where did he go? What the hell is he eating? I mean, logically, the snake survived in The Anywhere. So some kind of life could be sustained. It wasn't suicide, Koop is a survivor. But what was The Anywhere to him? R & R? A simpler life, where he didn't have to pull any triggers or tell any lies? I don't know. Sometimes in dreams I glimpse a strange land in a perpetual warm twilight. It looks like my idea of Ireland—a place I've never visited but I hear is green, rocky, and pleasant. What could that place be for Koop? A homeland where he could begin again? A family hearth? I honestly have no idea. I'm not family. I only thought I was.

For a long time I thought it was over. I wanted it to be over. Somebody said that grief doesn't get better, but, if you're lucky, you get big enough to contain it. So I got bigger, I guess. My belly sure did.

But part of me still had an itch that couldn't be scratched away.

One of the last things Koop told me: "Find the others who haven't escaped. Let them go."

Then one day I was half-napping when I saw a documentary about the Getty Museum in L.A., and they featured a manuscript from the fifteenth century.

They labeled it *A Cat with a Bishop's Crosier and Miter Sitting on a Circular Building*.

"You know what that looks like?" I asked June.

"The IF Pope?" she said.

"Yup."

Then they showed the Getty's beautiful garden. It was full of jumbo dandelions, or modern sculptures, or dozens and dozens and dozens of something else. Nobody else saw them. But I did.

I maybe would have left it there, but the woman who loved me was having none of it. "You got to finish it, Nuke. It's not over."

"I'm not brave enough," I said.

"Yes, you are," June said. "You closed The Way Out. You got to close the book."

"What'll I say to them?"

"You'll figure it out."

Thanks, Koop, I thought. Thanks a bunch.

Can I sleep now?

I am really fucking tired.

THE ENDING—2019

Did you ever notice how many love songs are about leaving? Being left? Separation. Goodbyes. Missing. I can't leave you alone. Don't leave me like this. I am lost without you. Maybe it's our first wound. The expulsion from our dark perfect unity with the mother into the hard light of self. There is embedded in the language of love the dread of loss. The hidden fear that no one will ever really see us. The hidden need that we dare not express, that we will always be alone. And finally, the hidden truth of the beloved we all must someday live without. That is the secret of love songs. The secret they taught us.

Those were my thoughts as I made my way to the central garden of the Getty Center where they had gathered like a field of pale flowers. Dead dandelions waiting to be blown away. The ones left behind. The ones that never made it out.

It's a beautiful place. Just don't look at the art. I mean, the art's fine, look at it if you want. But in a strangely ironic twist that no one saw coming, this breathtaking structure—sliced Italian travertine and flat white panels, aluminum and cacti and windows, windows, windows—beggars every painting, sculpture, Fabergé egg, or suit of armor on the inside; all that priceless, worthless art that all those ungodly wealthy white dudes donated for tax purposes because their personal assistants bought a new couch for their living room.

Ah, forget I said that. It's fucking beautiful.

I had put out the word through my invisible friend and he'd done the rest. I sat on the bluff overlooking them: the IFs sprawling among the stone paths, the green maze, and the garden. It was a Monday, so I knew the museum would be closed. I do recommend riding the white monorail that winds up the mountain alone, but I bet that was a rare treat reserved for me. In the distance caretakers ambled by occasionally—oblivious, as I knew they'd be.

The IFs all seemed to be looking down the mountain, watching the sunset over the ocean shedding a pink light on their concave heads, so that at times it looked like I was facing a field of Disney mushrooms. I took a deep breath, and like any Hollywood cowboy, I did what I had to. They didn't all turn to me at once. But, gradually, one by one, I could see their faces. I recognized some. The more I spoke, the more IFs turned, and my voice, which I admit was pretty shaky at first, got stronger and more confident.

I told them what they'd never been told before. I told them good-bye.

"You were loved once." A few heads turned.

"All of you. You were loved." A few more turned.

"You may not have felt it. You may not have believed it. The child who loved you maybe never felt love themselves, so they did not know how to pass it on."

I started saying their names as I recognized more and more of their faces. They were like strange little songs that tripped off my lips. Then one by one, the stragglers turned and faced me till a sea of black eyes spread out before me, watching.

"No matter what anyone says, you were loved once. That's why you're here. Because someone needed you so much, they made you.

"We gave you that gift of life. And you gave us your protection, your inspiration, your comfort. But now you must give yourselves something. The gift of goodbye."

A long, childlike moan swept over the crowd.

"A child is not a child forever. Your passage is over."

I stood up then. To make sure they could see and hear me clearly.

"You called me 'Flasher.' I am The Doorman. And I speak for all your children because they cannot speak for themselves. They may have forgotten you, but I have not. They may not see you anymore, but I do.

"Thanks for being our friends. Thank you and goodbye."

Yeah, of course I lost it. Wouldn't you?

THE OTHER ENDING—2019

The next day I was walking around a posh clothing outlet in Santa Monica—seeing what all the wealthy hipsters wear; a $5,000 belt buckle, a $800 T-shirt—when I saw a shadow. Something flitting on the edge of my vision. I knew enough by then to take it seriously and not to look at it directly, to trigger the wild beast flight instinct. And I knew who it was.

I guess I always knew Rudy when he was near. Sometimes it was like a bad smell you pass through on the way to clean air. Sometimes it was simply unbearable, like when you see a parent spank a child in public. And sometimes it was just a flinch of pain, like coming upon a frozen carcass of roadkill.

There was an arrangement of round mirrors in one corner of the store, and I knew the mirror trick would let me see him and give me the best chance of starting a conversation. Because I felt that, too; all Rudy really wanted was someone to talk to. Perhaps all evil starts that way and degrades inevitably through more and more neglect into something hard, and lonely, bitter and untouchable.

"Hey, Rudy," I said, not looking at him directly. "I thought you left with the others."

"You're not getting rid of me that easy."

"Who wants to get rid of you?"

"You do. You killed the others."

"If you were there you'd know that's not true. I said goodbye."

"Same difference."

"No, Rudy. I don't want to kill you."

He was silent after that and the mirrors were empty.

A short, amazingly beautiful salesgirl (at my age they are all girls) came up to me. Black bangs, round black eyes, and skinny skinny legs.

"Can I help you, sir?"

"God, I hope so," I said, but I couldn't afford anything she was selling.

So I gave Rudy some time.

A few days later I was sitting on the edge of the Santa Monica Pier watching the sun set. The scattered gulls squawking for handouts. The saltwater breakers rolling and foaming dark green under the pylons, and a bracing wind coming over the horizon. The mimes and sketch artists had cleared out of the boardwalk—God, I hate them. Envy, no doubt: I never could draw who's. Most of the tourists were gone. Just a few Latino fishermen and me—catching the last cool rays of sunset over the blue Pacific.

That's when I felt him, sitting next to me. You had to be careful with Rudy. He could always lash out like a feral animal. So I tried to be cool and watched a fat gray-and-white gull cravenly eyeing us both as if to say, You gonna eat that?

"Hey, Rudy."

"You don't wanna kill me?"

"No."

"Why don't you want to kill me? Everybody else does."

"Rudy. You don't have to be like this."

"Like what?"

"You don't have to have your dukes up all the time. Even when you're scared, you're not that vulnerable. Hell, you've lasted longer than any IF."

"I'll never be off duty," he said.

"What?"

"I was the soldier, the tail. Raleigh was the heart. The Other Guy was the brain."

I got those proverbial chills when he said that. I can still feel them running up and down my back and tickling the hairs on my neck. Was I his child? Was I the yellow starfish boy? That means: Rudy was my . . .

"You were my IF?"

"Don't call me that! It makes me sound like something you just made up."

After a moment I said, "PooMom?"

"That's your name for me. My real name is Ruddeganderfeet."

"I didn't give you that name."

"No, I gave it to myself. It's made of three words I like: Rudy. Gander. And feet. I never had feet. A bunch of geese is a gander. And I'm rude and I like it."

Poof! He was gone after that. For a whole day.

Our last meeting was pretty silly. I was watching a red northern cardinal bending over to admire his reflection in the deep blue pool at the hotel. Two fats crows started squawking in the palm trees that were just catching the first light of dawn. Then a hummingbird, I shit you not, flew into the courtyard, hovered a few seconds over the pool, then darted off. Jeez. What's with all the birds? They're everywhere I go. Just me and them, lounging poolside, reading the paper, sipping my morning coffee. No sugar, lotsa cream.

It was like a stray dog, black and wet and shivering, wandered over to give me a sniff.

"Hey, Rudy."

"I can see you."

"I know."

"I can hurt you."

"Yeah, you probably could. Listen. I wanted to thank you for helping me in the hallway by the portal."

"For what?"

"For making me invisible. That was great."

"That wasn't me. That was Raleigh. We travel a lot together."

"Really?" I looked around. "Where is she?"

"She's too smart to be seen. But the birds usually notice her."

We were silent for a long time, thinking about that invisible companion.

"Where's The Other Guy?"

"The Candy Cane IF who saved you?"

I took a deep breath, remembering the bloody bag of white that strangled the woman that creamed Koop. And died protecting us. I let out a deep sigh, remembering his tail gently pushing the book back into my chest.

"So. There's just us three."

We were silent for a time.

Finally Rudy said, "Why did you leave?"

"You know why."

"Growing up."

"Yup."

"It's like dying?"

"I suppose. But there's good stuff on the other side."

"Like what?"

"Well. I don't know. Music. Sex. Trust. Laughter. Pizza. A good beer on a hot day. Stuff like that."

"Stuff I'll never have."

I shrugged. I wasn't going start lying to him.

A breeze came out of nowhere, crinkled the blue surface of the pool.

"I thought I would find you, Doo-Dah. And tell you that I hurt the man who hurt you. The Koop who left you. And that would be my gift. My last gift to you. And you would thank me. But now I think it is something else. Maybe it is you who has the gift for me."

"We all get left, Rudy. Eventually."

"Yes. I see that. But not all are forgotten."

"I'm not forgetting you. How could I?"

"No. You were a bright light in a dark tunnel."

He smiled in my mind.

Then Rudy sighed and said, "Okay," like he had come to the end of a long journey.

"Okay?"

"Okay."

And I turned to him. And I saw him. Dear God. How can I tell you? He was like every child you've ever seen, the first time they know they can't have it all. I could only look at him for a short time.

"You can see me, Doo-Dah?" he asked.

"Yes," I nodded, trying not to cry.

He made a sound then that I doubt I can describe. Like an interrupted sigh or a short gasp of relief. It's the same sound the woman I love makes in the middle of the night. It's always my cue to take her into my arms. And then she relaxes.

"See me now," he said as if it was the only thing he'd ever wanted.

I turned my eyes to him and refused to look away. It's a horrible thing: loving. It's almost too much to ask.

He reached out to touch the scar on my lip with the tip of his tail.

"I remember the dog," he said. "I tried to tell you not to get too close."

I was looking at him, then I was looking through him, then I was looking at the shadow of a palm on the blue stucco walls of the pool.

Then the temperature of the day seemed to change and I knew he was really gone. Really, really gone.

The two black crows squawked down at me as if they had a point to make. They're smart birds but, really, they have absolutely no manners.

"Pipe down will ya?" I said. "I'm having a moment."

I fell asleep then, poolside.

THE ONE ABOUT THE LION

"Tell us the one about the lion, Koop!"

"I thought you were tired of that one."

"No!!"

"Okay. One day I went out for a walk in The Anywhere. There is much out here you cannot imagine. Dinosaurs. Dodo birds. Black taffy."

"Black taffy!" they repeated, then, "Ooooohh."

"And that's when I found where we are now."

"Where are we now?!" the IFs chanted.

"An old old church on a spit of land off a rocky coast so green it hurts your eyes to see it. All the windows are broken. And out every window you can see dark islands sprinkled along the gray horizon like seeds from a passing giant. A cold wind whistles in the rafters."

The high-pitched whistles of the IFs.

"And the air sparkles in the last light of day like magic dust from the tip of a wand. The sun is almost gone. And you know who I met here?"

"Whoo?" they said like baby owls.

"A lion."

"With big teeth?"

"Yes."

"And a big roar?"

"Yes."

"And big claws to tear you up?"

"Yes. But you know what?"

"What?"

"He didn't bite; he didn't roar; and he didn't tear me up."

"Why?"

"Because I did him a good turn."

"What choo do?" *Dooo, dooo* said the echo.

"In the rafters of a church, the lion leapt and leapt and leapt, and when he saw me he bared his terrible teeth and told me he would eat me."

"Nooooo!"

"He said I looked tasty."

"Nooooooo!"

"But I told him I wasn't afraid of him. That he would never catch me—I set records!"

"HE SET RECORDS!!!" the IFs chanted. "HE SET RECORDS!!!"

And just like that, he leapt and landed and braced himself on all four paws right before me. Crouched and ready to pounce. Right here. Right on this pale spar of wood.

He said, "Nothing can outrun me."

"My name is Koop," I said. "And I can."

"And I can!" the IFs echoed.

"You look like a flower," he said. "I like flowers. Hmmmmm—tasty."

I bopped his wet black nose and he blinked.

"Your problem," I said, "is not that you are hungry. Your problem is that you are hurting."

"Nothing hurts me. I do all the hurting."

"It is a familiar pain. So familiar that you forget that it hurts. Your problem is your collar is too tight."

"Collar?" the lion said. "I have no collar!"

"Oh, but you do," I said. "Let me fix it."

He held me with his fierce eyes—black dots floating in the middle of balls of gold. Finally he nodded, but he warned me, "If you hurt me, you are dead."

"If you hurt me you are dead!" the IFs repeated.

"So, gently, I reached into the thick, soft bush of his mane, felt down into the neck where the tight tight circle choked the lion. I found the rusty buckle that connected the cracked and sweaty leather strap. And you know what I did?"

"WHAT CHOO DO?!?!" asked the IFs.

"I undid it! And then the lion did the strangest thing. For a moment, he stood as still as a statue in the park. Then he shook his head. The mane became a dark golden bush whipping in a hurricane. Then the lion rolled over and lay down against the beam, twisting and twitching his spine, scratching and scratching his back, squirming in an odd little dance. His paws pumped the air, each taking its turn, padding an imaginary white ball that bounced up and down, up and down. Like a perfect hard-boiled egg.

"Then I looked at the leather collar in my hand. The edges were soaked with dried blood. And a little bronze tag read: RUDY. RINGLING BROS."

"Somebody loved you," I said.

The lion stopped his upside-down dance. "What?"

"Somebody loved you. That's what they do when they love you. They name you."

The lion closed his eyes.

"They called you 'Rudy.'"

The lion lay perfectly still. "Rudy?"

"You have forgotten. It was probably your owner."

The lion was on his feet so quickly it surprised me. I could see him stretching his great black claws. They slid out of his paws like black daggers from a sheath.

"Black daggers from a sheath," the IFs said.

One paw scraped four pale grooves in the thick wooden beam in the rafters; pale slivers curled up like the horns of a goat and toppled over. The lion's eyes sparked with gold as he came toward me. I met him in the middle of the rafter tie, and he ducked his great head into my chest and I was buried in a soft pillow of mane. And when the lion spoke, I could feel the rumble in his bones.

"I have no owner now," he said.

"Or maybe it was something you saw," I said. "A souvenir from the circus. A small small toy lion with a red red collar on the dresser in the bedroom of a boy who looked like a yellow yellow starfish. A shy boy who got a scar on his mouth that made him feel ugly for the rest of his life."

"In any case," I continued, "this is The Anywhere. You are what you are."

And the lion began to purr deeply; it echoed in the empty chamber and made the heavy spar beneath us shiver.

The IFs began to chant.

Short. Long. Wide.

Sleeping we are born like dreams.

Waking we are gone like dreams.

Living we are dreams come true.

Doooo Dah.

Doooo Dah.

Doooo Dah Do.

Then we sat up there together, the lion and I, side by side, on that sturdy old beam of pale white heartwood.

After a time my legs started swinging back and forth like the pendulum on a grandfather clock, and I could just picture how we looked.

Golden light from the last shard of glass left in the round window high above us cast a tint of flame on the dark brown tuft of fur at the tip of the lion's tail as it coiled and whipped, coiled and whipped in the shafts of drifting dust.

My IFs closed their eyes and continued to chant *Doooo Daaah-hhh! Doooo Daaaah!* and it echoed off the stone walls of the ruined church, and, as they always did, their white head cups began to tip back and forth, back and forth, like a field of flowers in the wind— easy friends, lost in trust, listening to a music conducted by the tail of a lion.

"People who shut their eyes to reality
simply invite their own destruction,
and anyone who insists on remaining
in a state of innocence
long after that innocence is dead
turns himself into a monster."

James Baldwin,
"Stranger in the Village," *Notes of a Native Son*, 1955

The Glossary

"I read the whole deck framed by his flattened palm. To this day I can never remember those notes without picturing them in the middle of a brown-pink hand. He sang each one. Each cursive little icon—part Arabic, part Japanese, part Walt Disney, part LSD, part over-the-rainbow."

A Align. The Allies. The Allegiance. The Anywhere. Ain't No Mountain High Enough.

B Bind. Bond. Bondage. Brother. The last word. Peeps. The people. Forbidden word. "No. No. No. Bodi." Pronounced "Bow-dee!" Usually screamed. Baby Love.

C Clowns. Caught. Cool Cats. Clear. Come See About Me.

D Disarm. Doodle. A little dab'll do ya. Dancing in the Street.

E Entrancing. Enter at your own risk. Exit. Extinct. Ask The Engineer: Is it Rolling? Each Day Is a Lifetime.

F Foster the fuck out of it. Flasher. Fingertips.

G Ghost. Goodie. Gobble it up. Drop the Gadget. Going to a Go-Go.

H The Key nobody remembers. The invisible key. Sometimes associated with notorious inventor Saul Lowe of "S.L.W. Enterprises" (who later admitted that a childhood friend, Milton Herzman, was the actual inventor of the Hold button—which Lowe claimed to have successfully marketed). In his last days Mr. Lowe told everyone he could (mostly African American nurses) about the theoretical physicist Dr. Shirley Ann Jackson, the first African American to earn a doctorate from M.I.T., the recipient of the 2014 National Medal of Science, and the actual inventor of the portable fax, the touch-tone telephone, the solar cell, fiber-optic cables, as well as the technology behind caller ID, and, not incidentally, call waiting. How Sweet It Is (To Be Loved by You).

I The Ichiban. The tops. The primo. The Big Daddy. The Infection. The Incredible Edible Egg. It Takes Two.

J The jackal's sword. Slice it thin. Do It Justice. Just My Imagination (Running Away with Me).

K The kernel. In the chicken coop. Plant it and it grows. Ask The Killer. What Key? Keep on Truckin'.

L Listen to The Lion. Lying. The Dirty Lowdown. Lay down The Law. Living we are dreams come true. Love Child.

M Matterhorn. Majestic, sheer and deadly. Goes straight down. Also goes up. Minstrel. Motown. My Girl.

N Navigate. Natural. You don't feel it, you don't play it. Nowhere to Run.

O The bass note. The open mouth. You sing it till it hurts. Till you know you feel. The Big Empty. The Momma Gate. The Omelas Constant: the minimum misery required to maintain a Utopia. Ooo Baby Baby.

P The cock. The rooster. The crow. You play this note, you stand tall and wake up the world. Please Mr. Postman.

Q Listen for your cue. The question mark. Nobody knows nothing, but only the fool dares to ask.

R Rock and Roll. RAM. Resist. Reach Out, I'll Be There.

S The Serpent of The Sleepy Place. Sister Twisty, Lordy can she get into the shit. Sleeping we are born like dreams. See the USA in your Chevrolet! Stop! In the Name of Love.

T Tempo. Tap it. Up and Down. Back and forth. Tip it all around. The Tracks of My Tears.

U Undertow. Understand. Udder. Utter? Uptight (Everything's Alright).

V *Esse quam videri.*

W White. The lack of color. The totality of color. Wait for the feeling. Wassup! Wonder where the yellow went. Waking we are gone like dreams. Where Did Our Love Go, What's Going On, War.

X marks the spot. You find the spot you mash it good.

Y Baby talk. They cry until you come. You come; they stop. Not what. Not where. Ask the Navigator why. You Really Got a Hold on Me, You Keep Me Hanging On.

Z Zero. Zilch. The Big Nothing. What's left after a flood? The Zoo. ("There are only two kinds of music: The Blues and Zipiddy Do Dah!"—Townes Van Zandt) The Living End. Zembla. A distant ancient Kingdom. A Brand New World.

THE AFTERWORD

You begin your life thinking the world is knowable. Like a novel.

51 took sixteen years to write. Ten years less than *The Gift*. I'm slow. Or as Harlan Ellison once said, "Slow? Christ! Glaciers are slow!" Yes. I have been insulted by Harlan. He called me "Science Fiction's J. D. Salinger." So I give him a pass.

It's not as if the plan reveals itself to me like a blueprint spread across a table. I scavenge. I collect stuff. Won't have any idea where it goes, until years later it's a cement block. Or a roof tile. Or a snarling white serpent.

It's like being on a riverboat in the jungle and you're supposed to narrate this dream cruise. You're the Tour Guide. Only this is your first time! You don't know if your pistol fires blanks until you shoot it. Your job is to charm the passengers and say something wry about the hippo. Welcome to my head trying to write a novel. You try working under these conditions.

The Anywhere was the remnants of a fairyland where I wandered for—I'm ashamed to tell you how long. In my defense there was a smart-ass talking dog. I gave his attitude to Rudy.

The poignant image of a little boy in bed reaching out to a closet of darkness. For what? Rescue? A friend? No one was more surprised than I when white creatures stepped out of the closet. They were newly drawn, just sketches of something stranger: a race who couldn't be seen. Symbiotes who cherished their mission: to sherpa toddlers through the transition into their terrible first dawn of consciousness. Doomed to be forgotten. I used the names of my eldest son's imaginary friends. I dreamt they thanked me for telling their story. I woke up and thought: Their story?

When you work the way I do, you get used to characters jumping out of the bushes. Changing genders. Hijacking the story. After all it's not my story. I'm just the guy who discovers it bit by bit.

I had these scattered people telling odd stories that didn't add up to anything. But they seemed true. I began to imagine a structure of tales and tellers who could not tell their story straight, who left the actual novel untold and left it up to the reader to construct it out of what was left out.

All these stories begged the question: Who were they talking to? A long way into it I thought of the cleanup man in the film *The Professional*. The guy you call when everything's fucked. Léon. What if my character was the ultimate disaster cleanup guy? The listener.

An expert interrogator. An executioner with a unique ability to erase memories. Koop. Nuke's most unforgettable character.

I have an old friend who is losing his memory. It's tragic, but it is amazing how much more he is than his memories. Even when his mind cannot remember the name of the forty-fifth president, he remains a kind, sweet, and thoughtful man. If we are not the sum of our memories, then who are we?

A breakthrough: ten years in I get the Big Idea. Boom, as Steve Jobs (my former boss) liked to say. Creatures who developed a curiously virtuoso form of camouflage. To blend until they are not noticed. They putz with memory, become forgettable. You may as well not have been there. Like my two colonoscopies. They could have happened to someone else and I wouldn't have been able to tell the difference.

To this day my wife will never tell what I said for the suspiciously long forty-five-minute gap of the ride home.

Gaps. That's what I do. I fill in the gaps.

Who invited the Presidents? I didn't want to write about Presidents! But, you know, they're like a late night snack—once you've had one, you might as well finish the bowl.

In the early nineties I met a stranger on the streets of Seattle who stopped me. Now imagine a slow pan up to a very I wanna say large man. He says my name. How do the homeless know about me? And then this hulk turns into my old friend. The best man at my wedding. So there. It happened. And sorry about the hulk thing, Timothy.

Big Secret: two men wrote this novel. Like that amazing foggy night when Tolkien dragged C. S. Lewis kicking and screaming from theism to Christianity. I started writing this novel as a theist and ended up an atheist. Maybe that's why I put the ruined gothic cathedral in the Anywhere. I now believe the arc of the universe bends toward entropy not justice.

51 was a working title for a stretch. Then it had a healthy lap or two as *IF. Forgettable* almost ran away with it until "WHOA MAMMA 51." Not a bad number. But if it was up to me, I would have gone jazzier. *77* maybe.

51 emerged from a long period of a personal chaos. I was often blocked. That changed when I was diagnosed with sleep apnea. Suddenly I could dream again. And I could write.

I should mention that I have a weakness for UFO stories. So Area 51 has been a sort of hobby for me for decades. No, I'm not one of the idiots who stormed it. I got over anal probes years ago. There's a lot of almost evidence. Some creepy film, lotsa knowing looks, but nothing conclusive.

UFO SIGHTING 1 (REDACTED)

UFO SIGHTING 2 (REDACTED)

Hey. I gotta leave something to talk to Terry Gross about!

When my mom was dying, she told my wife (her caretaker), "I finally understand what Pat was doing when he was reading all those Laura Ingalls Wilder books over and over. He was learning to be a writer." I adored those books. They were my introduction to literature. Tales of a brave lonely girl searching for a home on the Prairie, The Town, The Big Woods, Plum Creek, the shores of Silver Lake, through the Long Winter. To me these were sweeping adventures in strange worlds with violence as shocking as a bullwhip in a classroom, and love as subtle as an invisible inkstain, I had just moved from the country (which I loved) to the city. I understood Laura. Her stories had real terror, real courage, real laughter and joy.

I have seen things humans can't imagine. A New Zealand glacier shedding hundreds of waterfalls. A Bohemian castle with three brown bears in the moat. Flying peacocks in Octavia E. Butler's hometown. Snake charmers in Marrakech. The stinking sulfur inside a live volcano. I live in a constant state of being at a loss for words.

Hey. Thanks for reading.

PO
6/20/20

Patrick O'Leary is a poet, novelist, songwriter and photographer, Michigan born and raised. His first novel, *Door Number Three*, was chosen by *Publishers Weekly* as one of the best novels of the year. His second novel, *The Gift*, was a finalist for the World Fantasy Award and the Mythopoeic Award. O'Leary's third novel, *The Impossible Bird*, also received wide acclaim. His short fiction is collected in *Other Voices, Other Doors* and *The Black Heart*; his poetry collections are *The Wedding* and *The Black Gown*. His novels have been translated into German, Russian, Japanese, Polish, French, and more. O'Leary lives in Canton, Michigan, with his wife, the artist Sandra Rice.